THE
CHERISHED

THE
CHERISHED

PATRICIA WARD

An Imprint of HarperCollins*Publishers*

HarperTeen is an imprint of HarperCollins Publishers.

Library of Congress Cataloging-in-Publication Data
Names: Ward, Patricia Sarrafian, 1969- author.
Title: The cherished / Patricia Ward.
Description: First edition. | New York : HarperTeen, [2023] | Audience: Ages
    13 up. | Audience: Grades 10-12. | Summary: When sixteen-year-old
    Jo Lavoie arrives at the house she inherited from her grandmother, she
    begins unraveling dark family secrets and learns that the stories her late
    father told her are more real and dangerous than she ever imagined.
Identifiers: LCCN 2022001746 | ISBN 9780063235113 (hardcover)
Subjects: CYAC: Fairies—Fiction. | Kidnapping—Fiction. | Inheritance
    and succession—Fiction. | LCGFT: Paranormal fiction. | Novels.
Classification: LCC PZ7.1.W3674 Ch 2023 | DDC [Fic]—dc23
LC record available at https://lccn.loc.gov/2022001746

Typography by Jenna Stempel-Lobell
23 24 25 26 27 LBC 5 4 3 2 1
First Edition

For Zack

maur is gone. they put her in the ground yesterday. i wore the suit she got me when she found out she was dying. alls you do is stand there she told me. you dont have to speak. times like that no one asks for talk.

it was just like she said. hattie sat by me in the front. we were the family.

sam from morrow farm come and penny brought candles wrapped in paper and sarah come with flowers and hugged me too much. edie and all everyone else from town were there. the pastor said us all being together would help the healing.

it did not.

i keep thinking how she got at the end. it must have been the dying which means it could happen to me. she worried about everything. the garden the house the door. she got worked up id go. she said dont you take off out there in the world. you stay put right here. youll make do she said. that's what people do.

im not people i said.

its growing season. ive got greens cabbage
asparagus broccoli rhubarb and peas coming up.
ive got half a crate left of her soaps wrapped
in felted covers and tied with string. after she
got sick she quit making stuff. she said her
hands felt weak as wet wool.

its no matter now.

shes gone.

ONE

The fateful letter's lain on the entryway table for days, getting buried under junk mail until the morning of Nana's birthday bash, when Jo is exhorted to deal with the pile because her mom, Abigail, can't possibly think in this chaos, and why can't they be more tidy, and what has she done to deserve any of this?

She gets strung out every time they have to attend a thing at Nana's, especially if it's a holiday thing, or a birthday thing with such weight as Nana turning seventy-five and inviting half the planet to pay homage.

"It's not my mail," Jo grumbles. She's sixteen: nobody sends her mail. So it's not her pile or her job.

"Get that look off your face!" Abigail snaps.

She's a balloon, seven months pregnant, easily flustered, and ready to pounce on the slightest thing. Jo scowls and loads the mail up in her arms. "It's not my fault it gets like this. It's consumerism. Look, it's all ads and catalogs. It's disgusting."

"Oh, for heaven's sake." Abigail rolls her eyes at the ceiling. "Get on with it. Today's going to be awful."

Only because you make it that way, Jo fumes inwardly. She dumps the mail on the breakfast table, shoving aside the dirty plates left by her stepdad, Robert. Abigail says he can't help never cleaning up, it's how he was raised; plus, he's a man. So he gets to leave a trail of dirty plates and cutlery and half-finished drinks around the house, and they—or rather Jo, now that Abigail's increasingly ornery and tired—have to pick up after him the days the housekeeper doesn't come. Robert shouldn't be let off the hook. It's so patriarchal, not to mention lame.

She's been stacking junk mail on the right and bills and such on the left, and then she comes upon the letter, which is addressed, weirdly enough, to her: *Josephine Margaret Lavoie*.

It's so startling that she just stands there drinking in the strangeness. It's from a Nathanael Fletcher, Esquire., in St. Johnsbury, VT.

Vermont.

A tendril of unease snakes up through her belly into her throat. She tears at the envelope, unfolds the single sheet, and scans the contents.

"Mom?" she calls. "Mom!"

"What?" her mother screams from some other part of the house. "Why do you always yell? Why can't you just find me?"

"Where are you?" Jo hollers, now in the hallway.

"UpSTAIRS!" Abigail screeches.

Jo takes the stairs two at a time. Her mom is in front of her wardrobe mirrors, wearing the dress she spent hours choosing at Nordstrom while Jo died of boredom.

"I look like a whale," she says in despair.

"Gammy Maureen's dead," Jo says, holding up the letter. "She left me the house."

Abigail's mouth opens in shock. Their eyes hold in the mirror. Slowly, Abigail turns around. "She *what*?"

Robert takes over deciphering the legalese when he comes back from tennis. He stands in the front hall, pink cheeked and dripping, frowning down at the letter. Abigail peers over his elbow while Jo frets, watching, waiting. A whole house, left to her. She *owns* an actual *house*. Even if it's that one.

She feels a twinge of guilt that she's more focused on the house than Gammy Maureen being dead. But in her defense, Jo barely knew her. The last time anyone even heard from Gammy was two years ago, at the funeral. She showed up in an ancient Cadillac, having driven on her own all the way from Vermont. The gathering for Jo's dad, Enzo, was pitifully small, and when she limped in everyone stared. She stood out with her long gray braids and wrinkled linen outfit and leather sandals. She spoke to no one, just sat there with her hands clasped in a fist. At the end of it, on the steps outside, she stopped in front of Abigail and said: You ruined his life.

Abigail was too shocked to reply, and Gammy Maureen tromped down the steps to her boat of a car, threw her cane in the back seat, and roared off. In the moments after, Abigail feigned indifference, calling Gammy crazy as a sack of cats and an irrational old hag. But later that night, she blew up, storming around kitchen: So now *I'm* responsible for everything? she ranted. He chose me, and she never got over it! Crazy old cow! *She's* the one that drove him crazy, not me! Then she screamed at Robert and smashed a dish when he remarked that she was having more cigarettes than her usual two per day.

For her part, Jo couldn't believe someone so old—she had to be about eighty—drove all the way from Vermont and back in one day, alone. It was really striking, that determination, that abiding love. The mess of everything and the distance and the sadness encapsulated by this old lady's long, lonely journey, and the will she had to deliver just the one sentence like a whip—it was hard not to be impressed, despite her mom's humiliation. It was also amazing that Gammy hadn't changed at all from when Jo met her, like she'd stepped right through time in her same musty farm clothes, striding tall with no care for anyone's opinion.

In fact, now that Gammy's gone, Jo realizes she'd imagined her there on the farm just trucking along forever.

But she's dead. It's truly a shock.

And the house—that it's Jo's.

She was only eight the one time she visited. The trip wasn't planned; her mom was away, and her dad took her. The first days there were magical. She got to pet and brush the pony in the dim, breezy barn, swim in the pond, eat berries right off the bushes. Gammy taught her sewing and gave her tons of chocolate her mom never allowed. Then things took a turn. The grown-ups had a huge fight. Jo can't remember what happened—just that it was nighttime, and Gammy sounded so frightening, yelling over and over, *Get out!* Jo got badly hurt and still has ugly scars down her arm; Gammy hit her with a rake by accident, her dad later told her. She can't remember that or anything else, not even when he drove them off in a paranoid schizophrenic state. Her next clear recollection is of the blue wooden floors in the motel room all the way over in Maine and hearing the ocean crashing outside the window. He hid her there for four days before the police showed up.

Nana refers to it as That Incident With Your Father, dismissing the whole thing with disapproving amusement, like a punch line to the story of Abigail's disastrous first marriage. Jo can't bear it when Nana talks that way. She can still hear her dad and Gammy shouting, she can feel the darkness of the night all around. If she pushes herself back through time, trying to be there again, she gets clammy and anxious. Something awful happened. She knows it, but no matter how hard she tries, she just can't remember.

So thinking of the house, usually, is like tumbling into a black hole of sickening panic. But today, because of the letter, the house presents differently in her memory: bathed in sun, surrounded by waving green fields. She recalls the white clapboard siding, stairs with peeling paint, wind chimes singing on the front porch. Her years-old anxiety is swept away by excitement: *My own house!*

She gets enthralled by an image of herself in a convertible on a sunny highway, her hair flying, heading north.

"You don't really own the house," Robert interrupts her fantasy. "It won't be yours till you're eighteen. And then, gosh, we don't want this, do we?" He tilts the letter at Abigail with an amused look. "What a headache."

Jo's insides crumple in embarrassment at her dumb notion of driving off, alone and free. She only has a learner's permit: she can't even go down the block.

"Once the will's through probate, just tell him we intend to sell, and that's that." Robert flicks the paper as if it's a pesky insect.

"It's not that simple," Abigail says, taking the letter out of his hand. She folds it slowly back up. "He says she left a trust for the people living there. What about them?"

Robert's already halfway down the hall. "What are you going to do, take over supporting them? We've got to sell," he reiterates, leaning over the staircase railing. "Trust me, hon, there's no decision to make here."

Once he's safely out of earshot, Jo blurts, "I don't want to sell!"

"Oh, what do you know," Abigail says tiredly.

"So *he* gets to decide, even if it's *my* house?"

"Young lady," Abigail warns, going icy and stiff.

Jo glowers at her mother, who strikes a pose with her hands on her giant belly, communicating how much she dislikes disturbing

8

the gestational process. *Stupid amoebert*, Jo thinks nastily. That's her name for the baby, a combo of amoeba (formless, hideous, mindless thing) and Robert (annoying bore). If it weren't for the amoebert, maybe Abigail would wake up to how pathetic her marriage is, maybe then they could finally get out of here.

But no.

"He's right to be realistic," Abigail says. "Maureen's dumped a huge responsibility on us."

"It's on the lawyer, isn't it? It's not on us."

"That's just technical. I mean, the place is ours. Yours," she corrects, reading Jo's look. "But you're a minor, so it falls to me. I'm the one who has to deal with it."

The resentment in her tone smarts. "The letter says he'll take care of them. There's money for that. So what's the big deal?"

"But how much money? For how many years? What else do they expect from us? Jo, it's just not that simple. I mean, what happens if the roof needs replacing? Who pays?" She frowns at the paper in her hand, as if it might be signaling new messages. "I'll have to go—God, I didn't even think of that. But when?" she says in alarm, touching her pregnant belly. "It'll have to be now, in the next few weeks! I won't be able to deal with any-thing after the baby comes! My God, what a mess."

Jo's emotions are in such a whirl she can barely process her mom's words. The fantasy of her escape in a convertible has evaporated, but her mom going there instead feels all wrong.

The house is supposed to be hers. *She* should be the one to go.

But why does she even feel attached to that stupid house?

Because it was Daddy's.

The sudden revelation hurts so awfully that she bends her head, scared she's about to bust out crying.

"To think she had nothing, literally *nothing*, to do with us," Abigail rants, "and then she goes and dumps this on us! I'll have to go through her things. My God, that house was crammed with junk like a Turkish bazaar!"

A memory slides forth: the plaid couch in the TV room, sun slanting through the filmy curtains, dust in the air. The old brown dog on the ratty bed. An open box of candy, wrappers strewn across the table.

"I want to go with you," Jo hears herself say.

Abigail is startled. "Why would you want that?"

"It's my house. Why shouldn't I go?"

"I don't think it would be mentally healthy," Abigail says with clinical coldness. "Anyway, you have art camp."

"I don't want to go to art camp."

"Of course you do."

"No, *you* want me to go. *I* want to go see my house."

"Fine, then. Have a few sessions with Dr. Coletti, then we'll see."

The idea of having to sit in that chair all over again—this is going sideways fast. "Save the co-pay. I already know he'll tell me it's good to face up to things once and for all."

"Really?"

Jo isn't sure Dr. Coletti would say that, but it sounds good. "Absolutely. And I can defer art camp. They let you do that, you know."

Abigail considers all this, her eyes narrowed. Jo holds her ground.

At last, Abigail shrugs. "Well, all right, then, if you really want to. I could use the help taking inventory. And I might as well find a real estate agent. Maybe they can come take a look," she muses, as if it's her own idea, not Robert's. "The lawyer can figure out what to do with these people. We shouldn't have to have this burden."

"What about me? Don't I get any say?"

"Josephine, really. When you see it again, you'll be fine with selling."

"You don't know that," Jo retorts.

"Oh, Jo . . ." Her mom sighs, prequel to one of her laments about how Jo doesn't understand, how she's too young, how she's so obstinate.

"Whatever," Jo snaps, cutting her off. "I'm going to my room."

She leaves her mom standing in the hallway wearing her tragic abandoned-heroine look. Upstairs, Jo closes her bedroom door hard, communicating that Abigail better not follow the way she sometimes does. She waits a moment, listening. Nothing.

She flops onto her beanbag, arms thrown behind her head. The room is hot, even with the air-conditioning on and the blinds lowered against the pounding July sun. She wishes she'd snagged some ice cream from the kitchen before holing up in her room. She can't very well go down now; it'd be anticlimactic.

Her mom never listens to her, Jo fumes. If she's so bent on selling, why even bother going? She hated the house, says the time she lived there was a slice of hell. It was when she got pregnant with Jo and dropped out of college. Nana and Pops were so frantic they hired a private detective to make sure she wasn't being held captive by a cult. There was no cult, there was just Gammy. Whenever she comes up in conversation, Abigail makes the cuckoo sign at her temple and rolls her eyes. Gammy definitely had issues; it's why Jo's dad turned out the way he did—not because of genetics, since he was adopted at twelve, but just from living so many years with her.

Nana says Abigail let herself get silly with love instead of reading the obvious signs of looming disaster. Maureen was bad enough, but Enzo wasn't even her actual son, and his background was a total mystery because he couldn't remember it. Who couldn't remember anything, not even one detail? Someone severely damaged, that's who. Someone dangerously broken. Plus, he was dark-skinned, Hispanic looking. He could be from anywhere. He might even be Arab. Who knew what he'd done that he supposedly couldn't remember? This was who Abigail went and got pregnant with, a fellow with no lineage, no money, nothing to grab on to but his wild hair and big laugh. Abigail should have known he'd never fit in, and then, as if to hammer the point home, he ran off with Jo and ended up in the loony bin.

Sometimes, Jo feels a reluctant pride in that younger version of her mom. She went against everything for the sake of doomed love: her parents, their expectations, society. It's unreal, seeing her now. Look who she married the second time around, after all: just about the most conservative, bland, oyster-shucking, tennis-playing guy in a bow tie you might find wandering a Cambridge street. A stranger to their family would never for a single second dream Abigail once ran off with a schizophrenic in a farm truck. It's as if her whole Rebellious Phase, which is what Nana calls it, never even happened.

Jo is startled by the sudden rise of voices downstairs. She tiptoes across her room, cracks the door to listen. Robert and her mom are fighting about the Vermont trip. He doesn't want Abigail going, thinks it's reckless. She isn't giving in, though. It's weird, since usually she does when he gets this way, all logical and stern. Maybe her mom actually wants to go, deep down. Maybe she just wants to see, the way Jo yearns to. Like a final goodbye to the past.

She imagines the house on the hill, empty, silent, waiting for them. It's weird to think Gammy died and no one told her, even if it's not like Gammy ever called or wrote or anything. It hurts, too, thinking about her dad, how he's gone forever, and how he was young and happy there, once upon a time. She knows he was because she has pictures his girlfriend, Sue, brought over after he died, along with a bunch of stuff in his old canvas satchel. He wanted Jo to have it, Sue told her, and she was making good on her word.

Jo shuts her door, muffling the ongoing argument. The satchel's tucked in the back of her closet, and she has to drag out shoes, old puzzles, a sleeping bag, before she gets to it. She kneels on the floor, one ear attuned to the drama downstairs. The buckles are rusted, the leather straps floppy with age. Her dad carried it everywhere, laden with water bottles and snacks and random junk toys he bought at checkout counters. Now it's just got his old stuff in it, the stuff he wanted her to have. She hasn't looked at it in a long time. There's an envelope of photos and his old plaid shirt, the one she practiced embroidery on when she was little. There's one of the wooden boxes he carved with two animals inside, a fox and a bobcat. He made a whole forest of animals for her, and she'd line them up in a parade. There's his whittling knife, a Swiss Army knife, and a box of shining, pretty lures. He always said he would teach her to fish, but they never got around to it. At the very bottom, wrapped in an old linen dish towel, are the iron cowbell and chain. They always stayed in the bag, no matter what. She picks up the heavy, cold bell with both hands. When her dad took her to the motel, he made a tent out of sheets and hung this bell over where she slept. It would keep her safe, he said.

What matters, Dr. Coletti's words float into her head, *is that he did keep you safe.*

Sure, if being safe from imaginary creatures counts. Meanwhile, the bell could've fallen on her head and knocked her out.

Thinking of her dad lugging around these weird talismans and how he bequeathed them to her with this mishmash of stuff brings on a stifling tightness inside her chest. She forces herself to breathe through it, a trick Dr. Coletti taught her, then buries the bell back in its hiding place. It's just all so sad, and it'll never be any different.

She sinks back into the beanbag with the envelope of faded photos from his childhood. At least in that part of his life, he was happy and normal seeming. There's one of him and Gammy on the front steps, and another of him at the barn, holding a goat by a rope. Jo's favorite is the one of him in the field. She stares hard at the young man with his explosion of curly black hair and laughing eyes. The yellow field stretches far away behind him, the blue sky faded almost white. He looks like a regular guy in this picture, healthy, outdoorsy. Jo imagines herself in that field with her own wild hair blowing in the wind. She knows nothing about fields or goats. All she knows is every day, she wishes she were somewhere else, and that now, out of the blue, there's a somewhere else to be.

A loud clatter jolts her. Abigail didn't go for glass this time, Jo surmises. The copper fruit bowl hurled against a wall, maybe. Abigail hurling something across a room is the climax to every one of their arguments, like a shot fired to bring order. Now Robert will get all conciliatory and goopy, and Abigail will drag things out a bit longer, banging stuff around and complaining he never helps, till she finally burns out and they cuddle and make up. If Jo appears anytime before that phase, Abigail will zero in on her: Why can't you ever do your hair properly? Why do you have to be so sullen all the time? So she stays put, even though she's kind of hungry and could use a snack, but then that would provoke the lecture about watching her diet.

Jo sighs, maneuvering herself onto her back on the beanbag. She stares at the ceiling, waiting. After a short while, she hears the heavy footfalls and grunts that signal her mom's dramatic, pregnant ascent of the stairs. Soon, there will be a whole new eruption, because Abigail hates the dress she got and how will she ever look presentable and to think of all those people seeing her like this.

Jo holds up the photo to the light streaming through the shade. Her father appears as the ghost that he is, an outline against the yellow field, like he's floating in his transparent slice of heaven.

"Don't tell me you aren't even showered yet!" Abigail announces in the doorway. "We're leaving in an hour!"

"Not everybody takes an hour to get ready, Mom."

Abigail hisses disapproval and heads for her room.

If Gammy drove her dad crazy, Jo thinks sourly, Abigail probably finished the job.

TWO

They go to Nana's early so as to help set up, which involves Abigail going from one lavish room to the next and reassuring Nana that every detail has indeed been attended to. Jo hangs back in the kitchen and practices her Spanish with Valeria, the catering manager. *¿Cómo estás? Muy bien. Gracias.* Jo gets put to work folding napkins at the breakfast table while the cooks chop and prep. They speak in rapid-fire Spanish, briskly maneuvering around the kitchen. They've worked this house many times; Nana likes throwing Mexican-themed parties. When Jo informed Nana that actually, the caterers aren't from Mexico, she shrugged and said what did that matter. Jo hates these parties and the way everyone acts so cultivated and worldly. They're all fakes. She's not going to turn out that way. She might have if she'd been sent to some dumb boarding school, but she put up such a fight that Abigail finally relented and let her attend public school, mostly to spite Nana. Such acts are all that's left of her Rebellious Phase.

Other than Jo, that is, the living embodiment of Abigail's tragic mistake. She'll never fit in among the guests with her stocky build, olive complexion, and frizzy black hair. She's so out of place that people literally have no clue she's a member of the family. Abigail is the epitome of class, with long tan legs and honey hair and a fiercely toned bod due to a lifetime of tennis at the club; she even manages to look fit in her balloon form, energetically moving among the guests. Jo, on the other hand, hates tennis and any sports, really. She does just enough to pass in school, upending the family tradition of academic excellence. She doesn't have suitable hobbies like chess or violin; instead, she watches horror movies, which make her feel obscurely relieved. She does sew a lot, but no one likes her creations: bits of fabric patchworked with interesting stuff she comes across (a dried plant, fur trim, plastic). But what does it *mean*? Abigail always demands, exasperated, because she can't accept it means nothing, which is the point.

Chunky, olive-skinned, sullen, and a little too hairy all over—that's Jo in a nutshell. She wishes she could hide in the kitchen the whole time and not have to talk to anyone at all. She bends over the napkins, folding them corner to corner. Valeria hums as she works, and Jo watches from beneath her lashes, envying her. Maybe it's because she can just be who she is, and no one even notices her or cares. She doesn't have to go out there and get stared at and questioned: Oh, *you're* Abigail's daughter?

More waitstaff arrive and things get manic. Jo retreats up

the steep, winding back stairs to the second floor, travels down the hall, and collapses for a time on the window seat, texting Ellie, who's running late. Ellie's her best friend in the small, tight group they run with at school. Ellie and Jo stick together, scowling at anyone who stares. They trade notes in class and keep a list of cities where they're going to live when they're older: Paris. Rome. Marrakesh. When they turn eighteen, they'll get the same tattoo of a flying bird.

Abigail and Robert think Ellie's a "bad influence," as if Jo has no agency. They say it's because after meeting Ellie, Jo got her nose pierced, but Jo knows the real reason is Ellie's bi. It's so repressed and old-fashioned, and anyway, what have Jo and Ellie actually done that's so criminal? Nothing, is what. Apparently, it's all in their attitude. Except, hello, they're teenagers: they're supposed to be awful to their parents. Abigail doesn't buy this. She lectures that when she was a teenager, she was polite and always got As, conveniently forgetting how badly she went off the rails in college: at least Jo's getting it all out slowly, not in one major act of insanity. Jo threatened she'd refuse to come to Nana's party if Ellie wasn't allowed. What would Abigail do: drag her? Because she'd have to do that, literally drag her.

What's happened to you? Abigail said in despair. You used to be so sweet.

Jo hates being sweet or being thought of as sweet. The world is too wretched for sweet. Look what it did to her poor dad. Look at what it did to her mom: turned her into this

Stepford wife, vessel for the amoebert, clone of boredom itself. He'll probably come out all ready to go, complete with salmon-colored shorts and a polo.

The window seat has a view of the backyard where the mariachi band is setting up. Nana never spares any expense. Waiters swarm, flipping open white cloths and laying them across wooden tables. Out come the drinks and glasses and buckets of ice. A popcorn machine is rolled into one corner. The band tunes up, sending discordant notes into the maple canopy. Arriving guests hurry down the driveway and exclaim over the fun decorations and frozen tequila shots and the chipper band. Children rush the popcorn machine. It's all so delinquent. Especially when people all over the world are starving.

We give a lot, is Abigail's typical defense to this accusation. She's a vice president for the family foundation, always poring over grant requests and agonizing over scholarships. Still, that doesn't justify parties like this.

Jo waits as long as she reasonably can, calculating when her mother might notice her absence, from when she might start to get annoyed to when she'll definitely be seething. It's around then that Ellie texts she's arrived, and Jo dashes downstairs to find her.

The noise of glasses clinking and laughter fills the hall and rooms. All the guests are clad in cheery colors per the invitation's request. Jo herself is in a rust-orange linen dress and cream flats that Abigail chose at Ann Taylor. The hideous outfit is part of the Ellie bargain. Jo stitched up a cool headscarf to give the outfit some 1960s punch, but Abigail found the Pride rainbow in the patchwork and went ballistic about how this is no time to make a statement and what does she think and how could she and why must she always.

She never actually *does*, Jo retorted, because she's never actually allowed to.

Things look up now that Ellie's here. They grab canapés and virgin daiquiris and park themselves in a corner. They mock how everyone's dressed, especially Robert's slacks patterned with bright red lobsters, a nod to Nana's love of the Cape. He still looks boring: no pattern on the planet can save him. They mock each other's awful looks, too. Ellie's trapped in a silk top with a coupe-cigarette skirt, and her mom's taken a curling iron to her long brown hair, which is usually in braids. It's even pinned back with glittery barrettes. Jo hates how they have to fake who they are just to stand in this room with all these people. Maybe everyone's faking. Maybe when they go home they'll rip off their designer dresses and glinting jewelry and dance around like drunk ape-creatures, hooting and bellowing.

Never Nana and Pops, though. They're themselves to the bone. They hold court beneath the room's centerpiece, a giant portrait of Pops's great-grandfather who lost a leg in a skirmish during the Civil War. The painting shows the wounded colonel collapsed on a cot, saber heroically gripped in his fist, gazing resolutely at the Union flag billowing beyond the open tent flaps. In the shadows to the left, a medic in a white apron waits with a saw. Beneath this dramatic scene, Pops holds forth in his peach summer suit, waving a gin and tonic as he regales his audience with a story about a golf ball in a swamp. Nana and Pops are über-rich and influential, so people are always willing to listen, no matter how boring he gets.

"I can't believe you own a house," Ellie whispers. "We should have parties."

Jo hadn't thought of that.

"Andrew could drive. We could bring Erin, and Tania, and Di-e-go." Ellie singsongs the last, nudging Jo suggestively.

Jo twists out of reach, embarrassed. She got together with Diego at a party at the end of the year. They were sort of boozy, but still. He pushed up her sleeve and examined her scarred arm, and she wowed him with her crazy grandmother rake-attack story. They talked about horror movies for ages. She had to explain why the last *Halloween*s were so brilliant and what Jamie Lee Curtis was doing for the genre, but that was OK, it was a blip in an otherwise giddy night of making out. Then school ended and he went to the Cape. They've texted a few times, they follow each other on Instagram, that's it.

"I guess it would be cool to see him again," she says, feigning casualness. "But *Tania*?"

"OK, maybe not Tania."

"I should think not." Tania dumped Ellie so hard, Ellie cried for days.

"We could milk the goats, learn how to make goat cheese," Ellie sighs. "I wish we could just live there."

"Me, too," Jo agrees, because she's supposed to, but she doesn't really feel it. The house isn't a place for romantic parties and farming bliss. It was left to her because of her dad. It's imbued with the terribleness of everything that happened, and now, with the sadness of Gammy being dead, too.

Ellie should know this; it stings that she seems so oblivious.

But then again, of course Ellie sees the house as just a house. Jo's hardly ever mentioned Gammy or any of that stuff. Ellie doesn't carry the story of Jo's dad the way Jo does, a jagged lump in the throat, a sickness in the belly. It's really not her fault, so Jo rushes to suggest they could make maple syrup and skinny-dip in the pond, and Ellie says they could have miniature donkeys and potbellied pigs, and they grow the farm into a sanctuary filled with unwanted animals where people who hate the world can also go live and work and never have to go to parties like this one ever again. The cake gets wheeled out and Nana blushes and protests all the laudatory speeches, and then everyone gets refills, laughs turn to cackles, and the room gets unbearably hot. Ellie notices six texts from her brother, who's been double-parked down the street for a while and is threatening to call her an Uber. She dashes off, along with the rest of the now dispersing crowd. A dense weight settles in Jo's head, a yearning to be outside, away, alone.

As usual, tension erupts at the end of the night when the guests are all gone. Nana looks frazzled and undone by the long evening and too much champagne. Pops nods off in a corner, eyes flying open at every shift in tone. Abigail, the one under attack, holds a rigid pose, unlit cigarette in one hand, china cup of chamomile in the other.

"That woman leaves you the house, but there are people living there," Nana rants. "And to think the trust is for these strangers—it's a slap in the face, is what it is. Of course we told Henry about it! He can help!"

Henry's one of Pops's geezer golf buddies. He used to own a law firm. Nana and Pops told him about Jo's inheritance during the party, and Abigail's furious at this broaching of private family matters with "that old fart." But what she's really angry about, Jo knows, is Nana interfering at all.

"That money should be in trust for Jo's college," Nana insists, "not for strangers!"

"It was Maureen's to do with as she liked," Abigail says. "We don't even know how much money there is, anyway."

"Well, it should be Jo's."

"For God's sake, Mom, it's not like Jo *needs* it," Abigail snaps. "She can go to college six times over if she wants!"

"That's beside the point."

Pops grunts from his chair, and everyone turns. "We just wanted to help, honey."

"She apparently doesn't need our help," Nana retorts

bitterly, then swings back to Abigail. "How can you go there in your condition?"

Abigail chokes on her tea. "My *condition*? Is this the 1800s?"

"You shouldn't be traveling. It's not as if there's anything there worth keeping, anyway."

"It's not about that."

"You always went on about the state of that house. What about the dust, the dirt?" Nana expounds. "What if there's mold? You need to think of the baby!"

"Oh, so now I'm not thinking of the baby."

"Please, darling, I'm trying to help."

"You don't want to help," Abigail says icily. "You want me to do what *you* want, that's it. But I want to go see the house. I want to know what's going on up there. It's my right."

"Well," Nana straightens in her chair, "it's actually Jo's right, isn't that so?"

"That's why she's coming with me!"

"Despite the risk of another breakdown?"

Nana drops this small bomb with extreme calm, injecting all the awful layers of meaning in her delivery. Abigail stiffens, struck hard, and for once, nothing comes out of her open mouth.

Jo is mortified. Nana's referring to last year, when someone brought an old newspaper article to school and passed it around and then everyone knew about her dad, and they whispered and stared when Jo the Amber Alert girl came down the hall. Then came the gross rumors that her dad had molested her in the motel. Going to school became intolerable. She retreated to her room and closed the door. She lay in her bed with the shades down, refusing to get up or even speak. Abigail was frantic. That was when she booked Dr. Coletti the first time.

Recalling all that worry, Jo feels bad for her mom getting guilted by Nana.

"I don't even think about all that anymore," Jo says. They both look at her, startled. "I want to go. Dr. Coletti would agree. He always said I should face my past, not hide."

He actually advised her to put the past behind her, but Jo knows a call to Protestant boldness will appeal, and like clockwork Nana succumbs. She can hardly exhort Jo to run like a coward. She switches tactics. "But Pops and I will miss you awfully. If you don't come to Wellfleet now, you won't have another chance this summer."

"I wouldn't come anyway because of art camp."

"Oh, for heaven's sake, you're always so busy," Nana says, an extra dig at Abigail for overscheduling her child.

Jo drops her own bomb. "Anyway, like you said, Mom shouldn't go alone in her condition."

Nana's eyes narrow, sussing an impenetrable alliance, a losing battle. Jo feels kind of proud. It's not every day she teams up with her mom against Nana.

"Well, you're an adult," Nana sighs at Abigail, implying that her adulthood is far from ideal. "But a reasonable person would hire someone to take care of it all, from a distance, and be done with it."

"I can manage." Abigail takes a last sip and sets down her cup. "I just need to see the house, that's all. So I can be ready."

It's my house, Jo yearns to point out. But even in her own head, the argument sounds weak. It isn't hers except on paper. It's just a symbol, a way to dream of getting away, of being grown up and free. She doesn't even want to be free there. She wants to be in Paris or Rome, somewhere magnificent and truly far away.

Abigail kisses Nana on the cheeks. "I hope you had a nice birthday."

"It was magical until all this."

"Oh, stop." Abigail sighs. "Jo, you have everything? Let's go. We have to wake up Robert," she says, her voice turning cold.

"Now, you leave him alone," Nana chides. "You're lucky he puts up with you at all."

"Thanks," Abigail says flatly, and steps out the door.

On the patio, Robert stirs. He never partakes of family conversations, he just waits on the periphery like a chauffeur. Abigail approaches him and Jo can tell from her stance that the ride home will be the same old, same old, Why can't you ever back me up, how can you say it's not your business?

"All her life, she's been so difficult," Nana complains, hugging Jo tightly. "It just breaks my heart."

As far as Jo can tell, Nana's heart isn't so much broken as

bent out of shape because Abigail won't follow commands the way everyone else does.

"Happy birthday, Nana," Jo says, and hurries out into the night.

THREE

She's in pajamas, bare feet rooted to the floor. It's dark. Something's wrong.

Run, Jo-Jo! her daddy hollers. Run!

The air rustles softly. It sounds like paper flapping. She peers into the dark. There's something there, on the far side of the room. Not paper, she understands, her head muddy with sleep.

Wings.

Run! her daddy begs, but she can't make her body work right. He's so far away now. He's too far. Heaviness floods her. She can't move. She opens her mouth wide, wider—

Jo starts awake, rigid with terror, mouth wide open. Her eyes rove the room, but there's nothing here, nothing to run from. The night-lights cast beams across the carpet, the walls, the locked closet door. Her jagged breaths fill the silence.

She forces herself to turn over, sit up. She switches on the lamp. She stares around, ordinariness gradually asserting itself. The beanbag where she whiles away hours dreaming of another life. All the crap on her desk, school stuff she still hasn't cleaned up since June, empty seltzer cans. Her messy walls tacked all over with photos and memorabilia and her favorite horror movie posters, Michael Myers's white mask looming right over her bed. You watch too many of those movies, Abigail always criticizes. No wonder you have bad dreams.

Jo hasn't had one in ages, actually. She drags her blanket over to her beanbag and curls up there. Her whole body's taut, a spring about to explode. *It's just a dream*, she insists to herself. It makes sense she'd get nightmares again now, because of the house, because she's thinking about her dad so much. *You're just processing.*

That's the word Dr. Coletti used. She can't remember the awful things that happened because she was so little, but that doesn't mean they didn't affect her. She witnessed her daddy have a mental breakdown, after all. And then her family fell apart because of it. The dreams help her process the trauma.

Dr. Coletti told her once that trauma is carried in the body like an ember. One spark, and the ember goes up in flames. The image fits with the hot, metallic taste in her mouth now, the feeling of being all shook up inside. She can still smell the dream, weirdly. It's a cold, dark smell, like dirt. Her dad's shrill yells echo in her head. She feels sick, weak, like in the dream when she can't move. It's so real, like it's still happening even though she's awake.

It's frightening that her dad maybe felt this exact same way when he was losing his mind.

Dr. Coletti insisted the dreams didn't mean she'd turn out the same, but he just didn't get how real they felt, no matter how much Jo tried to explain. She learned pretty quickly to stop trying, and after five sessions he told her mom therapy was no longer necessary.

I'm so glad you saw him! Abigail proclaimed. Now maybe you can put all that behind you once and for all.

If only Jo were more like her mom, able to just sail right on as if nothing had happened. But she gets pulled back every time she looks in the mirror, sees her dad in her big brown eyes and mop of curls and tendency to plumpness. She can't help the creeping fear that one day, she'll be wide awake when she sees something flitting by, that she'll hear whispers, the crackle of wings.

And then someone will find out and lock her away, just like her mom did to him.

He got out eventually, she reminds herself dryly.

She's getting hungry, but the notion of moving through the still, dark house is too much to bear. She stares at her door, listening. The house is dead quiet. She travels through the rooms in her mind, her bare feet padding the gleaming wood floors, rounding the furniture with its tidy, folded throws. The tall windows give onto the dark night, where anyone could be crouched, watching. Like in that scene with Drew Barrymore in the kitchen, in the first *Scream*. If only Jo hadn't watched the kill count on YouTube first. But she can still appreciate the groundbreaking shock. There hasn't been anything quite like it since.

Thinking of the movie takes the edge off her tension, and she's able at last to drag her eyes away from the door. She wanted to put a lock on it, but her mom and Robert refused. It's good they did. She needs to get over this fear of the night, or she truly will end up like her dad. His illness, after all, started in his own wild imagination. For years he spun bedtime stories about children whisked to a magical, sunny place where fairies with golden eyes and dragonfly wings danced through fields and rivers and sang up into the trees. Jo-Jo loved those stories so much, and they made her daddy so happy when he told them. Sometimes she feels guilty, like she should have foreseen how they'd ruin him, destroy their whole family. Looking back, she can recognize the bits that weren't quite right, when the fairies didn't seem so benevolent after all. He'd tell her to watch out or they'd steal her away. She had to be aware of any spills or tracks around the house, because fairies were messy, and this was one way to tell if they were around. It was scary but fun, like a Halloween game. It's sad to think she was actually participating in his burgeoning illness, maybe even reinforcing it.

And then it happened, he unraveled completely, and the stories turned to horror and madness. *You have to hide, Jo-Jo,* he whispered frantically, ushering her into the tent. *Hide so the little ones don't find you!* Those were fairies that had turned evil, and they were out to get her. Jo was so scared she started to cry. He covered her mouth, hissing, *Be quiet so they don't hear!* She pressed against his chest, picturing small, winged figures with deformed, drooling faces and giant hungry eyes. She doesn't know what he saw in his own head. Whatever it was, he was terrified. His arm lay so tight across her chest she couldn't breathe. His eyes were wide, jittery, the whites glistening in the semi-darkness.

She hates remembering him like that. None of it was real, but he believed it so utterly.

Maybe Dr. Coletti was right, maybe she won't turn out the same as her dad. Her dreams leave her feeling gross, but she knows they're just dreams. And that's what counts.

She sighs, rolls off the beanbag. There's no way she can fall back asleep, so she might as well make use of the time. Her latest sewing project is laid out on the carpet, and she sifts through the fabric she hasn't used yet. The thing she's working on is dark, made from old black stockings, linen she dyed with wine and coffee, and a frayed skull T-shirt from when she was eleven. She basted the skull part to an indigo scarf her dad gave her years ago, which seems fitting. She's not sure what she's doing. Maybe she'll turn it into a skirt, or it can hang in front of her door if it gets long enough, like an extra barrier.

She spreads the fabric pieces out, considering which to use. They're mostly dark blues and grays from various clothes she picks up at thrift stores. There's also some black denim from an old pair of her own jeans, stamped with tree shapes in faded silver acrylic. She chooses the ones she wants, pins them in place around the central skull image, and starts sewing. The needle moves swiftly, joining the swatches with tidy, soothing rows all around the skull. She's been making a lot of dark, broody pieces like this. Ever since her dad died, she's been preoccupied with death. The finality of it. The black end, the nothing. She has a habit of closing her eyes and trying to feel being dead. She empties her mind as much as she can, hollowing out the dark spaces, emptying, breathing, but there are always thoughts floating by in the darkness, like the squirming lines under a microscope slide. They never stop. They are the basic proof of life, these mismatched errant images and words. No matter how still she lies, no matter how black her clothing, how filmy and gauzy and soft (clothes of a long-dead person, lying in stillness, in darkness), the thoughts come.

Her dad, before he died, lay in a white hospital bed. His eyes were vacant, staring. All the life was gone from him and the room hummed and beeped and whirred. If he had thoughts flitting through the dark bowl of his mind, there was no way to know. His huge wood-carver hands lay docile on the folded sheets. When she touched his hand once, it twitched, as if it sensed her. But his face did not move, and she could not know if the thought of her, *Jo-Jo*, had sparked through the darkness.

She told Abigail that she wants to be buried in a mushroom shroud to give back to the earth and not take up space. Don't be ridiculous, Abigail said. She asked why Jo can't be normal, why must she talk about dying, and couldn't she just wear some color for once.

Jo's answers were: I'm just not, Because I must, and No. She told Abigail she'd better be prepared because she herself was definitely going into a mushroom shroud: she'd suggested it to Robert, and he liked the idea because it was economical. Snap.

She knots the last few stitches and bites off the thread, drags the sewn collage away from the scattered mess of fabric. Alone out on the floor, it looks vaguely sinister. Like a shroud, she realizes, amazed. She can save it and leave instructions to be wrapped in it, then the mushroom one. Or maybe she can sew in the spores herself.

She busies herself for some moments imagining a company that provides personalized mushroom shrouds. They could be printed with images from the dead person's life, or embroidered with passages from their diaries. *Ashes to ashes*, she thinks. She likes that phrase. Her family's not religious at all, though they went to church regularly when she was little, because that's what you do.

Her dad's voice wells up through the clutter of her thoughts: *God does not love the little ones.*

The memory is sharp, clear. They were in the tent in the motel. She strains to remember more, but all she sees are her arms reaching up to hug her daddy because he was sad. *I'm sorry, Jo-Jo*, he said, over and over, because her arm hurt and it made her whimper. When he changed the bandage, she looked away, eyes squeezed shut.

It wasn't like that all the time, though. They played cards on the smooth blue floor to the lulling sound of the ocean, and she watched lots of TV. She got to eat popcorn, Pop-Tarts, chocolate bars, and hot dogs with ketchup so she'd get a vegetable. She stayed up as late as she wanted, fell asleep when she was tired. It might have been just an odd, fun camping-in-a-motel trip, except the whole time, there was an Amber Alert and everyone was searching for them. It's so sad, because all her dad wanted was to protect her. When the police finally broke in, he refused to let Jo go. *It's not safe!* he screamed, keeping her tucked behind his legs. She can still see his blue-striped pajamas and big hairy feet.

She smooths the shroud and carefully rolls it up. She feels exhausted now. It's three a.m., and there's no use looking backward. Dr. Coletti used to say, It's in the past. He made it sound so simple, as if the whole story were something tangible, in a box labeled "Past." Things did get better for her dad, she has to remember that. Even though he died so young, it's like his girlfriend, Sue, said, Jo mustn't grieve because his life was made complete when she came back into it. He died happy, and Jo must hang on to that fact.

She gets back in bed, leaving one light on in addition to the night-light, in case she has the dreams again. She lies still, focusing on keeping her eyes open, which she's discovered makes them heavy with sleep all the sooner. She finds herself wondering how Sue's doing, still chain-smoking or finally quit, and if she's still in the same house where her dad lived those last years of his life. Jo rarely got to see him because he'd "ended up in New Haven," which was how Abigail put it, as if he'd taken a wrong turn. It was so far that they'd meet at a rest stop halfway. Abigail waited in the car while Jo and her dad ate at McDonald's, sitting across from one another, divided by the linoleum smoothness. *My beautiful girl!* he called her, every time, embarrassing her because he spoke so loud. She got to go all the way to his house just once, for his birthday. She can see in her mind's eye the tidy green lawn with the plastic outdoor set, her father perched proudly on a chair under the umbrella, telling her about his job at Home Depot. Sue cooked on the grill and the three of them ate out there next to the potted plants interspersed with garden figurines of little children carrying flower baskets. Her dad wore a loud Hawaiian shirt, though he'd never been to Hawaii, and awful white shorts, stiff and new. He had blocky, hairy legs, huge feet in a pair of rubber flip-flops. At the end of the meal, he lit a cigar. When he fell ill, a rapid-moving cancer that depleted him, he stopped going places. They spoke on the phone, then she went to the hospital once, and then, so quickly, he was gone.

Jo wishes she could have sewn him a mushroom shroud. He's in a coffin, stone-cold still right in this moment as she lies in her bed, breathing, wishing. She wonders if he did this, too, when he got scared of the things in his head. If he lay awake at night the way she does, with the lights on. She stares and stares, forcing her eyes to stay open till at last, her thoughts become incoherent and slow, like being dragged through syrup, and sleep finally comes.

FOUR

A package arrives from the lawyer with papers Jo has to sign and return, which makes her feel important. There are a ton of documents, a copy of the will, and a sealed envelope addressed to Jo in sloping cursive. The will lists everything Jo is going to inherit when she's eighteen: 190 acres, farmhouse and outbuildings, and all possessions therein. It names the tenants who live there and should stay on: Tom Pierson and Hattie McDougal. Mr. Pierson is named as Hattie's guardian.

"Are you going to see what's inside, already?" Abigail urges.

Jo doesn't want to open the envelope in front of her mom, but she can't find a way to refuse. Abigail is right there, going through all the documents line by line. Reluctantly, Jo slides the opener through, making a neat tear. There's a single folded sheet inside. She withdraws it, hunching to hide its contents from Abigail, who's craning her neck, practically falling over the table.

"Come on, Jo," her mom cries impatiently. "What does it say?"

The letter's about as weird as Jo might have expected:

Dear Josephine:

If you are reading this, it means I am dead, which means you now own the Lavoie house and land. It'll come as a shock, seeing as we have nothing between us other than your father, and the loss of him to your world near destroyed me. You've had the wrong of it all these years, it's just plain fact. You'll need to face up to that now. You are the Lavoie, and your place is here.

Don't you dare take this responsibility lightly. Don't think you can sell and walk away. There is down and dirty work to be done here, necessary work. If I had someone else to ask, I would, but all there is is you. The house has to stay in the family. Ask my friend Edie if you have questions, or Tom and Hattie, but in the end the work is yours alone.

Tom can run the farm, but don't you forget he'll never belong. Tom is guardian of Hattie because you are too young to name. I expect you to care for Hattie as if she were your own sister. You are to be patient and kind and you are never to abandon her, for she is Cherished.

There will come a time when what must be done, must be done. You remember these words

from me, and you remember them well: You have
no choice.

    Gammy

"What did I say?" Abigail huffs, tossing the letter onto the table. "Crazy as a sack of cats!"

But Jo can tell the letter's disturbed her mother. How could it not? *Responsibility* and *down and dirty work* make Jo nervous: she has no clue how to farm or take care of animals. And then she's supposed to take care of Hattie? It makes no sense.

Abigail gets more riled as the letter sinks in. "What is she thinking: 'responsibility'! As if my daughter's going to move to some grubby little farm in the middle of nowhere and drive a tractor and kill chickens? Necessary work, my ass!"

Jo giggles a little, enjoying her mom's outrage.

"You think it's funny? You know what she did once? Called me out to watch her chop off a rooster's head! My God, the blood everywhere and the poor thing banging around in a bucket! I can still hear it!"

"Ugh," Jo shudders.

"And then to go and burden you with this *girl*—I mean, of all things! You do *not* have to take care of her, do you understand?"

Jo is relieved, though she also feels guilty seeing as how Gammy truly expected her to. "What do you think she meant at the end—the part about 'what must be done'?"

"Who cares? You're a kid in school: What was she thinking?"

Jo wishes she could be as dismissive as her mom. The words bother her, they sneak under her skin and stay there, scratching at her. *What must be done. No choice.* The words bring back her dreams: Gammy's rage, her father's hoarse shouting.

Jo swallows, choking down the anxious lump in her throat. The letter doesn't make any sense. Gammy was nuts, just like her father. Jo's only down and dirty work is to make sure she doesn't end up the same.

She wants to keep the letter to read again later but doesn't want her mom to notice, so instead, she folds it back into its envelope and sticks that inside the manila folder with the other documents. She snaps a rubber band around the folder and drops it on the To Vermont pile in the foyer.

Abigail goes into a frenzy packing for the trip. She piles her clothes in rows on one of the guest room beds. She shifts items from one pile to another, or onto the Do Not Take pile on the other bed. She lines up sandals. Her feet are too swollen for shoes.

"I'll need boots," she laments. "I have to go shopping. Dammit."

"Boots," Robert scoffs. "What do you need boots for? It's July."

"It's a farm," she retorts, scathing.

Robert loiters in the doorway or in the hall, peers over her shoulder as she scribbles lists. Jo senses his increasing animosity toward this trip, mostly because it excludes him and involves knowledge he doesn't possess.

"You should take the Audi," he proposes magnanimously one morning. "It's safe."

"The Audi would get wrecked on those roads. I'll take the Subaru."

Robert tries to recover. "That Subaru's already a wreck!"

"They last forever. I'll have it tuned up."

The Subaru once belonged to Abigail and Enzo: they drove it from Vermont all those years ago. She drove him back and forth to the mental institution in it. He kidnapped Jo in it. It's like a time capsule of a previous life, complete with jam stains and scratches and Dora stickers. It stays parked in the spare garage at Nana and Pops's. Abigail refuses to get rid of it, arguing it's a good car and Jo can use it for college and why create waste and think of the planet.

"Don't blame me if it breaks down," Robert warns.

"Why on earth would I blame you?"

Her feigned surprise, the nasty undertone. Robert exiting in a huff.

These flare-ups exhaust Jo. Robert blames it on hormones, pampers Abgail with sugary crepes and massages so she collapses and says sorry, and then the whole circus starts again. It's amazing that her mom can't see his excruciatingly boring patience is a form of control, further enmeshing her in a marriage she can't actually want. Jo knows her sour moods and cranky remarks aren't just hormonal; the amoebert gives Abigail cover to finally let loose. The reality is she should have listened to Jo, who, even though she was just a kid, knew right away this

42

liaison was a bad idea. She hated Boring Robert the second he strolled in bearing good credit, a cottage on the Cape, and season box seats at Fenway. Abigail, who'd never watched a game in her life, went mad over watching baseball with waiters in attendance. It was embarrassing. Plus, Robert was old, fourteen years older than her mom: ugh.

Abigail insisted he was a perfect match, no pun intended: they'd met teaming up for doubles at the club. Her trust fund had been drained by Enzo's medical care, and Nana and Pops weren't about to replenish without evidence of mended ways. She needed this marriage, Abigail explained. They needed the stability, and Jo needed a father, as if the one in New Haven didn't count.

Nana and Pops were over the moon about Abigail's marvelous new husband. Robert was tall, Teutonic, tan, versus Enzo's robust and unsourced darkness. He was perfectly bland and polite, versus Enzo guffawing at the dinner table. He came complete with two children of his own who might help Jo "come into her own," though how Jo might ever mirror these preppies with white-blond hair and snobby affects, no one could actually define. In those early days, Jo regarded her stepsiblings across the Ping-Pong table, granite counters, the pool. She kept the mass of things between her and them, sure they would eat her alive should she come too close. She'd been only twelve, and they in their teens: mean and dismissive. In hindsight, they were probably equally horrified by this union, but the three of them never got close enough to bond over it. Jo's never even lived with them. Robert Jr. and Natalie were away in boarding school when Jo and her mom moved in, and now they're in college. They show up on holidays, breezing through required parties and dinners and then ducking out early, like strangers who stopped in at the wrong address. Jo envies how they get to do that. She dreams it'll be like that for her one day, just passing through, older, independent, free.

FIVE

The day before they're due to leave, Abigail again calls the law-yer, Nathanael Fletcher, Esq. It's the third time she's tried to reach him, so she comes at the task on edge. She arranges herself at Robert's home office desk and dials on speakerphone. Jo sits in the leather armchair opposite to listen. The man who answers sounds old and frail. He responds to Abigail's brisk introduc-tion with an apology. He was away up north, he explains. His daughter has a cabin up on Lake Memfa-something—Jo can't understand the name—because it was his birthday, and the whole family was there.

Abigail listens to this meandering explanation with undis-guised disapproval. She finally interjects that she has gone over the documents and the house must be sold.

"Well, hmm, I see," he says, switching tack on a long, slow turn. "I understand, but Maur didn't want that, you know."

Abigail widens her eyes at Jo. "Perhaps she didn't," she says, "but we need to sell."

"Nothing can happen till Josephine comes of age," he replies. "She may not feel the same when the time comes."

"Of course she will. What on earth would she want with that house?"

"Maur wanted her to have it."

"I appreciate that, but Maureen is gone."

Jo flinches. There is a silence. She imagines Mr. Fletcher as an ancient man in a sagging suit in a run-down office, his nice family getaway fast receding. Gammy must have been a friend, the way he refers to her.

"The law is the law," he sighs at last. "Josephine will be free to do as she likes when she turns eighteen."

Abigail presses on, asking about the finances, the bills, what if the roof fails, what if the hot-water heater needs replacing. She loops back to the matter of a minor inheriting: Is there anything that can be done to speed things up, do they really have to wait two whole years? And then back to what if the house needs repairs, are there enough funds to cover emergencies, and what if those people have medical needs?

When Robert gets back from work, Abigail lays in about the lawyer's unprofessional attitude, how he seems more concerned with those tenants' interests and not Jo's. Jo loiters in the hallway, spying on them. He pours their cocktails, Abigail's virgin given her condition, which makes her even more testy. Her righteous annoyance turns to flip jokes. She gets merrier and louder, unconsciously mimicking inebriation. Jo is ashamed for her. Ashamed that she married this stuffy, boring guy, and that she decided to have a baby with him after all. Jo's life with them is a suffocating weight on her chest. She doesn't belong here. She just needs to grow up, get away. Two more years: she'll be eighteen and out of the house, never to return.

She slips away to her room, pokes through her open suit-case, remembers there's a pond, and adds her bathing suit. Her dad's satchel is coming, too, stuffed with the skull sewing proj-ect and wads of material she might add to it. The bell and chain are still buried under all that; she can't bring herself to take them out. Her dad never went anywhere without them, they've been in there for a whole generation. Maybe she can find a spot at the house, set up kind of a shrine.

Dr. Coletti would probably approve of that since it's a laying-the-past-to-rest sort of activity. Maybe she'll finally move on, the way he kept saying she was supposed to. She hopes so.

She curls up on her beanbag and texts Ellie a picture of the suitcase and satchel: **pretty much packed.**

Several minutes go by. She grows irritated, wondering where Ellie is, what she's doing. Then Ellie answers: **omg road trip with your mom!**

i know shes totally insane! Jo hesitates, thumbs poised over the screen. She taps: **i'm getting nervous.**

about what?

About everything, she could say. About being there. About what it might make her feel: she's already roiling sick in her

47

belly, every time she thinks about it. Maybe her mom was right, maybe she shouldn't be going. Her whole body is so taut she could just crack to pieces.

i dunno, she types. just all of it.

i wish i could go! i love goats!

Jo sends the goat emoji and a heart. Ellie sends a heart with echo. Jo smiles at the exploding screen, sends a goat with echo. Ellie sends back lol. Jo types that she wishes Ellie could come, then, seeing the words, she realizes it's not true. Swamped by guilt, she quickly deletes the message and says: gotta go.

hattie keeps me up nights worrying what if the door opens. she says airs coming through and whatll we do. its not our work i told her. she checks every day anyway. to be prepared she says.

prepared how. shes scrawny and distresses easy at blood. shell get hurt.

i told her leave it be its nature but she dont listen to me like she did maur. nothings natural she screamed. she screamed a lot. she said she wished i was dead instead of maur. then it was time for weeding and we did that and she was quieter.

later she said she didnt want me dead. We made a pie from raspberries and rhubarb.

maur said shed suffer grief more than me and id need patience. this must be how she meant.

SIX

Abigail drives one-handed and fast in the left lane. They stop three times to pee, Abigail cursing her bladder. The third time, Jo munches on a granola bar while her mom fills the car. The sun beats down on the asphalt. She's in a black lacy tank and a long wraparound she dyed black and stitched with random patterns that ended up looking like bloodstains. Abigail hates it, she calls it her dead-girl skirt. Right now, Jo hates it, too, because the dark material's sucking in the heat, cooking her. She texts a pic to Ellie: i'm dying. She wishes she had Snapchat, but Robert read some article about bullying and that was that, for her own protection. Whatever. She's boiling. She wishes she'd worn her shorts. People park, get out, go in, come out, drive away. Their faces blur. Families, guys, women. Everyone going somewhere, blank faced and sweaty. She wonders if their journeys mean as much. She realizes she must look the same, sticky and grumpy, tucked into a slice of shade under the eave.

"Come on!" her mother calls from the car, waving impatiently.

They do look the same, for sure. No one could ever divine the gravity of their mission, or suss the letter tucked into the old satchel (it's her letter, after all), or the knots in her stomach causing her to throw away the granola bar only half consumed.

"Why do you buy that junk when Robert packed muffins? They're the blueberry ones you like."

"I already had one," Jo reminds her.

"We've still got an hour and a half," Abigail announces, peering at her phone, then comparing what she sees with the car's ancient navigation system.

Jo sinks into her seat, hands tucked under her thighs, grateful for the air-conditioning blasting across her face.

"When we get there," Abigail says, "you let me do all the talking, you understand? I don't want you engaging those people."

"Those people" is how she's come to refer to Gammy's tenants. It has a cold ring to it. Preparation for informing them that in less than two years, they will be sent off into the unknown, homeless and penniless. Jo can't figure how else it will go. Neither Abigail nor Robert will stand for giving them a stipend or finding them a house. But how will they survive? According to the lawyer, they've been living off of Gammy, working the farm in exchange. Jo doesn't think it's right to kick them out, but Abigail is resolute, citing Robert's analysis that there is no advantage to maintaining a subsistence-level farm in Vermont.

Time passes. There is the noise of the AC and occasionally traded phrases about hunger or needing to pee or the temperature. The radio stays off because their tastes lie wildly apart.

They drive and drive. The highway empties and green fills out the landscape. The views are astonishing. The land is lush and endless. The mountains in the distance look purple. Jo stares hard out the window, trying to remember the trip all those years ago with her father. She has a faint image of herself packing her Dora backpack and her dad's loud laughter, but that could be any trip. Of that particular car ride, there's nothing. She imagines herself asleep in the back, her whole body tilted to one side, held by the seat belt, her wiry hair a complete mess the way her dad always left it because he hated her screams when he worked the tangles. She can see this clear as day, because there's a picture in the album of her asleep on some other trip. He'd have been singing as he drove, the way he always did.

"I can't believe there's no traffic," she tells Abigail, to stop the spiral of her thoughts.

"Wait till you see where we're going." Abigail glances at her, adding, "You remember the house, don't you?"

"Some of it," Jo says, put off-balance by her mom opening the topic. It feels like a heavy door swinging open. Her mom standing at the top of the stairs, staring down into the depths.

"You might get upset again, being in that place," Abigail says in her clinical voice. "Are you prepared?"

"I guess."

"We'll only be there a week or so."

"I'll be fine."

"I hope so. I can't take any more drama."

Silence follows. Jo's voice shutters up, sunken. Talking to her mom is futile. It always has been. Abigail flings darts with indifferent precision, clueless as to their effect.

"It's because I care, you know," Abigail blurts, angry, as if the caring is an unwanted burden.

"I know."

"I just want you to be strong."

"I am."

Abigail clamps her lips, staring straight ahead.

Be strong, not like your father, Jo thinks the unspoken. Because this is her mother's deepest worry. That the daughter, who looks the same and sometimes acts the same, will turn out the same: crazy as a sack of cats. Except Abigail's actual worry probably is that then everyone will know, everyone will stare. The gossip. The social torture, relived through the daughter.

Jo turns her face to the landscape rushing by with dizzying speed. If only she could open the door and hurl herself out. Fly into the green and blue, carried by the wind.

They cross the New Hampshire border into Vermont. The welcome center is decorated with pictures of moose and bears. Jo peruses the brochures while her mom goes to pee yet again. She gathers a bunch, unable to resist: a giant corn maze; Cabot cheese; kayaking. Abigail rejoins her, shaking her damp hands to air-dry them. "What are you doing? This isn't a vacation, you know."

Jo leaves the brochures in a pile on top of the shelving.

After about an hour, the phone directs them off the highway onto a route that winds north past fields of new corn, swathes of tilled earth, meadows scattered with grazing cattle under the vast blue sky. Abigail mutters at the phone, checking the screen constantly. She was led off course once in Boston and now has no faith. After what feels like eons, they make a left turn, and there the asphalt road gives way to dirt. The narrow road climbs and drops with alarming pitches. Thick forest on either side darkens their view. There are no other cars. Abigail goes slower. Jo starts to see some houses, different sorts, not like the neighborhoods she's used to. A tidy Cape with a bit of manicured yard, followed by a set-back trailer on blocks surrounded by metal junk, followed by a ranch with a pool. She sees trees nailed with NO TRESPASSING signs and, occasionally, NO HUNTING. They come in and out of the forest, the abrupt changes into bright sunlight causing Jo's eyes to smart. Farms roll away into the distance. At one, some sheep graze with a large white dog in attendance, a Pyrenees. At the end of the driveway is a cute farmstand with a hand-painted, colorful placard listing available wares. It's like something from a storybook. Jo cranes her neck this way and that, taking it all in, wondering if they're going the right way but smart enough not to raise the question with her mom, who's leaning forward, both hands white-knuckled on the wheel, staring without blinking.

At last a small sign indicates they are two miles from Laddston. Jo knows she shouldn't expect too much—Abigail made that clear—but it's still thrilling to see the sign. The road winds up a hill past a farm. A river runs alongside the road, shallow and rocky, sparkling clear.

"Ah, glorious Laddston," Abigail announces. "Hasn't changed a bit."

They roll slowly into the village, if it can be called that. The town hall is a decrepit colonial with peeling pink paint, a dark encroachment of moss creeping up its sides. There's a park next door with a statue in the middle, and a graveyard and little white church next to that. On the left is the Country Store, which looks a little more well-kept, with two gas pumps out front.

"This is it?" Jo says, craning her neck to look all around.

"This is it," Abigail confirms. "Still a pit stop on your way somewhere else. At least that place got a makeover," Abigail points farther down the road. "It used to be a diner, a real hole-in-the-wall."

If Jo were a tourist, she'd be on her way elsewhere, too. At least the diner turned café looks OK, the sort of place she might see back home. Pink lettering on the door reads LOLA'S SWEETS & SANDWICHES. The window's strung with Buddhist flags and plastered with flyers. There's a wicker bench out front with paisley cushions and a drinking bowl for dogs.

Abigail pulls in at the Country Store. They need to stock up on the basics. The big supermarkets are all at least half an hour away, she says, and she doesn't want to have to go after this drive. She gets out, groaning about her back and her feet. She pops the hatch and roots around for shopping bags. Jo waits nearby. Her mom's brisk knowing of this place is both a relief and a source of bewilderment. She's never actually pictured her mom living here that summer, all those years ago. To the point that she knows about the store and supermarkets, to the point that she can identify the changes in the village.

She wonders if her mom is thinking about that time, too. It doesn't seem so. She's got her bags under her arm, and she's waving Jo to come with her on the stocking-up mission.

The store's divided into two areas, one a typical small market, the other woodsy and stocked with souvenir items like honey and syrup and T-shirts with moose on them. Abigail goes up and down the market aisles, methodically filling the minuscule cart with way more than what they'll need. She tells Jo the shelves are way better stocked than they used to be, and they might not have to go to Greensboro at all. Jo hopes they don't. Their pantry at home is ready for a nuclear holocaust, and it looks like Abigail's going to set up Gammy's the same way.

They approach the counter. There's a guy in overalls buying some stuff, so they have to wait. Jo notices an old man in the corner next to the coffee station, sitting on a chair reading a newspaper. He's like a Santa Claus with a puffy gray beard and sizable paunch straining the buttons on his plaid shirt. He examines her up and down over the newspaper, clearly disapproving of her attire. She turns away, her neck stiff with discomfort.

The guy at the counter's taking forever, telling the cashier about a camper van that went over in a ditch and how he had to haul it out and what were they thinking, traveling these roads after rain. The cashier, a stringy-haired girl not much older than Jo, slouches at the register, chewing on her nail and sliding glances. Jo grows aware of how different she looks in her black lacy top and dead-girl skirt. At least the cashier's got multiple ear piercings, too. Finally, the talking guy grabs his bag and heads out. Abigail starts to unload.

"Well, well . . ." An older woman comes up to the register, wiping her hands on her stained apron. She's been chopping up sandwich fixings; there are cutting boards on the back counter, tomatoes and onions and lettuce in piles. "Abigail, is that you?"

Abigail goes still, jar of pasta sauce in hand, then she slowly lowers it to the counter. "Yes, it is. How are you, Edie?"

This must be the friend Gammy mentioned in the letter. Her fingers are bent with arthritis, and her skin's wrinkled and brown from the sun. "Same old, same old," she says. "It was a sad day, Maur's passing. You weren't at the funeral."

"No one informed us about it."

The woman ignores Abigail's frosty tone, peering closely at Jo with bright blue eyes. "And you must be little Jo-Jo, all grown up. You look just like Enzo. Spitting image. He brought you in for sweets all the time, remember?"

Jo shakes her head.

"Not surprised. You were little, and all that happened. So, Maur went and left you the house?"

Jo flushes at the skepticism in her tone. "Yeah. We came to check on it."

There's the noise of rustling paper, then the old guy in the corner mutters, "I'll be damned."

Jo and Abigail turn in surprise. He eyes Jo with an expression of disbelief, then asks Edie, "Is this for real? You're telling me that's the Lavoie?"

"Shut it, Amos," Edie snaps. "It was for Maur to decide."

His bushy white eyebrows go up. He mutters something and snaps the paper up, concealing his face.

"Don't listen to him," Edie dismisses Abigail's incredulous look. "Everyone's been concerned, is all. Now, last time I saw you, this one was on the way. And now another. When are you due?"

"Seven weeks," Abigail says, angrily unloading groceries onto the counter.

"Well, Maur wasn't known for her good timing." The joke is delivered with an odd twist of a smile. Jo isn't sure it's even meant to be funny. "You'll find the house the same, pretty much. Tom and Hattie take proper care. I can come by later and walk you through things."

"It's all right, we can manage."

"As you wish," Edie shrugs.

The cashier scans the groceries, listening with blatant curiosity. Jo wonders what a teenager around here does for fun. Abigail hands the cart off to Jo to park with the others. "The store's well stocked now," she remarks to Edie. "Did you build that campground after all?"

"Nope. We get tourists coming through on their way to Greensboro. Canadians mostly."

"I never understood why the select board said no to that developer. This town could really have taken off."

"They had their reasons."

"Well, it was shortsighted," Abigail mutters.

Jo cringes at her mom's casual criticism. She offers Edie an apologetic look. "We've had a really long drive."

"Travel is never easy," Edie says blandly. "Come by for a visit when you can. I'm always here. Live upstairs."

"OK," Jo says. "Thanks."

Jo picks up the laden grocery bags, studiously avoiding Amos, who's scowling at her over his newspaper. Abigail's silence is huge and furious until they are out of the cashier's earshot at the car.

"You can go see her if you want," Abigail says, every word clipped with anger. "But I can guarantee all she'll tell you is how awful I am. I wasn't at the funeral, my ass!"

"Mom!" Jo exclaims, spinning to see if anyone heard, but they're the only ones around. "What's the matter with you?"

"I don't want to talk about it right now," Abigail snaps.

"Jeez, you brought it up!"

"You don't understand, OK? You don't understand how hard this is for me!"

Abigail pulls out with her hands at five and ten, knuckles white. Jo fixes her stare on the world outside the window.

They pass the little café and a few small ranch houses, and then Laddston is behind them and the trees bend over the road, casting shadows all around.

"It's hard for me, too," Jo says into the whirring air of the enclosed space.

After a moment, Abigail replies, "I know. I'm sorry."

This clipped, short apology is the sum of what Abigail is ever able to offer. Jo shrinks into her seat, Edie's wizened features floating in her mind. She'll go visit, just like she said. She doesn't care about her mom and everything that happened way back in the past; she wants to find out about her own story, about when she was here.

"What did that guy mean, what he said about me?"

"I don't know. Nosy old fart."

"He called me 'the Lavoie,' like Gammy said in the letter. It's weird."

"Trust me, everyone's weird here. Where the hell are we now?" Abigail says, examining the phone map. "It never took this long from town!"

As if on cue, the phone dings and melodiously announces they have arrived at their destination.

"You see? You see?" Abigail exclaims. "I hate this thing. There used to be a yellow house, that's where you'd turn. There's nothing here. Where's the house?"

Jo squints at the screen: there they are, a blinking red dot, surrounded by empty green space. The fields are indeed empty.

Up ahead stands an ancient, collapsed red barn. It seems familiar to Jo, though maybe it's because they've passed a number of ramshackle barns already.

"Maybe it was up there, with the barn," Jo suggests, pointing.

"Maybe."

Abigail inches forward at five miles an hour, hunched and peering right and left. A little ways after the barn they see a rutted dirt road heading off through the meadow and disappearing into woods.

"That's it," Abigail says with relief, turning the steering wheel hand over hand. The dirt road hasn't been graded in a while, and the wheels thud, clattering their teeth. "They must have taken down that house, that's why I got confused. But I remember now. It's a little ways from here. It wasn't so bad in the truck."

Jo flashes an image of her young parents together in a truck, on this road. It seems so impossible.

The car bounces hard, causing Abigail to huff in discomfort. The meadow on either side is dotted with wildflowers, orange, white, purple, so many colors filling Jo with amazement. After several minutes, she sees a wooden bridge up ahead. Jo rolls down the window as they cross, looking down at the water flowing over the rocky bed. It's cold as anything, she suddenly knows: she glimpses her sun-darkened feet distorted in the water, the hem of her dress pulled up, the old brown dog panting on the bank. There is also a part of the river somewhere farther up that's deep enough to swim in, sort of: she'd paddle on her belly, pushing herself along the pebbles with her hands.

She's shocked by the clarity of the memory, as if she were here just recently. This is how it will be, she realizes, memories resurfacing at every turn.

They emerge from the trees into sunlight again, and see at the top of the hill a large, rambling white farmhouse, outbuildings, and a giant red barn.

"I'd forgotten how big it was," Abigail says.

Jo had, too. Not just the buildings, but the land itself rolling away on all sides. One hundred and ninety acres, the will said, a mix of forest and meadows, with river frontage and a pond. It looks endless. It feels like they're the only inhabitants of this big green world.

They climb the hill and roll slowly onto the gravel drive. The tire swing still hangs from the maple over to the left, except the tire is now gone. All that remains is an ancient, frayed rope bending in the breeze. Her dad took to spinning Jo so hard on that tire that she barfed. Chocolate barf, because she'd gorged on candy all the time and no one cared.

Abigail parks in front of the detached garage where Gammy used to keep her Cadillac. Now the garage door stands halfway up, the concrete floor within empty and clean, and visible against the back wall is a tool bench and drawers.

Abigail switches off the engine. "Wow," she says, staring at the house and shaking her head. "It's just . . . wild to be here."

They get out, the car doors slamming loudly in the hot

silence. Jo pulls out her phone from her back pocket to send Ellie some pics.

"Oh my God," she says, staring at the screen in horror. "There's no service here?"

"We're in the middle of nowhere," Abigail points out.

Jo feels rising panic. "Do you think there's Wi-Fi?"

Abigail gives her a bored look, probably happy Jo's being cut off. "Does this place look like it has Wi-Fi? You can go back down the road or to town if you have to text or Instagram, or whatever it is you're doing these days."

"This sucks."

"You wanted to come."

"Whatever." Jo shoves her phone back into her pocket.

There is a sudden quiet after their spat, then the twitters and buzzing of summer, the rustling of leaves. The heat is aggravating after so much time in the air-conditioned car. Jo pulls her hair up off her neck and twists it into a knot. She squints in the sunlight, shading her eyes with her hand. There's no one around. A dirt road leads left, up the slope to a greenhouse and tidy plots of vegetables and flowers: she'd go with Gammy to eat cherry tomatoes right off the vines. To the left of that is a cottage under a stand of pines. Jo remembers the green shutters and low stone wall out front; it hasn't changed.

The day feels heavy with heat and stillness. Their shoes crunch the gravel as they approach the house, which looks dilapidated close up, in need of repairs with paint flaking in strips and some areas just bare wood. There's a screened wraparound porch, the door on the inside wide open. Some chickens peck at the grass around the steps, clucking softly and strutting. Next to the porch, an apple tree shades a picnic table with an unfinished checkers game and an empty pitcher.

"Jesus," Abigail mutters. They stand at the bottom of the sagging wooden stairs. A row of potted geraniums lines the right side, competing with the metal junk strewn on every step. "I'd forgotten how bad this was. Look," she points to a scatter of objects nailed above the screen door: horseshoes, a giant pair of scissors, files, and other unidentifiable objects that look like parts of farm machinery. "Iron's supposed to ward off fairies. You see where your father got it from?"

The iron junk looks sinister to Jo, laid out in such careful rows on every step. "Gammy said never to touch it," she says, remembering.

"And how. She was always checking it was all in place. God forbid you move one little thing!"

Jo can tell from her mom's tone that she must have done just that.

The heat and the silence and the spaces tended by others make Jo feel like an intruder. "Are you sure we can just go in?" she asks.

"It's your house now," Abigail says. She stretches her arms, grimacing at her huge belly. "Get the bags? My bladder's about to go."

Abigail heads up the stairs, grasping the railing and huffing. Jo doesn't want to be left alone out here, nor does she want her mom going in first, though it's too late to stop her. Annoyed, Jo hurries back to the car and pops the trunk, hauls out the two suitcases, her mom's full-size and weighing a ton. She loops the satchel over her shoulder. It bounces against her butt as she drags the suitcases along. Her mom is already inside, the screen door slammed behind her. Jo hauls the suitcases up one at a time, her skirt bunched in her fist so she doesn't trip. She almost yells when she stubs her toe on an old-fashioned weight, the kind with the ring for picking it up. *Don't touch or move anything!* Gammy's warning echoes in her mind, one of the many weird, strict rules Jo had to follow: No loud laughing. No shouting. No going anywhere alone. Everything feels exactly the same, down to the rickety screen door, which is stuck. Jo has to put aside the bags to dislodge it, and when it finally flies open, it almost sends her falling backward.

She dumps the bags on the porch. Her burst of activity finished, silence dominates once again. There is a desolate feel to the place, maybe just because she knows it was Gammy's, and Gammy is gone. To the right of the door is a wicker sofa with faded cushions where Gammy must have sat to read the paper; there's a pile of them stacked on the side table. A calico cat lies on a hook rug so old the colors have all gone gray. It stares up, then utters a single meow. Jo crouches to pet it, but it takes off, expertly weaving through furniture legs to vanish around the corner.

She stands up, disappointed by the rejection. Farther down the porch, another wicker table is piled with magazines and more newspapers. Empty boxes lie strewn on the floor. A pair of work boots are parked on newspaper. They look huge. They could have been Gammy's; Jo remembers her as imposingly tall. A memory floats up, hazy like an old movie reel: Gammy with her long gray braids, a baby goat peeking over her arm. *Can I hold it?* Jo-Jo begged, and the goat was lowered into her embrace, warm and snuggly. It happened here on this porch, Jo is pretty sure.

She steps into the kitchen, and recognition rises with the same clarity as when she crossed the river. The giant wood-stove on its brick platform, the raggedy hobbyhorse nearby. The shelves with their rows of knickknacks, vintage farm stuff, an ancient butter churn. The lino floor that she skidded on when her feet were wet, rushing toward the yellowed rusty fridge. She'd fling open the door to the interior freezer, root around for those Welch's grape juice concentrate cans. She'd make a whole pitcher and sit out on the porch drinking it. Like the pitcher on the picnic table now.

She opens the fridge. It's stocked with some greens and veg-etables. The door's filled with suspiciously crusty condiment jars and bottles, along with two mason jars of syrup. Gammy would pour so much syrup on the pancakes, it formed a moat around them. She made the syrup herself from her own maple trees.

Jo gingerly opens the ancient toaster oven where she'd cook her Pop-Tarts. It's still filled with burned bits and crumbs. Gammy and her dad let her spend her days like a wild animal, sleep whenever she wanted, eat whatever she liked. It's obvious now that her dad picked up his terrible habits from Gammy, the lassitude about schedules and treats and cleaning that drove Abigail nuts. Jo can still remember their fights over laundry piles and dishes.

Nothing's changed, even with Gammy gone. Dirty dishes sit on the table, which is speckled green lino with silver legs, a retro treasure that would go for a fortune these days. Jo would trace animal shapes out of the specks while she ate her cereal in the morning. At the deep porcelain sink, she discovers more unwashed plates and silverware, crusted with old food. The lawyer said Tom Pierson lives in the cottage; maybe this is the girl Hattie's mess. She runs the tap and drinks deeply from her cupped hands.

"Jo? Is that you?" her mom calls. "For heaven's sake, do you see toilet paper anywhere?"

Jo looks around, the map of the house forming in bits and pieces in her mind. Her mom must be in the bathroom off the kitchen, the one in the narrow corridor just past the fridge.

She finds the pantry in the hallway leading to the dining room. Rows of jars line the shelves, neatly labeled: pickles, peaches, tomatoes. On the floor there's torn plastic wrap with two rolls left. She passes it to her mom through the door held ajar. The bathroom is poorly lit and unadorned, the purely functional space of a busy farmer. Dirt crusts the broken grout and tiles. There's no curtain to the shower stall, which serves as storage for an assortment of buckets and other odds and ends.

Back in the kitchen, Abigail stands with hands on her hips, taking it all in. "I can't even imagine," she says. "How the hell do we clean all this out?"

"We have two years," Jo says a little snarkily.

"It'll take ten!" Abigail retorts.

Jo follows reluctantly as her mom circles the kitchen, then moves down the hall to the dining room, a heavy, dark place with built-in cabinets displaying china crockery and figurines in rows. The faded wallpaper between the cabinets shows bucolic scenes of trees and cows. Ancient framed photos have gone yellow on the walls, on shelves, on the sideboard. The mahogany table is covered with a thick blanket to protect its surface. Jo is sure they never once ate here, and probably no one ever did; Gammy was hardly the type to host parties.

Abigail pushes open the lace curtains, loosing a cloud of dust motes into the streaming sunlight. A ratty ottoman sits under the window next to yet another butter churn.

"This has to go," Abigail frets. "This has to go." She picks up a photo, then sets it back down in despair. "This is worse than I remembered."

Jo is kind of enjoying how much her mom hates this house. It's the opposite of their house in Newton with its pristine white pillows and folded throws and shining pine floors. On the other hand, the stress probably isn't good for the amoebert. Abigail's cheeks are a high pink, her gait tight and stiff, and now she suddenly freezes, gesturing Jo to do the same.

Jo becomes aware of the unmistakable murmur of a TV. Abigail widens her eyes, finger to her lips.

She goes first, which Jo now doesn't mind.

They exit the dining room into the house's central hall. The front door at the far end stands wide open, sunlight pouring across a faded hook rug. There's an umbrella stand in the corner next to an ornate mirror. The screen door creaks on its hinges in the lofting breeze. Stone steps lead to the yard, a rich green expanse dotted with daisies. A pair of flip-flops has been kicked off on the floor, one upside down. Jo surmises from the flowery pattern that they must belong to the girl, Hattie. She wonders where the girl sleeps—surely not alone in this house, now that Gammy's gone? But does that mean Tom Pierson stays here as well?

Her mom moves forward and Jo tiptoes behind her. The TV noise gets louder as they approach. They edge up to the doorway adjacent to the dining room and peek in. It's as Jo remembers: the brown shag rug, the dog bed in the corner, the old photographs in their dusty frames. The behemoth TV in the tall walnut cabinet has been replaced with a flat-screen, which is jarring as it doesn't fit with Jo's notion of Gammy Maureen.

Sesame Street is playing. A girl watches from the old plaid couch—Jo feels a reflexive itch on her legs, recalling the scratchy wool upholstery. The girl's surrounded by pillows like a bird in a nest, focused on the screen with rapt attention, her mouth open, a doll tucked tight to her chest. Her arms are skinny and bony, her knees knobby bumps under the faded blue sundress. Her long, stringy brown hair hangs uncombed around her narrow face, making her staring eyes look huge. The lawyer said she was thirteen, but she looks no more than ten, she's so malnourished and small. Jo exchanges a look with her mom, who is equally appalled. Still, judging by the detritus, Hattie isn't lacking for food. A scattering of crusty plates litters the coffee table along with crushed seltzer cans, cups, and utensils.

"Hello," Abigail announces.

The girl jumps in terror. She's got the biggest green eyes Jo's ever seen. She disentangles herself from the blankets and leaps from the couch as if to dash out.

"Please, stop," Abigail puts out her hand. "It's OK. I'm Abigail, and this is Jo."

The girl's arms tighten around the doll, a creepy, old-fashioned thing made of cloth and porcelain. It's got no clothes and the painted hair's almost all worn off. The huge blue eyes click with every motion. Jo wonders if the doll can make cries. *Mama. Mama.* It's unsettling, seeing as Hattie should be too old for dolls.

"Weren't you expecting us?" Abigail asks. "Didn't Mr. Fletcher tell you?"

Silence.

"Can you speak?" Jo asks, perplexed.

The girl nods, staring and tense, flight-ready.

"Are you Hattie?"

"Yes."

"Hattie," Abigail repeats. "I've never met anyone with that name. It's nice."

Hattie's staring hard at Abigail's belly, clutching her doll. "Is that a baby inside?"

Abigail exchanges a quick look with Jo. "Yes, it's a baby."

Hattie chews her lip, eyes narrowed, clearly distressed. She looks Jo up and down, fixes on the embroidered patterns down the skirt. Jo squeezes her mom's arm, and Abigail says, "Is Mr. Pierson here?"

"He's gone to town."

"Can you show us around?"

Hattie glances back at the screen. "I have spelling."

Abigail is thrown for a loop. "You don't know spelling?"

"It's twenty more minutes," Hattie ignores her, backing away and sinking onto the couch. "I can't miss it."

"You don't go to school?" Jo asks.

Hattie casts her a suspicious look. "I'm homeschooled. It's allowed."

A flat, rehearsed statement, meant to put off anyone who might pry. Jo's skin creeps with discomfort.

"She can stay here," Abigail tells Jo quietly. "Let's go."

Hattie doesn't even look up, immersed once again in the bright chatter of the show.

They retreat to the hallway. "That was weird," Jo whispers.

"Tell me about it," Abigail whispers back.

They just stand there a moment, as if the encounter has left them rudderless. Finally, Jo says, "Should we put our bags upstairs?"

"I guess. We can look around after. Can you get them?"

Her mom's milking this pregnancy for all it's worth. Jo trudges back to the porch to get the suitcases. The cat has returned, and this time it doesn't run off, just watches from its perch on the wicker sofa. Jo drags the suitcases back through the house, and they set up the stairs, which still have the ancient runner nailed to them, the scrollwork pattern almost invisible from the passage of time. At the top is a landing with a white railing. A number of balusters are splintered into pieces, as if something crashed there. The hole's been patched with a piece of cardboard, and Abigail rolls her eyes, muttering about repairs and getting the house to code.

Gammy Maureen's room off to the right is the largest, with its own bathroom. It's just how a dead person's room should look, with the curtains drawn, the bed stripped with a comforter folded on top, and a layer of dust everywhere. There are bookshelves and dressers and a small sofa and chair and a multitude of carpets. The armoire is still full of clothes, causing Abigail to tsk disapprovingly. Jo spies Gammy's wooden cane propped against the wall, and she turns it in her hand, studying the carved wolf-head handle that she used to stroke and talk to like it was a pet. Gammy limped because her leg got mauled fighting off a bear. That's what she said, anyway, chuckling at Jo's amazement. It can't have been true, Jo surmises now with a touch of indignation that she was tricked.

On the round bedside table, Jo finds a framed photograph of her dad when he was young, grinning in overalls, holding a pony by the halter. Jo imagines Gammy here in her last days, next to this photo. She senses acutely the close, musty air of a room gone over to disuse, the curtains blocking out sunlight. It feels like a tomb echoing absence, gone-ness, the finality of Gammy being gone and her father being gone, forever. She chokes on the tightness in her throat, aware through her haze of grief that Abigail is not feeling the same way at all as she peruses the room, running her finger across surfaces and inspecting the contents of drawers.

"I guess they didn't see fit to prepare for us," she says, briskly wiping her hands together.

Jo swallows hard, turns away from the picture. "Maybe they made up another room."

But none of the rooms have been made up. Next door to Gammy's is a small room with a rumpled twin bed and clothes piled on the floor. Jo supposes it might be Hattie's room, except it, too, is dusty and feels abandoned. The next one down the hall might have been a guest room at one time, but now the bed is piled with empty boxes and folded things and other junk, including a rusting, broken birdcage that Abigail pokes with distaste, stating they will need a dumpster when the time comes, for sure.

The room at the far end of the hall, though, isn't cluttered at all, and Jo recognizes it instantly: it's where she stayed that time. It's really long and narrow, spare compared to the other rooms, with gray floors and two twin beds, a table in between. A three-drawer dresser stands against the far wall, and the same watercolor of a fox hangs between the beds. Two dormer windows overlook the backyard and outbuildings. She used to kneel on the window seat at night, watch the meadow under the moon when the coyotes were yipping.

She drags the satchel off her shoulder and sets it on the floor next to the suitcase. She looks out. All is desolate and silent in the hot July sun. The goat pens next to the barn are empty. Wood is stacked in neat rows under a lean-to, and in the adjacent shed are farm tools and a small tractor. Then there's what Gammy called the Old House, standing kitty-corner to this one with a few yards of scrubby grass between. The front door is barred with a two-by-four and padlocked, the same as back when she visited. It was in the will that it should stay locked. The house is more of a wreck than Jo remembers, a dilapidated, sagging structure with warped dark brown siding and undersized windows, all shuttered tight except for where one shutter's fallen into the weeds below. The window glass is the old-fashioned kind, opaque with swirls. A memory wells up: standing on tiptoe trying to peek in, hanging on to the splintered window frame. The Old House was off-limits, but she couldn't help it, she wanted to see. Suddenly Gammy showed up, hauled Jo out of the weeds, and spanked her bottom, making her cry. Then she got mad Jo was making so much noise. Jo can still feel the rigid, calloused hand clamped over her mouth as she was half carried, half dragged back into the house.

She'd forgotten about that. Unnerved, Jo backs off the window seat and moves to the bed. The springs squeak under her weight. "I can stay here," she says. "You should take Gammy's room."

Abigail gives a dramatic shudder. "I'd never have imagined."

"Where did you stay when you lived here?"

"Your father's room was in the attic," she points at the ceiling. "It was a furnace up there. He had fans blowing all over the place. I couldn't take it, so we ended up in the cottage. That Tom Pierson fellow is using it now. The lawyer said."

"So you'll be in Gammy's room, and I'll be here," Jo says, to affirm.

Abigail wipes her forehead with the back of her hand. "We have to make up the beds."

Jo hears something in her voice, and notices how drawn her mom looks, how pale. The drive has taken its toll, along with the heat. And she is really, really pregnant, after all.

"I'll make them later," Jo said. "You can direct."

Abigail smiles a bit. "How are you doing?"

Jo shrugs. She feels numb, mainly. All that buildup, and now that she's here, whatever happened all those years ago seems unimportant. It's just an ordinary house filled with the stuff of someone gone. It's sad in a way she hadn't expected. In the silence of this house, the rooms cluttered with things Gammy collected over her lifetime, Jo feels guilty for all the negative talk back in Newton. Gammy didn't need to leave this house to Jo, but she chose to, and all she's gotten in return so far is nastiness. Abigail's always said Gammy was to blame for her dad's mental illness, and sure, she had some strange ways, but it also doesn't fit that the owner of this messy, cozy house drove anyone crazy, let alone the boy she adopted and raised whose picture remained near her pillow right up till she died.

Her mom looks disheveled and sweaty and upset. Jo wonders if maybe she's realizing all the same things, too. She's just shaping the words of how she might ask, in a way that won't provoke disdain, when Abigail gets to her feet with her exaggerated I'm-so-pregnant sigh and says, "The sooner we get started, the better. Chop-chop."

She's not capable of feeling subtle, deep things, Jo thinks with sullen resignation, following her mom down the hall. She doesn't understand anything, really. She doesn't get Jo's sewing, or art when they're at a gallery, even with the little cards describing the artist's intentions. She's like one of those perfect, hard plastic dolls, penetrable only with a knife or fire. And if she did feel something, she'd never admit it: it's just not done.

Unless it's anger, Jo amends. That, her mom excels at.

SEVEN

When they go back downstairs, Hattie is gone. The TV's still on, the mess untouched. Abigail is annoyed. "She'd better shape up while we're here. A teenager and not cleaning up after herself? I mean, really."

Jo leaves her mom tidying up and wanders across the hall. The door opposite opens onto a room with a sewing machine and piles of fabric. Jo runs her hands across the materials, her mind stitching and shaping patterns. There's so much here she can use. It was Gammy who taught her to sew. She remembers sitting in this room hunched over a project, working the needle with her young, clumsy grasp. The window looks over the yard full of weeds and daisies and dandelions. It's pleasant in here, warm with the promise of satisfying labor. She pauses a moment, drinking in the memory of the sewing machine whirring and clunking as Gammy mended curtains. She leaves the door open, as if to guarantee her later return.

The rear hallway leads back to the kitchen. She'd run

around and around the first floor, chased by her dad. Now everything is silent and dusty. Her mom marches in carrying Hattie's dishes with tight-lipped disapproval. She retrieves a pink tub from under the sink and dumps all the dishes into it, as well as those already sitting there. She runs the water hot and squirts soap. "This is unbelievable," she criticizes. "It's like a frat house."

"Gammy was always messy like Dad," Jo says, elbows on the table, chin in hands. "I remember my feet were always black going through the house."

"I know. It drove me batty."

"Maybe she just had too much to do," Jo offers. "She was always outside, working."

"Well, whatever the case, Hattie should pick up after herself!"

Jo checks quickly to make sure Hattie hasn't appeared in the doorway. They've barely been here a few hours, and already her mom's commandeering the household. It feels wrong and rude, even if she's right about the lack of hygiene.

They go around the first floor opening cupboards and drawers and checking all the rooms. The locked Old House bothers Abigail; there must be keys somewhere, she says, and that becomes the focus of their search, but they come up empty. At the back stairs off the kitchen, Jo notices some wasps flying jagged circles near the window, and hastily clambers down. "There are wasps," she announces.

"Shouldn't that Tom Pierson be taking care of those things?" Abigail says. She sits at the table with her hands to her face. "I can't deal with this. I can't."

"Why don't you just leave it the way it is? I mean, who cares?"

Abigail looks up, irritated. "You don't understand. You're too young."

She's always too young, and Abigail's always snapping, as if it's Jo's fault she went and got pregnant and turned into a sweaty whale.

Jo leaves her there to stew, wandering down the narrow hall toward the light pouring in from the attached three-season sunroom. Gammy kept her office in the hall; there's an antique secretary desk, a file cabinet, some chairs, and piles of old seed catalogs. Framed photographs cover the walls up to the ceiling, barely any space between. They're really old, all in black and white, showing people and places over the generations. Gammy's family goes way back in Laddston. Jo knows some of the family history: Josiah Ladd came from England with just the clothes on his back, so the story goes. He landed in Boston and took a train north, and things went well enough that the village is named after him. It's kind of crazy that Jo's descended from a town founder. She's calculated that Josiah Ladd was her great-great-great-great-grandfather, albeit by adoption. He had a bunch of kids, and one of his daughters, or maybe it was a granddaughter, moved up to Quebec and married a Canadian, which is how the name Lavoie came into the family. Gammy came from that Lavoie line.

All the people memorialized in the photos must be Ladds and Lavoies from different eras, standing in stern rows with hats and gowns, or posed as babies in frilly christening outfits. There are newspaper clippings, too, yellowed behind the glass. One is about the statue in the park, the one they saw on the way in; it turns out it's Josiah Ladd. Another headline reads, "Ladd Dairy Closes, Herd Sold to New York." Only the first paragraph of the article is visible, the rest folded under, but from this Jo gleans the sale wasn't a happy event. A morose-looking man stands in front of a barn, his hand resting on a cow next to him, the cavernous black of the barn depths behind them like a metaphor for his loss. In another frame is Henri Lavoie's obituary. The picture is of a young man in a bow tie gazing into the distance. He resembles the old man with the cow, but just barely. More pictures. Three children at stiff attention in frocks with ribbons, the house behind them. A woman in a dark dress, schoolmarm with round glasses and a book, seated in a chair, sunlight pouring across her. Jo wonders if one of the kids is Gammy. She can't see a date anywhere to do the math.

Farther along the wall, the pictures turn to color as they move ahead in time to when Gammy ran the farm with Enzo. There's a copy of the picture Jo has of him with his hair blowing against the blue sky; it's been better preserved behind glass. At the very end of the wall is a newer group of color pictures in black plastic frames. It takes a moment for her to recognize that they're from when she was here. She stares in amazement at her grinning eight-year-old self sitting bareback on the paint pony.

She's never seen a single picture of that trip. Sometimes she's found herself wondering if it happened at all, because of the sheer craziness of how it ended. But it did happen: here is evidence. She remembers the solid, round warm feel of the pony's frame, her hands twisted in its thick mane. And there she is with her daddy, smiling in the sun, leaning against the hay, and there she is again, hugging the panting brown dog. In the last, Jo sits tucked close to her daddy on the front steps.

"We should keep going," Abigail announces behind her, grim and resolute, as if on a polar expedition.

Jo almost points out the pictures, then refrains. They're hers, she needs to absorb them a little longer before her mom tugs the magic out with a negative comment about hanging on to the past. The walls in Newton are painted light gray, decorated with carefully curated pieces of art. The only pictures of family are professional: on the Cape at sunset, everyone in matching white and khaki; formal graduation photos; the wedding. Certainly there are none of Jo and her real dad. It saddens her to think of Gammy hanging up these pictures with her son in jail, or maybe he was in the hospital by then. Maybe Gammy thought he'd move back one day, or Jo would visit again, but in the end, Gammy only ever had the pictures.

Jo follows her mom into the screened sunroom, a place of mismatched chairs and spindly tables, lamps, and shelves filled with books and things. In the center is a wingback chair with an unfinished quilt piled up on it. Sewing needles and scissors and thread tangles clutter the side table, along with a box standing open stuffed with bobbins, baggies of embroidery thread, more needles, a teacup with the bag ossified on a plate next to it. There's mold inside the cup, which causes Abigail to make a face. All this in the afternoon sun with the dust across the tiles and a different cat now rising from its perch and arching a deep purr, and in that instant, Jo remembers her small self there at the arm of the chair, watching Gammy sew.

"Look at this thing," Abigail mutters, lifting the quilt and examining the multitude of shapes. "Who has the time to do this?"

This is amusing coming from someone with so much time on her hands, but Jo doesn't have the energy to make a quip. She feels soggy with tiredness, dizzy from the light glancing off the windowpanes all around. The cat rubs itself along her leg and vanishes silently into the dark hallway from where they came. She can see Gammy's veined hands working the needle, deft and quick, and she feels a yearning to be sitting in peace and quiet, doing the same. When she was little she sat on the otto-man right there. She bent over a patch of material, intent upon sewing a row of stitches. *Keep them straight*, Gammy reminded without looking up from her own work.

"Should we just burn it all?" Abigail wonders, holding up the quilt in question.

Jo, startled, can only stare at her in shock.

A noise, and they both wheel about to find Hattie on the step, the doll dangling from her fist. Her face white, her mouth an O of concern. Her eyes big and wet. "Tom's b-back," she stammers.

"She won't," Jo says quickly. "She won't burn anything."

Hattie looks wildly from Abigail to Jo, then whirls and runs off, her bare feet slapping the floor.

"How could you?" Jo accuses.

"For crying out loud, I had no idea she was there!"

"Even if she wasn't!"

"Oh, stop it," Abigail retorts, but Jo can tell she feels bad, withholds further criticism. Abigail looks pasty and totally drained. She seems barely able to make it over to the screen door. She stands there, staring out over the yard and meadow. "It's just too much, Jo," she sighs. "It's like everything's the same as the last time I was here. I was pregnant, it was just as hot. I can blink and it's the same: the yard, the barn, the sky."

She says no more. The things that are not the same hang in the hot stillness of the room: Gammy gone. Enzo gone. Everything utterly changed.

"We can't burn it," Jo says, worrying again.

Abigail's shoulders sag, and she leans her forehead against the doorjamb. "We'll have to do something."

Jo doesn't know what that might be. She doesn't want to touch or move anything here. It's a shrine, she understands now. A shrine to Gammy, maintained by Hattie and Tom. Down to the teacup with the mold, probably the last cup she ever drank. And they've bumbled so shamefully into this quiet, holy place and messed it all up. They shouldn't even be here at all. The feeling is deep and terrifying. They should leave: they should leave at once.

84

She shouldn't be here!

Jo's heart pounds, remembering. It was dark. Outside. *She* meant her, Jo, she knows it.

That is all. The memory recedes, swift as a wisp.

"Let's go find Tom," Abigail says tiredly, and she steps out, the screen door clattering in her wake.

They cross the yard, past the fountain that used to sparkle and tinkle with goldfish moving in the depths. Now it's dried up and filled with matted leaves, the desiccated corpse of a bird among them. Abigail makes her way under the hot sun with increasingly slow, labored steps, sweating and breathing heavily.

"You sound really out of shape," Jo comments.

Abigail gives her a dark look, wasting no breath on a reply. They trudge up the slope and come to the greenhouse. A truck is parked there. The moist, hot space inside the plastic tent makes Jo drowsy. Green vines climb thickly, tendrils reaching out between the rows, obstructing their passage. "Cucumber," Abigail says when Jo winces at the prickly leaves.

They exit out the back. A dog starts to bark. They see it farther up the slope, a fluffy shepherd mix standing guard at the vegetable plots. Hattie comes into view, a set of long-handled shears dragging at her arm. She shushes the dog, who promptly sits, panting and staring expectantly at the newcomers.

Hattie waits for them, swinging the shears. She points as they get closer. There's a tall wire fence around the vegetables. A man is crouched near the bottom, working with pliers.

"Hello!" Abigail calls out.

He swings upright instantly. He's weird looking, in the sort of way that makes Jo want to stare. Close-set eyes, a sharply jutting brow, his face planed and angled like a carved wooden puppet. He's in a pair of shorts and work boots, no shirt. He's all ropy muscle, thickset as a stump, and his arms look too long, like they kept growing when the middle part of him was done. He squints at them a moment, then heads their way with a jolting, fast walk.

Abigail stands taller and puts on her imperious face, which means she's nervous. Jo can't blame her. He comes right up to them and abruptly stops. His eyes are gray, flat, unreadable. His face is riven with deep furrows. He could be forty, fifty, a hundred.

He looks Jo up and down, then says, "You Josephine?"

Jo nods, embarrassed by his sweaty odor and hairless chest, thick as a barrel and sunburned. *He should use sunscreen*, Jo thinks.

"I am her mother," Abigail states, claiming authority.

He shifts his narrow, slanty gaze to her, then his eyes drop to her belly. He looks displeased. "How long you staying?"

The lawyer said he's a little off and not to pay it any mind. That he's a solid worker, he's been Maur's right-hand man for years, and that's all that should matter. But it's hard for Jo not to get creeped out by how fixated he is on her mom's belly and how rude his question is. She cringes, expecting her mom to deliver some snark, but Abigail is perhaps too off-balance herself to lash out. Instead, she just says, "About a week, that's all."

"Good," he affirms. "Can't have a baby here."

Abigail's cheeks flare pink. "What right do you have to say that to me?"

He stands there, evidently surprised by this, his long arms dangling. He's still holding the pliers, and Jo notices his hand with dismay: he's got stumps where his fourth and pinkie fingers should be. There are scars up his forearms, like he was in a knife fight. Or maybe Gammy whacked him with a rake, too. He says, "It's the truth."

Hattie approaches from behind, plants the shears point down in the dirt. "Only a week?"

"We just need to put things in order," Abigail explains.

"Ain't nothing out of place," he counters.

"We'll be the judge of that."

He frowns. "I told Hattie to tidy up."

Hattie bites her lip and makes a worried face. He shakes his head at her. "Ain't right, with guests," he rebukes.

"We aren't guests," Abigail reminds him.

Tom Pierson receives this with a blank expression. Jo wonders if he even understands. It's like the meaning of things just goes one layer down, blocked by a solid, dull mass.

The discomfort between them feels thick and heavy. Sweat runs down Jo's sides, tickling her. Abigail, drawing on years of training at cocktail parties, exudes total obliviousness to anything being out of the ordinary. "It's so hot," she remarks. "Is it always this hot?"

He stands there, slowly absorbing the change in topic. Then he says, "Heat'll break when the storms come. There's a box fan in Maur's closet. She used it at the end."

The words stir sadness in Jo, evoking how it must have been, Gammy Maureen getting sicker and sicker till she couldn't move anymore. She probably lay in bed for days or weeks, unable to go about her work anymore, and then she was gone, the bed made up, the fan stored in a closet.

"No need to shop," he nods back at the field. "Everything you need, we got here. We'll bake bread in the morning, bring you a loaf. There's chicken in the freezer."

Abigail is flustered by this generosity. "Thank you, we appreciate that, but there's really no need. And what do you mean, *we*?" she adds after a moment. "Doesn't Hattie stay at the house?"

At the sound of her name, Hattie pushes herself into Tom's arm and lifts it around her shoulders, hanging on to his maimed hand. Tom says, "She moved on over with me after Maur was gone. Got scared alone."

Abigail wants to object but refrains. Jo understands why; they're here for only a week, and who are they to judge? Gammy named him Hattie's guardian, she must have known what she was doing. Though that is increasingly in question. This guy is beyond strange, and hardly seems capable of raising a girl who is without a doubt disturbed, never mind educating her when she doesn't even know how to spell.

"You're welcome to stay back in your room while we're here," Abigail suggests, but Hattie quickly shakes her head.

"All right, then, whatever suits you. By the way, I need the key to the Old House."

"Not supposed to go in there," Tom says.

Abigail is taken aback. "Well, I have to open everything up."

Hattie presses closer to Tom, her face pinched with worry. The sun beats down on them, the dog panting and staring. One of its eyes is blue, giving it a shocked look. Tom says, "I don't have the key."

Abigail turns to Hattie. "How about you? Do you know where it is?"

The girl shrinks under the pressure. "She isn't supposed to go in," she pleads with Jo.

Jo enjoys a small thrill at being seen as the one in charge, until she notices her mom's glare. "It's OK," she says hurriedly. "You can tell her."

It's clearly not the right answer, given Hattie's expression, but Jo could hardly do otherwise—her mom would kill her. Hattie says glumly, "It's in the top right drawer next to the sink."

"But I looked there," Abigail says, exasperated. "I'll look again, I guess. Thank you."

She turns and leaves. Her pointedly ungracious exit is somewhat diminished by the tense, shuffling gait down the slope, her whole body striving to prevent a fall.

Jo hangs back, hesitant. "Sorry," she offers. They both look at her. "Um, by the way, can I ask, where are the goats?"

"Was Maur kept the goats," Tom says flatly.

His meaning unfurls slowly in the silence. The goats were hers. She died. He got rid of them. It doesn't seem right. "Couldn't you keep them?"

"We got enough work without adding on."

"They're expensive, too," Hattie adds. "Maur said to give them to Sarah. She's our friend. She gives us milk and I make yogurt."

"Oh. I'm sorry," Jo apologizes, ashamed. "Thanks, anyway."

She gives them an awkward little wave, hurries to catch up with her mom.

Abigail is even more strung out and pasty after this encounter. Things aren't going to go smoothly this week, not with Abigail already in this state.

"Did you see how he looked at me?" Abigail hisses. "Telling me I can't have a baby here!"

"Super weird," Jo agrees.

"The way he spoke!" She shudders. "There's something *off,* Fletcher said? Talk about euphemisms. Can't have a baby here, imagine!" Abigail laughs suddenly, high, nervous pitched. "As if what, as if I'm planning to give birth in the clawfoot? Do you know that Maureen said the same thing to my face? She told me to just get out, leave Enzo, just go. And now here I am again—"

Her voice cracks. She's in tears, Jo notices in alarm. The outrage has veered off course to anguish. Hormonal, Robert always says, but in her mom's words, Jo can hear the hurt from all those years before.

"That sucks, Mom," Jo says. "Maybe he just meant because it's unsanitary."

Abigail gulps a teary laugh. "You're kidding, right?"

Jo is relieved her mom's outburst has been interrupted. "I mean, look at this place. No one could have a baby here."

They are standing next to the dead fountain, staring up.

"God, can you imagine," Abigail tries to joke, but it sounds flat.

On impulse, Jo takes her arm and says, "It'll be OK."

They stand there awkwardly, until Abigail suggests they change and settle in, and Jo gratefully darts ahead to open the door.

EIGHT

They dig through the linens in the hall closet and find sets that fit their mattresses. Jo's skirt is suffocating in the heat, so she changes into shorts before making up Gammy's bed while Abigail pulls open curtains and windows. The sun and fresh air do little to cheer the room.

"I don't know how we'll get everything done," Abigail sighs, her head falling back in the chair, arms and legs akimbo as if squashed by her giant middle. "I can't believe I forgot how bad things were. It'll never be ready."

"For what?"

"There's an agent coming to take a look on Saturday."

"What? We just got here!"

"Don't be that way, Jo. It's just a first assessment for when the time comes to sell."

"But—"

"Don't start about keeping the house again," Abigail snaps.

"Do you seriously see yourself becoming a farmer in the middle of nowhere?"

Jo doesn't, not really, but that's beside the point.

"You think farming is petting goats and ponies, but it's hard work, and dangerous, too! Don't you remember Maur's ear?" Abigail shudders. "Some farm implement did that. Just imagine."

Gammy's mangled ear resurfaces in Jo's memory, hazy and gross. She'd touched it with her fingertip even though she didn't want to, like when you touch a worm or a frog. *Can you still hear?* she asked, and Gammy laughed. She seemed fine, and maybe Jo could become a farmer also, but she'll never be able to find out, will she. She stuffs a feather pillow into a case, slams it on the mattress a few times to puff it up. There's no use arguing. Robert's hand is all over this, and Abigail won't budge. She thinks of Hattie nested on the couch surrounded by crumbs, learning her letters. Where will she go?

Jo works hard on the bed, pulling and tucking and smoothing.

Once they've wiped down the bathrooms and dusted a little they go back downstairs. Abigail sits at the kitchen table with her notebook open, making a list of tasks they need to accomplish. The list is long; she licks her finger and flips the page. Jo stands at the stove, waiting for the water to boil in the ancient kettle. The counter needs cleaning, and there's a layer of grime on the stove back and hood. A sprig of lavender hangs from a cabinet knob, as if to ward off the decay and inattention. Desperation snags at Jo: she can't call or text Ellie, she can't check her Instagram. She's marooned in this depressing place with her mom, whose list is frantic and unreasonable and unachievable.

"We can't do all that," Jo complains.

"We have to."

"We don't, actually."

"Drop it, Josephine."

Jo pours boiling water into the mugs. Both teabag strings get whirlpooled into the water, and she has to fish them out with a spoon.

"First and most important is all the stuff just lying around," Abigail says once Jo is seated. "The place needs to be as tidy as possible to make a good impression."

"It'll just go back to being a mess when we leave," Jo points out. "Why not wait till it actually matters?"

"Stop being so negative. We also need to go through that desk—the filing cabinets, my God, did you see them? There were bills from the nineties in there. We need to go around each room and see what needs to be done before the house gets listed, too. Repairs, painting, floors . . ." Abigail counts on her fingers. "So that means probably three months before, we'll need to come back and hire people. My God. It's just too much."

"You look really sick."

"I feel like hell. It's the heat."

It's more than that, it seems to Jo. Her mom is pallid, with bright pink splotches on her cheeks. Her voice sounds a little hoarse, too.

"We should eat," Jo suggests. "Should we just do pasta?"

"Sure." Abigail's bent over her list again, frowning and tense.

Jo digs through the shopping bags to find pasta and sauce. She puts water on and then opens up the pantry to put away the rest of her mom's nuclear stockpile. The pantry's full already. Jo picks up a bag of lima beans. It expired two years ago. She slips the rubber band off an open bag of Doritos chips: they're so stale they reek. Jo says, "Ew," and tosses the bag in the garbage. The rice stored in a large plastic container looks suspiciously infested; she hastily pours it all into the garbage, too. Now she sees what was hidden at the back: a stash of candy in large-size bags. Lollipops, chocolates, licorice, toffee. The sight brings back a memory of sitting at the table, candy wrappers strewn everywhere, her tummy hurting. Gammy was so weird to hoard all this candy. Maybe she had some kind of addiction. Jo drags out the heavy bags and drops them in the garbage along with the other expired goods she finds: cereal, nuts, potato chips. The tuna and sardines are still OK, at least. Sighing, she refills the shelves with all the stuff Abigail bought that will expire in turn when they leave. *The cycle of pantry life*, she thinks sourly.

"I threw out so much when I moved in here," Abigail says. "I think it was one of the first things that pissed her off. Me invading her kitchen. I guess I shouldn't have. I was just trying to help, though."

Her mom's voice is muffled, and Jo turns to see she's hidden her face in her arms on the table.

"I think you're getting sick, Mom."

"You may be right."

"Do you still want to eat?"

"I don't know," her mom mumbles.

The noise of footsteps on the porch catches their attention. Abigail groggily lifts her head. Tom Pierson stands in the doorway, wiping his boots on the mat with slow swipes, one, two, one, two. He's wearing an old T-shirt now. Hattie slips in from behind, barefoot. She's done her hair up in a messy bun on top of her head, strands hanging down in disarray. She's got her doll tucked under one arm, and with her other hand she holds up a mason jar tied with ribbon. "Fresh milked. Sarah brought three jars."

"Oh, how nice," Abigail says, surprised. "Thank you."

"I'm making yogurt with the other milk," Hattie says. "Good for the baby. Can I touch?"

Abigail draws her arms protectively over her belly, shielding it from Hattie's outstretched hand. "I actually prefer people don't," she says.

Hattie's expectant expression collapses with disappointment. She draws her shoulders inward. She says, "You look sick. There's echinacea in the pantry. Maur dried it last year."

"We don't want to be no bother," Tom steps into the kitchen

at last. "Just seeing you're set for food and all."

Jo can tell her mom's tensed up, and she has, too. His presence in the room charges the air. He's not normal, with his long arms and planed, bony features and his weird stillness. Like there's a coil in him that might spring at any moment. He seems to have more to say, but rather than speak, he just stares.

"What is it?" Abigail says, turning in her chair, sitting taller.

"I called Nate," he says.

"Nate—?" Abigail queries.

"He's the lawyer."

"You called him? Why on earth would you call him?"

"He's our friend," Hattie answers. "Are you gonna sell? That's what Nate said."

Tom lays a hand on her shoulder. She goes abruptly quiet. He says, "Nate told me you're gonna sell."

It's jarring how he states so flatly what's already been said. He's like a machine, steady and potent, but somewhere inside, a nut's come loose.

"It's an option," Abigail says. "Now, it's hot, and I'm not feeling well—"

"Maur didn't want you to sell," Tom interrupts in his stubborn, toneless voice. "She said she'd put it in the will."

Abigail glances at Jo, conveying her shock that he is pressing on like this. "It'll be a few years at least, all right?"

"Wasn't supposed to be ever."

He evidently can't grasp how inappropriate he's being. Hattie can't, either, clinging to his arm and drinking in their every word, her mouth an anxious O.

"The request not to sell was in a separate document appended to the will. It's not legally binding," Abigail says. "The house *can* be sold."

Jo is grateful that her mom doesn't add, *When Jo turns eighteen.* She wants nothing to do with this. He seems perplexed, which was obviously Abigail's intention, to disarm him with big words. Jo feels queasy and ashamed. She makes a quavering sound, trying to speak. They look at her. "It means we don't have to do it," she says shakily. "It means the law can't make us not sell."

In his hatchet face she reads the first signs of distress. "But she said."

"She said many things," Abigail says sharply. "We don't need to discuss it now. If that's all, we need to have our dinner."

A silence follows. Jo stares miserably at the jar of milk with its pretty ribbon.

Tom turns on his heel and strides out. Hattie runs after him, and Jo, without thinking, barges around the table to follow, almost tripping.

"Josephine!" her mom barks, but Jo lunges out the door to catch up with Hattie, grabbing her arm at the bottom of the steps. Tom is already crossing the yard, his boots punching the earth. The dog waits, looking up with its alert, blue-eyed stare.

"I'm sorry," Jo says, words tumbling in a rush. "She's not, you know, she's sick, I guess."

It's not sickness, it's just Abigail, but Hattie doesn't know that. She nods, accepting the excuse. But her white freckled face is furrowed with worry. "Are you really gonna sell?"

"She wants to."

"Can't you tell her not to?"

"I can try." It feels like a lie. "They won't listen to me. I mean her and Robert, my stepdad."

Hattie squinches up her eyebrows, truly perplexed. "Why won't they listen?"

"I don't know. It's just the way it is. Because I'm the kid, I guess."

"That's dumb. They have to listen. You're Maur's grand-daughter."

There's a weight to her words, as if she's just named Jo president of something. "I don't think they see it that way."

"They should."

Jo doesn't know what to say to this. "What's his name?" She points at the dog.

"Loco. Maur said he looks crazy because of his eye, so she called him Loco. That's 'crazy' in Spanish."

Jo bends to pet the dog's head. He licks her arm. Hattie giggles. "He just ate poop."

Jo yanks her arm back. "Eew!"

"It was coyote poop," Hattie adds, as if this makes it better. "I like your shorts."

She's pointing at Jo's needlework on her old jean cutoffs:

embroidered scrolling patterns and flowers. "Thanks."

"Maur was teaching me sewing."

The girl sounds so wistful, Jo feels like she should offer to teach her instead, except she's not sure she actually wants to. "Just keep practicing," she says.

"I'm glad you're here," Hattie blurts, and then her freckled skin turns red with a deep blush before she dashes across the grass to join Tom. She tugs on his hand, and he swings her forward into the air. She squeals, her doll flying high at the end of her outstretched arm. He swings her again. Loco leaps, trying to catch her. Jo retreats back to the kitchen, where Abigail is putting the pasta in the pot with studied concentration, looking like the effort might kill her.

"Mom, sit down," Jo begs.

Abigail shuffles to the table and sits. "He's starting to scare me," she says in a low voice, as if they might be lurking outside, eavesdropping. "Who knows what he might do. I wish Robert was here."

Robert wouldn't stand a chance against Tom, but Jo doesn't bother pointing that out. She's torn to pieces inside. There's definitely something wrong with Tom, and with Hattie, too. She can't sort it, but their worry about the house being sold has gotten under her skin. She feels an obligation rising in her, but how can she argue her mom's decision, which is basically Robert's? Even once she's eighteen and it's her right, they'll make her life miserable. Just the thought of going against them gives her hives. What if they get so mad they don't pay for college? That's what Nana and Pops did to Abigail: cut off all funding till she did what they wanted, marry someone right and settle down properly.

"I should call Robert," Abigail says.

"There's no service, remember?"

"Landline," Abigail points.

An old-style rotary phone, faded blue, hangs on the wall.

"I wish I could call Ellie," Jo complains, stirring the pasta.

Her mom points at the phone with a *Hullo?* look.

"Seriously?" Jo says. "I won't be able to see her or anything."

"Really, your generation. You can bike to town in the morning. The café must have internet." Abigail, already dialing, glances back and notes Jo's confusion. "There were always a few bikes in the garage. You'll need to pump them up, I expect. I'm sure Hattie can show you."

Jo prepares two bowls while Abigail answers Robert's questions about the drive, the house, those people. She makes the mistake of mentioning how cluttered the house is and how much work it's going to be. Jo can make out his criticism over the phone, vindicated in his opinion: see, she shouldn't have come, how is she supposed to take care of all this, she can still hire someone, why does she ignore his good advice.

When they sit down to eat at last, Abigail looks more drawn than ever, even ready to cry. Jo hates it when she gets that way, all strung out from being in a shitty marriage, because she never actually does anything about it, just suffers, and then she takes it out on Jo.

"Why do you look so grumpy? It's such a downer," Abigail

remarks, on cue. "You'd better be ready bright and early to help, is all I can say."

Jo studiously winds pasta on her fork. Indifferent silence galls her mom the most.

"Really, Josephine," Abigail mutters.

Really, Jo mouths in imitation, making a face. Her mom is tapping Parmesan over her bowl and doesn't notice. She stands her fork upright in her bowl as if staking territory. She twists methodically, exuding displeasure. She says, "I don't like Hattie staying with him. It's inappropriate."

Jo recalls Hattie swinging up through the air, laughing. "I don't think it's what you're thinking."

"I suppose I'll have to try and find a proper home for her, too."

Jo's skin crawls at her mom's martyred tone. *She has a home,* she wants to say, but it's futile. Once her mom gets something stuck in her head, it's all over, she's a train barreling down a single track with a broken brake. Which sums up her marriage to Robert, basically.

Jo eats without speaking, letting her mom's rambling litany of worries wash over her. When they're finished, she picks up the bowls and takes them to the sink. The sky outside is darkening, and the view from the window is dominated by the Old House. In the waning light, the walls look black.

Abigail comes to her side. "Ugh, that place," she scoffs. "Maureen wouldn't let me near it. Probably has a fortune buried there and didn't want anyone to know!"

Her mom is joking, but Jo's throat is blocked up. "I don't think so."

"What's the matter?"

"I just don't think we should go in."

Abigail barks a laugh. "What, you, too? Well, we have to show it along with the rest of the place, so that's that. It probably needs to be torn down. It's too much, it really is."

By which she means, all the work she's made for herself, for no reason. Jo would point that out, but she's so distraught she can hardly breathe. The Old House can't be torn down. It mustn't be touched, not ever. The knowing swamps her with panic.

"What's the matter with you, for heaven's sake?"

Jo stares blindly at the window, the house blurring to a blot against the fading sky.

"Jo! Speak to me!"

Jo's gaze readjusts, finds her mother staring irritably at her. Abigail will do whatever she wants. She'll barge right in and hire bulldozers the next day, if she decides it's warranted. "There's no point," Jo says, her voice shaking. "You never listen anyway."

"Josephine!"

Jo ignores her. She makes a show of tossing the towel over the rack and leaving the room as if she could care less what her mom says, which she actually couldn't.

Late into the night, Jo still can't fall asleep. Her body's a stiff tangle, her heart thudding the mattress. She's on the bed she used when she was little, the one against the wall. She could never sleep in the other bed, stranded out in the center of the floor, emptiness on both sides.

She remembers lying here staring up at peeling, cracked plaster, the globe light fixture strewn on the inside with the dark shapes of countless insect corpses. She remembers the sheen of the gray-painted floors, the shadowy vaults of the dormer windows set deep into the sloped ceiling. The half-moon shines dimly through these small windows, casting the flat tidiness of the unused bed in gray shadows, beyond which the gloom darkens to pitch black at the far end of the room. She can just make out the hulking shape of the dresser. The closet doesn't stay closed: she propped her empty suitcase against it to seal the crack of darkness.

She knows she was scared back then, the way she's feeling now. She tried to yell, except her voice didn't come out, like in her dreams. Where had her dad slept? He must have been in Hattie's room, or in his old room in the attic. The dog slept with her, though: she remembers it barking, the sound shattering the night.

Her eyes go dry and scratchy staring at the darkness beyond the other bed. She can hear every sound: a creak in the wall, the trees rustling outside, the distant, shrill cries of a bird. She waits in agonized paralysis, minute after rigid minute, and then suddenly sits up in a rush, breaking the awful spell.

She switches on the bedside lamp and places her bare feet on the floor, hands tucked under her thighs. She rocks a little, trying to settle her anxiety. She has dumb fears carried over since childhood, habits she follows automatically now, without thinking, but here in this new space they stand out. The closet door, deformed from years of damp and cold, and how she labored to make sure the sliver of dark would not edge open again. The lack of curtains on the windows, how it upsets her. She needs the windows covered at night. She also needs a nightlight, but she forgot to bring one.

She listens hard, but there's nothing. Just the house with its myriad noises, scratching, creaking, settling for the night.

She forces herself to get up. She rounds the bed to kneel on the window seat and look out, the motion deeply familiar, except it's harder to fit into the narrow space now. The meadow back then was yellow under the moon; it was later in summer. Now it's dark, the green absorbed by the night. But its movement is visible. The trees sway against the sky, too. The world never ceases motion. She might be still as stone, but everything in the world outside flutters, sways, shivers. Perhaps that's what always frightens her from falling asleep, the knowing that when she lies unconscious, helpless, there is ceaseless motion all about. Life, continuing without her, changing, moving. Only the farm buildings stand still against the motion of the night, shaping a dimly colored world of red barn, stacked wood, latched shed doors. All color disappears into the Old House, the walls are so dark.

You better not go in! Gammy hollered, the hard smacks stinging little Jo-Jo's bottom till she cried. *Fall down the well and no one would hear you! You'd die starving!*

Her recollections of Gammy are benign overall, but in the

end, what kind of person threatens a kid like that? Maybe Jo did something wrong—maybe *that's* what the shouting was about, why her dad took her away? Had she gone in? Was Gammy yelling for her to get out?

Her mind whirls with the effort to recall, but nothing more comes.

Gradually, a sadness wells up in her, for what she doesn't know. For the wreckage of an old, rotting house doomed to be torn down; for her father; for memories lost and gone forever. Her throat is dry and raw, jaw aching from being clenched. She retreats to her bed, placing the bedside lamp on the floor, a makeshift night-light. She lies with the sheets twisted in a heap next to her, the heat heavy even this late into the night. Her sadness must be because of missing her dad, and maybe even Gammy. Or maybe it's because for all Gammy's effort, here they are, going against her wishes. It's her mom's fault. Jo wouldn't bother with any of this, if she had her way. She'd leave it all as is, come back when she's older. She certainly wouldn't put Tom and Hattie out onto the street, no matter how weird they are.

She turns onto her side, her melancholy replaced by the bitter mental listing of her mom's bad traits: stubborn, demanding, insensitive, wrong. Abigail will get exponentially worse when the amoebert comes, a whole scenario that feels almost fictional, lying here in this strange bed, so far away. Maybe she can just stay here when Abigail heads home to give birth. There's a thought. She can skip the whole part of her life where she has to be big sister to Spawn of Robert. She can get some dogs, fill the fountain and stock it with goldfish.

Though she'll need to get Wi-Fi, she realizes with alarm, and drifts to sleep ruminating on how this would be accomplished and what if it can't be.

it was the girl laughing and squealing and calling up her own fate so i oughtnt have been punished. it was a crime what maur did and she never said sorry. not once. she said it wasnt the girls fault for being merry.

wasnt my fault neither i said.

she said whats done is done. she wont remember maur told me. she wont know right off. she might not even come at all and if that happens then you take care of hattie and the farm and dont worry about the rest.

i dont worry about it i said. its not my work.

its hers.

NINE

It's barely eight a.m. when Jo wakes up, which is hideously early, but the air's too hot and sticky to sleep longer. She drags on shorts and a tank, rinses her face, then wipes a cold washcloth over her arms and neck as well. Marginally refreshed, she's about to head downstairs when she hears her mom croaking her name. She turns back to find the door open, the room dim with all the curtains drawn. Abigail's propped up against a mound of pillows with more under her knees. She gazes at Jo, her eyes barely open.

"Uh-oh," Jo says, keeping her distance. "What's going on?"

"I got up to work on the papers. Couldn't stop coughing. Hacked up half a lung," Abigail whispers. "Yesterday I thought it was just the trip, how hot it was, you know. But I'm sick as a dog."

"Do you have anything you can take?"

"I hate to. Can you get me water? And look for the thermometer."

Jo waves assent. She goes into the bathroom and digs through her mom's elaborate toiletry bag hanging next to the sink. The bathroom is spacious and filled with morning sunlight, white lace curtains floating on the breeze, a clawfoot tub. The blue pine floor is worn to bare wood in places. In front of the hand-painted dresser is a small carpet, a real Persian, Jo knows from Nana's house. Gammy must have gotten it on her travels when she was young; among the silver-framed pictures on the dresser, Jo sees the pyramids in Egypt. She bends closer to look at the faded black and whites, finds a young woman in an ankle-length skirt and white blouse standing in front of a donkey. She recognizes Gammy's long nose and narrow cheekbones in the youthful face. It's weird to imagine her in such an exotic place. To imagine her young at all.

"Jo?" her mom calls weakly.

She runs the water till it's cold and fills the glass on the sink. Back at Abigail's bedside, she withholds the water. "Temp first," she instructs, as her mom has done so many times to her.

Abigail obediently sticks the thermometer under her tongue.

"I think you should cancel showing the house," Jo says. "There wasn't time to get ready anyway, and now there really isn't."

Abigail stares fiercely, the thermometer clamped between her lips.

Jo uses her two minutes to the fullest. "How'll you even take someone around? I can't do it. I don't know what you're supposed to say or anything. You'll be sick for days. You know you will. Every time you get this hacking cough, it's like that. It's because you smoke, you know. Your lungs are damaged. When the baby's born, you should stay quit."

Abigail pops the thermometer out. "God, Jo. You have a terrible bedside manner." She squints at the reading. "It's low, but it's a fever. Dammit."

She drops her head back, leaching frustration. Jo feels bad. It does suck to be sick, plus it's so hot. The room feels suffocating and dark. Abigail's a beached whale, sweating in a sauna.

"You should hang out downstairs," Jo advises as she goes around opening curtains to let in the breeze. "It's going to be a cooker again today."

"I just want to sleep some more."

"Should I call and cancel?"

Abigail slowly turns her head. Her eyes are glazed, her skin damp with sweat. "Honey, I know you don't want to sell. I get it. It's the first thing that's really yours." Her eyes drift shut. "But we have to. You need to realize that."

"Because Robert says."

Abigail's eyes flutter half-open.

"If it was just you," Jo presses, buoyed by her mom's weakness, "maybe you'd think about it, at least. But the minute he says something, you just say OK."

"It's not like that, Jo," Abigail sighs. "He wants what's best for you. We both do."

"Whatever," Jo retorts, feeling guilty and angry all at once.

"But you'll have to show them around yourself."

At the door she looks back. Her mom hasn't moved. She really does look miserable. Jo regrets attacking her in her helpless state. But it's not fair. Either her mom has no time, or she gets angry, or she's suddenly too sick. It doesn't matter what Jo says or thinks, ever.

She closes the door harder than she should, a final retort. At the landing she stares down over the banister, recalling how she'd drop things down onto the hallway floor: marbles, stuffed animals, a sandwich. There's a faint creak, the distant tinkle of a chime. The silence of the house feels strange, but thrilling, too. She has it all to herself, at least for a while.

Downstairs the light pours in through the narrow windows on either side of the front door, which they locked last night. Jo opens it and props the ceramic cow doorstop in place. The air is filled with birds chirping, the unmowed yard bright with daisies sloping down to the narrow, rocky river. In the distance is the empty road, and beyond that the forested hills. She always thought their backyard in Newton was so spacious; it seems tiny now.

Heading for the kitchen, she imagines herself older, living here in her very own house. She's got a car and a job and maybe even a boyfriend. In the afternoon, she swims in the pond. She has a dog. Robert is allergic to dogs, so she can't have one. She could get two or three with all this space.

Her dreamy state evaporates in the kitchen. She isn't living on her own with a car and a dog and a boyfriend. There's a fresh loaf of bread wrapped in a linen towel on the kitchen table, along with a carton of eggs and a jar of pickles. Nearby is a note in large childish handwriting: *Good morning. Hattie.* The pen strokes look labored, pressed hard. Jo imagines her bent over the note in concentration. The image touches her, and also leaves her ashamed for sleeping while this girl was baking bread and gathering eggs.

She opens the carton and sees the eggs haven't been cleaned. Gammy would scrub them with her fingers under running water at the sink only when it came time to eat them. The carton was stored on the table, room temperature, just as it is now. It's all coming back.

She finds jam in the fridge and unwraps the bread. Her mom already had a slice. Hattie and Tom were probably up at five or six, laboring away. The routine Gammy followed is a jumble in her memory. Weeding and harvest; the chickens; and back then, the goats and the pony.

She wipes the crumbs from her dish into the compost bin on the counter so as not to mess up the septic. As she turns on the water to rinse, a motion catches her eye: Hattie's crossing the meadow, Loco bounding ahead. Her hair is loose and she's in a sleeveless dress. Jo watches a minute and then turns around, sighing. She isn't sure what to do. There's no sound from upstairs; her mom must have fallen asleep again.

The list Abigail made is still on the table, the notebook

folded open to the second page. At the top, emphasized with three stars, is *Go through papers.* Her mom already started that, apparently. Jo flips the pages: *Decide what needs to be chucked. Clean out basement. Clean out attic.* The list is crazy. A bunch of dirty, difficult tasks her mom has dreamed up as necessary, even though they're two years out from selling. It's so typical of her mom to engineer urgency, to manufacture projects she can oversee and control. She does it all the time at home, whether it's painting a room or cleaning out the shed or whatever. Everyone always has to be doing something. It's just a way for her to avoid living in her own head, is what it boils down to. A way to ignore the rut that's her life.

Well, Jo's not doing any of it, and her mom's too incapacitated to make her. It doesn't look like she needs much help anyway. Gammy's secretary desk in the hallway is already half-gutted. A bunch of the little drawers and cubbies have been emptied out, and the file cabinet, too. Manila folders are piled high, papers spilling. The wastepaper basket brims with odds and ends. Jo fishes out a clip in the shape of a bouquet of flowers. The paint is worn. Gammy must have used it a lot.

Even though her mom warned she'd do this, it feels unbearable, all this stuff that was precious to Gammy getting tossed in the trash. Surely Gammy hadn't intended for someone to dig through her things and throw them away? Jo puts the clip back in a drawer and closes it. She can't believe her mom came down, destroyed everything, then went back to bed. The space was already cramped with the desk and filing cabinet, the chair rolled off to one side on the uneven floor, and the general clutter of books and papers piled along the wall. Now it's a disaster zone. Gammy spent evenings here bent over paperwork with a cup of tea. Jo would sit on the spindly wooden chair next to the desk, now piled with old seed catalogs, watching as Gammy went through bills and letters. She trailed Gammy all over the place; she has memories from all different areas of the house and farm. Gammy couldn't have been so awful, or she'd not have stuck with her like that.

Jo pokes disconsolately through the files. Electric bills going back to the early nineties. Goat sale bills, feed bills, vet bills, roof repairs, the purchase of two new water barrels, the ones now standing outside on concrete blocks under the eave. Folders stuffed with ancient newspaper articles and letters, more bills. It's overwhelming how much there is, and then there are the cards stacked all over the desk, probably pulled out of all the drawers.

Dear Maureen, one flowery notecard reads, *Thank you so much for the pie, you are a godsend.* And another: *My dearest Maur, I hope you recover soon and you'd better rehome that nasty buck or I'll come do it for you!* There are countless such notes from over many years, tied with rubber bands, and more stuffed into drawers and nooks. Jo opens tiny drawers to find a hodgepodge of artifacts her mom didn't get to: buttons, bits of paper with lists, stickers from mailers, photographs, mostly of people and places she doesn't know. Sometimes there are dates scrawled across the backs, all from long before she was born.

She flips through a small stack, comes to one of a young couple, laughing in front of a waterfall.

Then the shock of recognition: her parents.

They're so unbelievably young, in cutoff shorts and T-shirts, barefoot. They've got their arms around each other, and they're grinning. The picture's faded, but sunlight still dances off the rushing water behind them, creating a glare on the lens that almost wiped out her mom's delighted, smiling face.

Jo's never seen a picture of them from that time. Her mom keeps the pictures from her first marriage tucked away in a shoebox, but they're from after Jo was born. They mostly center on the baby—on her dad's lap, or set between them like a prop, or on a high chair with her pudgy arms stretched and mouth open. The few pictures of her parents together never really registered, they're so ordinary, snapshots of any couple sitting at a dinner table or standing in front of a house.

This picture tells a whole other story. They look so alive, so bright. Her mom's honey hair messy and long, her dad grinning, at ease. They would have met just a few months earlier, at Island Pond, the fateful day her mom and some friends drove up from Middlebury. He was like Tarzan, her mom said once, jumping out of the woods just like that and straight into the water, half-naked. Jo thought, *Eeew*. Who took this picture? she wonders. One of the friends from college? Her mom doesn't talk about that time in her life other than to recall how much of a mistake it all was. But they were happy. They laughed and hugged at a waterfall, they had a friend along with them.

They sure don't look like a mistake.

Her surprise turns acid. Her mom lied. Everyone did, even her dad, with all his protestations and apologies, as if the entire past had been a disaster he caused. Jo stares bitterly at her mom's wide smile, the loose sundress and bare feet. The person in this picture doesn't exist anymore. No wonder she's always so angry. She's like the living cliché from some novel they're forced to read in school. The heroine who gambled and lost and then lives her life in misery. Look at what she gave up: it's right here in the picture. She's living Jo's own worst nightmare. That all her dreams to get as far away as possible from her life, to be an artist living in a van with a dog and a boyfriend, or whatever—they'll all be crushed. Instead, she'll go to the right college and take the right classes, then she'll get married, and then one day, she'll find herself in a cocktail dress on a patio chatting with strangers.

It strikes her that she herself might be in the photograph, a tiny speck floating inside her happy, carefree mom. Jo peers closely at her shape: the belly flat as a pancake, the cutoff shorts dangling strands. It's inconceivable that they were once these two totally alien, happy people. That she, Jo, comes from them, and not from the people they turned into.

Maybe it's always like that, she wonders. Maybe one day she'll have a kid looking at a picture of her, thinking, *What happened to her, how'd she become such a complete loser?*

Jo tosses the picture onto the desk. Let her mom find it. She'll chuck it, most likely. She'll throw all this stuff away, and the desk and the chair and the pictures and everything, so why bother going through it all to begin with?

Jo pushes back the chair savagely, and it crashes into the wall, shattering the quiet. She doesn't care. She hopes it wrecked her mom's sleep. She stomps down the hall and out the sunroom door.

The door bangs behind her. Chickens cluck worriedly, halted in their hunt for grubs and seeds by her sudden arrival. The sun beats down: she can feel her skin turning red, sweat sticky under her tight tank top. Sighing, she kicks at the dry dirt, sending up dust. The sky is huge and pale blue. The shrill peeping of a hawk echoes in the distance. The day yawns ahead, weighed down by nothing to do. She stares disconsolately out at the empty goat pens, the worn plastic bins and toys where the baby goats used to frolic. It's too bad there's not enough money to keep up the farm. She wonders if there were more animals that Tom got rid of when Gammy died, and if he regrets their loss. Not likely.

She digs out her phone, feeling grumpy and bored. She thumbs through her playlists, then remembers there's no cloud here. There's very little stored on her phone thanks to Abigail refusing to buy her an upgrade. She's only got like five or six albums to choose from. She scrolls down to Of Monsters and Men and tucks in her earbuds. It's been a while since she's listened to them. It's satisfying walking the dead zone of the yard and empty barn with the haunting melodies and lyrics playing in her head. The barn's like a scene from an end-of-the-world movie, with tack gathering dust along the wall and stall doors ajar, bits of hay blowing in the breeze down the worn floorboards. She pauses where the paint pony used to live. She braided its mane one day. It looked pretty sloppy, but Gammy took a picture. Maybe it's buried somewhere in all those papers.

She comes out the other end and gets smacked by the hot sun. She shades her eyes, staring along the edge of the meadow till she finds the opening, the grasses crushed by deer. She went that way with her dad; she remembers him telling her to slow down, that she might trip on the roots. She ran and ran, delighted by the flowers and the giant sky overhead. Now she's hot, sweat trickling down her back and sides, and she's fretful about the tall meadow grass brushing her bare legs, the threat of ticks. Gammy brought her out here to gather flowers that she'd dry out in bunches all over the kitchen, but Jo can't identify the plants that Gammy taught her anymore.

She follows the path out of the meadow and enters the cool shade of the woods. The treetops are so high up, the branches forming patterns against the blue sky. She plucks out her earbuds and turns off the music. Now she can hear the birds and the rustling of leaves, the creaking and cracking of tree trunks. It's both silent and filled with noise inside the forest.

Don't go in too far, her daddy whispered.

They were here, in the forest. She remembers her sunbrowned feet in sandals, the pine needle floor, her daddy's big hand squeezing hers. She must never come here alone, he warned. She might get lost: the forest was gigantic and endless and she was too small to navigate it. He made Jo promise to stay away unless she was with him.

She misses him suddenly, a wistful hurting that presses against the backs of her eyes, welling tears. Everything here reminds her of him: the house, the meadow, the forest. Her daddy said it was called a sugarbush. The term delighted her. *Sugarbush! Sugarbush!* they sang. He told her how he tapped the maple trees, carried the heavy pails through the deep snow back to the tractor. The farm once had a big syrup business; by the time he lived here, it was shut down, too much for Gammy to manage on her own. Jo runs her hands up the rugged bark of the giant maple, counts the plugged holes: there are three. *When you cook the sap*, he told her, *the sky fills with white sugar clouds.* He walked these woods his whole youth, he filled the pails and cooked the sap in the sugar house. She wishes he could have shown her how, just once.

She wends deeper into the forest. She's older now, she won't get lost. She tries to keep to a path, but soon she's clambering over mossy rotting logs and picking her way through tangles of dried-up dead branches. She crosses a thin stream bordered by lush ferns and mushrooms. The stones glisten through the clear water, worn smooth and slick. The forest floor feels soft and ancient, and the air smells earthy, rich with greenery. There's no path at all now, but she can still see the meadow through the trees, so she decides to just go with it; she'll find her way back out at some point.

She picks up a branch, snaps off the twigs to make it more

comfortable to use as a cane, and forges on. After a short time picking her way upslope, she comes upon a clearing. Hacked stumps ring the area, trunks and branches piled to form low walls between them. It could be a campsite, Jo supposes, though there's no firepit or any sign of anyone using the area at all. The grass grows lushly on the uneven ground, and the whole place has an air of abandonment. Jo walks out to the center of the clearing, looking around, perplexed. She doesn't remember coming here with her dad; they never climbed through the chaos of rotting mossy logs and deadwood like she has today. She's glad she did because it's kind of cool here. She turns in place, snapping pictures on her phone. She examines the pictures, but they don't capture the desolate, haunted feeling of the place. Ellie won't really get it. She resolves to come back, maybe even put up a tent. It can be her own private escape, secret from her mom. Not so far from the house that she'll be gone too long, but not close enough that her mom would ever find her.

There's a huge boulder near the branch fence. She climbs onto it and lies down, enjoying the heavy feel of her legs hanging down the cool stone. She stares dreamily up at the treetops. They move ever so slightly, like breathing. She closes her eyes, listening to the trunks creaking gently, the distant rush of water over stone, insects flitting and buzzing.

She comes to with a start: she must have been almost asleep. A noise roused her, something in the trees. She sits up, rubbing her eyes.

Listen, her daddy said, finger to his lips, worry in his eyes.

Jo freezes, utterly still, not breathing. He held her hand tight. They left the forest at a run, though he made it like tag. She squealed happily, ignorant of his worry, but she recognizes it now, she can hear it in the memory of his voice.

She hears rustling noises, then a cascade of giggles, so faint and gone so swiftly, she thinks she was mistaken.

Then again: a tripping, clutching, giggling sound, like children hiding in the bushes, mocking her.

"Who's there?" she yells. It comes out a pitiful croak. She scrambles off the boulder, staring into the forest on all sides. The thick jumble of trees and rot looks menacing now. For a panicked moment, she can't remember which way she came from.

The giggles erupt again, then catch, then she hears a high-pitched cry. No, not a cry. Singing. Some kind of singing. A bird, maybe. Except it doesn't sound anything like a bird.

Jo grabs the stick she used as a crutch, turning in place, scanning the trees. There's nothing to see. The trees creak, louder than the far-off, mournful cries. She stumbles a few feet, dumb with fear, not knowing which way to go. She can't remember what they heard, that time with her dad. Was it this?

The sound fades. Her own noisy breathing fills her ears. Her palms are a sweaty mess clutching the branch, which looks pathetic and useless. She needs to get out of here. The uneven ground causes her to trip. She sees a clump of dead flowers, dried up and brown, an ancient bouquet tied with faded ribbon. She stares at it in confusion. There's another one, and another, spaced far apart.

The fence woven out of branches, the protected, desolate space—God, what if she's standing on graves? What if she's standing on dead bodies? Why else would there be bouquets lying around?

A burst of laughter erupts from behind her. She whips around, but all she can see is the underbrush, the wall of tree trunks, and the darkness beyond.

She turns and runs, tossing aside her branch. Her legs sting, scratched on tangled sticks and prickly bushes. She grabs at the slender trunks of young trees to keep from falling as she hurtles down the slope, keeping her gaze fixed on glimpses of the sunny meadow. At the bottom of the slope she runs into the stream, wider here with no passage, so she just charges through the icy water, losing a flip-flop. She almost doesn't go back for it, then reason prevails.

Within a few minutes of frantic scrambling, she bursts out of the forest at last, the meadow providing wide-open, bright relief. She sucks in her breaths, trying to quiet down, to listen. She can't hear anything now, other than the noises of nature.

She half jogs along the meadow's edge seeking a path across, then finally plunges into the tall grasses. By the time she gets to the scrubby dirt yard behind the barn, her legs are an itching mess and she's sweating profusely. The barn's cool shade is such a relief that she just stops there for a few minutes, catching her breath. It seems like ages ago that she sauntered through here, clueless. *What the hell was that?* she wonders. Birds, or some other animal, it had to be. So why was her dad afraid? He grew up here, surely he could identify forest sounds.

Then again, he wasn't exactly stable.

She forces herself to get moving again. She'll have to check on her mom, probably deal with another argument. *Back to reality*, she thinks sullenly. She steps out the other end of the barn and practically walks right into Tom.

He just stands there with his dour stare, long arms dangling. He's holding a knife. The hot, buzzing silence is deafening.

He squints at her. "You all right?"

"I—I was in the woods."

He turns his gaze in that direction. The heat pounds Jo's head. She feels dizzy. He says, "Best not to go too far in. Could get lost."

"I know." She hesitates. "I saw a place, like maybe a grave-yard or something?"

He gives a loose wave with the knife. The blade glints sharply in the harsh sunlight. "Was Maur's. Couldn't bear to let 'em creatures go without rites."

Her goats and chickens, Jo realizes. She's touched at the thought of Gammy mourning her pets. She almost asks about the weird noises she heard but doesn't want to appear foolish.

"You got too much sun," Tom tells her.

"I'm fine. Just hot."

"Storms'll break the heat soon," he says, and turns his back.

It's only now, in slow motion, that the pieces of the scene fall into place. He's standing next to a row of three cones screwed to the barn wall. Nearby, a metal pot filled with simmering water stands on a kerosene burner. One of the cones has a chicken in it, upside down, its little head poking out the bottom. It's looking around, docile and silent. Jo gazes in dismay: the talons curled up, pointing at the sky, the body cocooned in metal, the little head tilting this way and that, the red comb flopping.

Tom says over his shoulder, "Rooster's been pecking hard at the hens."

His flat words thud into her one by one. "OK," she says.

He grabs the rooster's head, which disappears in his huge, gnarled hand with its missing fingers. A year ago, Jo was vegan for a while. She'd lecture her mom and Robert about how divorced people are from food production, but she's never seen it herself, except on YouTube when she was researching a paper on animal rights. Jo stares in horror, unable to look away. It takes only an instant, one blurred swipe of the knife, and the head's off.

Blood spurts down into the dirt. The rooster's body bangs around inside the tin cone. Tom peers at it, waiting, like a machine on pause. He seems to have forgotten his audience.

Jo backs away, then hurries into a jog. She looks back once she's in the sunroom. Tom is lifting the rooster out of the cone. He turns around to deposit it in the hot water. A cloud of steam rises into the air. Tom stares down into the pot, waiting, motionless. A thick, rotten smell drifts across the yard on the breeze, making Jo gag. She retreats farther into the house. She needs to check on her mom, figure out what to do with her day. *Just don't think about it*, she orders herself. *You're on a farm, aren't you? This is how it's done.*

Necessary work, she recalls with a shudder as she goes up the stairs. Maybe her mom's right about selling. Jo would never, ever, be able to do something like that.

TEN

"I'm dying," Abigail whispers from the bed, indifferent to Jo's story of the rooster. Jo hangs back sullenly in the doorway, waiting for instructions. "You should clean up Hattie's room and get things in the laundry."

"Seriously? Why can't she do it?"

"Oh, God, Jo."

"It's just not fair, is all."

"They're obviously not capable," Abigail whispers, trying to raise her scratchy voice. "God knows what's crawling around in that room!"

"Oh, great," Jo fumes. "So I get to deal with it!"

She stomps to Hattie's old room and strips the bed, releasing clouds of choking dust. She lays the sheet on the floor and dumps clothes onto it: a few sundresses, a sweatshirt, underwear (eewww), a wraparound skirt from like 1960, and one sock. She looks around for more, finds a T-shirt lumped under the bed. There's a ticking sound when she shakes it out. She bends down to find teeny things scattered on the floor, like black rice: mouse droppings.

Revolted, she tosses the shirt onto the laundry pile. The idea that there might be mice scuttling around her own room when she's sleeping makes her frantic. She bundles the sheet and carries the load downstairs. The washing machine is in the kitchen. There's no dryer: she recalls running between the wet sheets when Gammy hung laundry with wooden pegs. So she'll have to hang up Hattie's stuff, too, unless she can track her down and make her do it.

Downstairs, she digs around under the kitchen sink, looking for detergent. She regrets not wearing gloves, ugh, her fingertips come away sticky from the sliding rack, which of course doesn't budge. The rack is packed with old rags, cans, and other junk that's been there for a hundred years. There's no detergent she can see, but in the way back she spots an interesting-looking leather thing with a bone clasp. She drags it out, surprised by how heavy it is. It makes a clanking sound when it hits the floor. There's a worn embossment on the front: *P. Lavoie.* Gammy was an *M*, so *P* has to be from sometime before, her dad or granddad, maybe. She undoes the clasp and unrolls the leather.

Yikes.

A tall, curved knife—the name of it wells up from movies: machete. There's also a small axe. A piece of rebar, the end flattened and sharp. And a length of chain.

The sight of the chain fills her with unease. It recalls the heavy, wrapped-up dish towel nested at the bottom of her dad's satchel. She gingerly lifts one end, then lets it drop. *It's not the same*, she tells herself. Which doesn't even make sense. Of course it's not the same. But it's a chain nevertheless, and her dad had one, too. That time in the motel, he laid it on the floor between them when they slept, one end in his fist at all times. He said it was for protection. But from what?

Jo cautiously picks up the machete. The blade is shining and clean. She can see it was oiled before being put away. So was the axe. Her dad had a chain, but not the rest of this stuff. Abigail always says it was Gammy who made him so sick in the head. It's starting to look like she was right.

Jo rolls the tools back up in the leather and fits the clasp back in place, leaves the package on the middle of the table so her mom won't miss it if she comes downstairs. Maybe she saw it back when she lived here and can explain what it's supposed to be.

The detergent's in the bathroom, as it turns out. There's barely any left. It's the one thing her mom didn't stock up on. She measures out the powder, calculates there's enough for one more load, maybe.

The laundry running, she heads for the cupboard under the main staircase, lifts the slender latch. She'd play tag with her dad through this hall, around and around they'd go from the kitchen through the rooms she just passed, around this staircase and back into the kitchen, and then she'd hide in this cupboard, convinced he had no clue where she was. The same canister vacuum is still there, a relic from probably the 1950s. She hauls it up the stairs to her bedroom. Sure enough, there are droppings along the walls under the bed. She pops in her earbuds and cranks ABBA. The vacuum works, which is a relief; it's kind of cool, actually, that Gammy kept this thing running all these years. It's like the total opposite of her mom's rampant consumerism, a new robot vacuum practically every six months because Abigail needs one for this room or that room. One old vacuum should be all people need. *Money money money*, Jo mouths, swaying her hips as she works, *it's a rich man's world*.

Jo vacuums till the floor is spotless, then moves into Hattie's room. There's satisfaction in sweating so hard and getting so hot and tired from the work, and she's not unhappy with the result. The room looks empty and tidy. It's a nice room, with a big window overlooking the lush yard behind the Old House and out to the road and hills beyond. Her mom was right to insist on cleaning the place up a little. At least it'll be nicer for Hattie once they're gone. For like a week, anyway.

She peeks in on her mom, who's slept through the vacuuming racket. She must really be doing badly. Jo resolves to try and be nicer.

She leaves the vacuum out to do her mom's room later, peels off her soaked clothes to have a shower. The water pressure is weak because the washing machine's running, but it's still a relief to rinse off the sweat and dirt. She lies on her bed in her towel for a little bit, drying off and enjoying the fan blowing across her. She likes her room. It's long and bare with those cool dormer windows and gray-painted floors. If she lived here, she'd keep this as her room instead of using Gammy's. She'd fill the barn with goats and ponies and build a cute farmstand at the top of the driveway; why isn't there one already?

It's pointless to think this way. She'll never stand up to her mom and Robert, the main reason being that it's unrealistic to live here. After school she has college, then she has to find a job and become self-supporting so she can be free.

Gammy was self-supporting.

She gets up abruptly, hunting for something to wear. Sure, Gammy was self-supporting, but look how she lived. Barely any money. The roof in need of shingling, the siding stripped to bare wood, the house a perpetual mess with a mouse infestation. Never mind upside-down roosters and blood everywhere. No, thanks.

By the time she goes downstairs, the laundry cycle's complete. She finds a mesh bag of pegs under the sink but no basket, so she carries everything in her arms. The line is out behind the Old House, stretching from the far corner to a beech tree. She finds a nice-looking clump of grass and sets everything down. As she pegs the laundry, the cool, damp material flaps refreshingly against her face and arms. She steps back to survey her work, the colored clothes and the two sheets neatly in a row, billowing in the sunny breeze. When she turns around, she's struck by how miserable the Old House looks by comparison, looming darkly over the bright scene. Maybe it should be torn down after all. Just because Gammy was so fixated on preserving it doesn't mean she has to be. The crooked, sagging brown clapboards are all dried out, the window frames rotting. She rounds the corner and picks her way through the weeds up to the one exposed window, standing on the fallen shutter to look inside, just as she did way back when. There's nothing to see, just a bare stone floor. She feels a creeping unease, which annoys her, so she marches up to the door, tugs at the padlock on the off chance it'll open. It doesn't budge.

She hears a sound, turns, and is astonished to see Hattie running straight at her, her thin arms pumping, the doll bouncing. "You weren't going in, were you?" she exclaims, out of breath.

"I was just looking," Jo says, a little irritated. "I don't have the key on me."

"I already looked yesterday."

"What do you mean?"

Hattie's eyes narrow in suspicion. She doesn't answer. Her hair is wet down her back, sundress clinging to her bony frame. Jo smells the dank, cool scent of the pond seeping off her in the sun, and she suddenly envies Hattie's carefree ways, not even bothering with a suit, just jumping right in by the looks of it. "I did your laundry, by the way," she says. "You're welcome."

Hattie's oblivious to the implicit accusation. "Rain's coming in," she points out. "Won't dry by then."

"So it'll get washed again," Jo retorts, but this only causes Hattie to giggle. "What's with this place, anyway? Is it locked because of the well? That's what Gammy told me when I was a kid."

Hattie's laughter dies abruptly. She lifts her doll and folds her arms around it so it's looking right at Jo, too. Hattie's gaze has gone as disconcertingly bland as the blue glass eyes. "Yes. It's because of the well."

The lie is so obvious it's almost laughable, except for Hattie's unnerving expression and the annoying doll perched in her arms, its eyes clicking with every motion.

Jo says, "There's no well, is there."

Hattie sets her jaw. "Yes, there is."

Jo wants to keep pushing, but the girl's white, pinched face makes her nervous. The whole thing is just weird and stupid. "Well, I don't care, so whatever. Is there a bike I can use? I need to go to town."

"Why?"

"There's no service here."

Hattie frowns, uncomprehending.

"My cell." Jo pulls it out of her back pocket, like evidence. "I need to use it."

"There's a phone in the kitchen."

"Yeah, and it can't send texts or pictures."

"What?"

Exasperated, Jo shoves her phone back in her pocket. "You can come with me, and I'll show you," she says, killing two birds, because she doesn't really feel like going all alone to a strange place, anyway.

Hattie shakes her head. "I can't go to town without Tom."

"Why not? You're old enough, aren't you?"

"It's the rule."

Jo's neck prickles. The girl's pale, freckled face and strange ways are getting on her nerves. How bony and malnourished she looks, her stained, crooked teeth.

"Hattie, where did you live before here?"

The question has an immediate effect, like poking a hermit crab. Hattie's shoulders turn inward and she drops her chin. "I'm not supposed to talk about it," she says.

Jo feels bad; what if the girl was abused or something? "It's OK," she says. "How about telling me how long you've been here?"

Hattie scrunches her nose. She stares out across the meadow, thinking. "I dunno. A year, a little longer, maybe."

"A year," Jo repeats. "Wow. Cool. Do you like it?"

"Yes."

"So it's better here."

"I can't remember."

Something crawls across Jo's skin. "What do you mean, you can't remember?"

"I just can't."

Jo's about to press more, but Hattie's retreated once again behind that blank look, twin to her doll. "You wanted to go to town," she states. "There's a bike in the shed. Maur used it before she got sick. I can lower the seat for you."

She abruptly sets off as if Jo agreed.

Jo looks out across the meadow, where Hattie kept looking, but there's nothing there, just empty fields and then the forest, which goes on for miles. *Maybe she comes from the woods*, Jo thinks sourly. *The Mowgli of Vermont. Barefoot, illiterate, raised by moose.*

She trudges after Hattie, and when she steps into the thankfully cool shade of the garage, she finds the girl wresting a bike from behind some folded plastic chairs. Jo wants to tell her she can take care of the seat herself, but Hattie's on it with fiendish focus. The bike is ancient, with broad curved handlebars and giant wheels, and Jo feels a mounting horror at being seen on it, even in the empty little town she's headed to. There's nothing to be done now; she can hardly say no when Hattie's doing all this work wrenching the seat this way and that to drop it several inches, glancing at Jo as she works to gauge.

"Try that," she instructs.

Jo obeys, stepping over the seat, testing it. Her toes just touch, which seems high, but Hattie pronounces it perfect and gives the nut a few more twists to be on the safe side.

"I think you should come," Jo says, because now that the expedition is nigh, she's nervous.

Hattie shakes her head, holding her doll. Jo's annoyance spikes at the sight of the scrawny girl with her dirty doll and bare feet. It isn't right. She's being kept here like a prisoner, working all the time and never allowed out.

"I'm telling you, you can come," Jo says sternly. "Gammy told me to take care of you, you know. You should listen to me."

Hattie casts a furtive, greedy glance at the other bike, which is outfitted with pink ribbons and a basket. "There's market today. We have to load at one thirty."

"We can totally be back by then," Jo insists. "I need you to show me the way, anyway."

"It's straight," Hattie points.

"Don't you want a treat from the café?"

At this, Hattie brightens. "Chocolate?"

"Sure, whatever they have. I'll get it for you."

There is a moment of hesitation, during which Jo wonders if she's made some kind of big mistake, but then it's too late, Hattie darts over to her bike and plops the doll in the basket. She grins as she wheels the bike out into the sun, her excitement palpable. Jo suddenly feels like her liberator, like she's doing just what Gammy wanted her to do, treat Hattie like she's her little sister.

"It's going to be awesome," she promises.

ELEVEN

Jo hasn't ridden a bike in a while, and after the first short incline she's sweating. If she remembers right, most of the way is downhill, which is a relief; but judging by her performance so far, coming back will be painful. Hattie, on the other hand, rides merrily along, ringing the bell every so often, her thin legs pumping the pedals. When they come to the main road, she sticks her legs out and coasts, hair and ribbons flying. The doll somehow doesn't fall out of the basket, and Jo, seeing Hattie adjust it every so often, resolves to help her sew a little dress for the grubby thing sometime in the next few days, just like a big sister might do.

She lets out a laugh, relieved to be coasting down the hill, the wind in her face. There's no one else around, just fields and trees providing swathes of cool shade as they ride along. She even sees a rabbit nestled at the edge of the road. She snaps pictures with her phone; she'll send them to Ellie, along with those she took of the house and her room. Thinking of her friend gives her a boost, and she pedals to pick up speed. She can't wait to show Ellie where she is; it's just nuts, so far from everything, but also kind of beautiful. The world feels so big here. Back home, she can't step out the front door without running into cars and people and noise.

The town appears at the bottom of the hill with its white spire and cluster of buildings. Hattie rides next to her, ringing the bell to announce their arrival. A couple of people lounge on the bench outside the café. A camper van laden with bikes is parked just ahead; on their way somewhere, just as her mom described. Jo's thirsty and hot and can't wait to get inside. They ride up and wedge their bikes into the stand. Hattie gets her doll from the basket, wraps it in her arms.

"Do you need to take that everywhere?" Jo asks, embarrassed by how filthy it looks.

Hattie nods as if the question were not rhetorical. Jo notes how worn her strapless sundress looks, the lace hem torn in places. Hattie's legs are bruised and scratched, her bones jut in angles. But it's too late to worry what strangers might think. The bells jingle against the glass as Hattie goes inside.

Jo slips in behind her. The blast of air-conditioning is an immense relief. Hattie's already over at the display, poring over the baked goods laid out on trays. A couple sits in the corner, their toddler in a high chair waving a spoon. They're talking in French; they must be visiting from Canada.

"Hattie, what are you doing here?" A woman leans around the register, looking worried. Her hair's in a bandanna, and she's wearing an apron embroidered with a chocolate cupcake and the logo LOLA'S SWEETS & SANDWICHES.

"Hi, Lola!" Hattie points at Jo, then goes back to her perusal.

"I'm Jo," Jo explains. "Maureen's granddaughter?"

"You're the Lavoie?"

Jo bristles at her dubious tone. "Yeah, I guess. Or you can just call me Jo."

"Who said you could bring Hattie out?" The hostility in her voice is at odds with her merry apron.

"No one. But it's fine, she's with me."

"You keep a tight rein, you hear? Hattie, what're you getting? It's on the house."

With that, Jo is dismissed. Smarting, she pretends to examine the pastries. She's sure the Canadians heard the exchange. As did the young woman in the kitchen pulling trays out of the oven. She's got dark hair with dyed pink streaks pulled up in a messy ponytail, her eyes heavy with liner. She must be the Nazi Baker's daughter, Jo thinks rudely, because there's no way she'd be here voluntarily. Whatever. Jo can just get what she came for and leave.

She orders a chocolate croissant and a fizzy lemonade. It's not on the house for her. Lola hands back her change with a scowl. Jo can't figure out what she did wrong. Hattie's fine. She's sucking on her chocolaty fingers and staring up at all the notices on the board as if she's never seen the like. It's good for her to get out.

Jo tucks herself in at a table near the window, checks her phone. She's memorized the Wi-Fi password and plugs it in. Within moments she's hooked to Ellie, fast-typing her news: the house, the weird-ass tenants, the crazy amount of stuff, the lack of goats. She pops onto Instagram, and her heart lurches at Diego's message: When you coming to the Cape? She scrolls swiftly through his posts. Eating ice cream, sunbathing, night party with a fire. Not coming, she writes with a pang of regret. She adds, In VT dealing with inheritance, which sounds important and intriguing.

She's so absorbed chatting with Ellie that she doesn't know how much time's gone by, no more than five, ten minutes, surely, but then Hattie's high, thin voice penetrates through the rapid back-and-forth messages.

"If you stand still in the woods, you can hear them sing."

Jo lowers her hands, the phone still vibrating with Ellie's barrage.

"What do they look like?" the biker woman asks in her rich accent. She sounds amused but kind. "Are they big or small?"

"They can be big *or* small," Hattie says.

She's right next to them, swinging her doll by the arm. The toddler waves his chubby arms, gurgling at her. She reaches out to touch his cheek. She says, "If you don't watch out, they'll take him."

The parents smile at each other. "Don't worry," the mom says. "We'll be careful."

"Nothing you can do if they want him," Hattie says gravely.

She draws her doll into the tight fold of her arms. "They'll take him and he'll forget you and when they don't want him anymore they'll send him back."

Her voice cracks at the last. The mom grasps the back of her son's high chair, as if ready to pull him out of Hattie's reach. "You have been reading very scary stories!" she says brightly. "You want to go sit with your friend?"

Hattie's back is to Jo, but she can just picture the girl's pinched expression, her scrawny muscled arms clutching the weird doll. Jo gives the mom an awkward, apologetic look. "Hattie, come on, come over here."

Hattie rotates her body side to side, refusing. "They don't get it."

Her voice is choked up with anger. Jo gets up and takes her by the shoulder, tugs a little. Hattie doesn't budge. There's a moment of quiet, full as a balloon. Then it bursts. Hattie whips around, her face horribly contorted. "Don't you understand? He'll be ALONE!"

The mom scoops her toddler out of the high chair and shuffles backward, shocked. The dad starts gathering up their stuff—maps, sunglasses, diaper bag.

Hattie drops to her knees right there on the floor, heaving sobs, clutching her doll.

"Hattie, get up," Jo begs, too scared to touch her again. "What's wrong?"

The people from outside crowd the doorway, watching. The Canadians shoulder their way through and out. Then Lola hurries over, scoops Hattie into her arms, and carries her out past the register, the countertop propped up by her daughter. The counter slams back down and they vanish into the back.

The air trembles with the awfulness of what just happened.

Jo cringes under the curious looks. She can hear the Canadians rattling off their story, and faces turn aghast, gawking in search of the little girl who had a fit. Instead, they see Jo, standing there in dismay.

"What happened?" someone asks. "Is she OK?"

Jo shakes her head, conveying confusion. On impulse, she darts across the room, lifts the wooden counter as if she does it every day, and runs to the back, away from all the prying eyes.

There's a screen door at the rear of the kitchen. She stops up short, hearing agitated voices outside.

". . . what Maureen was thinking, must've lost her marbles from all those meds!" Lola is saying. "Let that girl come here and do as she pleases!"

"Mom, stop, you're making Hattie worse."

"It's not me who did that, it's that girl, and Maur should've known better than to leave things to an outsider!"

"Mom!"

Lola whirls around in surprise. Jo didn't mean to come into view, but somehow she edged over to the door, transfixed by what they were saying, and now she's been caught. "S-sorry," she stammers. "I was just—"

"Listening in on private conversations," Lola snaps, trudging up the stairs and opening the screen door. She pauses to glare down at Jo. "I hope you're pleased with yourself, young lady!" She shakes her head in disgust and stomps by.

Hattie's at a picnic table, head in her arms. Lola's daughter sits opposite with a boy next to her, about three years old with wild, curly brown hair. The air is full of the noise of a brook rushing over stones. The place looks so peaceful and homey, except for all that's happened.

Lola's daughter gives Jo a tired wave. "I'm Amanda. Come sit."

Her rueful smile conveys apology for her mom's meanness. Jo forces herself to walk over, trying to seem indifferent to what just happened. She sits down next to Hattie and pats her back. "Are you OK?" she whispers.

Hattie's muffled, thin voice emerges from the cave of her arms. "I'm sorry."

"Mason's on his way," Amanda soothes.

"I don't want to go with Mason."

Jo asks, "Who's Mason?"

"Edie's grandson."

"I want to stay with Jo," Hattie says. "I know I'm not supposed to talk. I'm sorry, Jo—" She sobs into the doll's head, hunching over.

"Hey, it's OK," Jo comforts, patting her back awkwardly. Hattie looks so frail and pitiful. Her hair needs washing. Her elbow has a wicked scab on it. *Not supposed to talk.* Jo's stomach feels sick and cold deep inside.

"So, anyway," Amanda says, drawing Jo's attention. She

flicks her hand, conveying boredom with the whole thing, as if she's way past it all. "You just got here, right?"

"Yesterday," Jo says, realizing she hasn't been here even twenty-four hours. The little boy's playing with a wood-carved truck. He sets other carved objects in the truck bed and drives them in a circle, making engine noises. The antiquated toys add to Jo's sense of displacement. "My mom's gotten sick. A cold. She's in bed. I just wanted to . . . you know, check my phone, do something. I thought it'd be nice for her to get out."

"Yup. Well, now you've been there, done that."

"Your mom's really mad at me."

Amanda shrugs. "She's old-fashioned. She's got a thing about 'outsiders,'" she air-quotes. "So, like, I want to move to Boston with Lukie," she says, touching the boy's head, "and she's freaking out and saying how can I want to go down there so far away . . ." Her voice trails off in a sigh. "I just get bored here, you know? There's nothing ever going on. Except for this stuff"—she juts her chin at Hattie with a wry look—"which I could live without. You're lucky, you know."

"I guess," Jo says.

"Come on—you get to be near *Boston*. You have no idea."

"It's not like I do anything cool. All I do is school stuff."

"Huh," Amanda dismisses this. "But when you're finished, you could do anything. I'm twenty, and all I do is make cupcakes and clean. I want to *do* something."

Jo nods in sympathy, not sure what to say. She notices the tattoo on Amanda's chest peeking out from her frayed T-shirt collar. Something with leaves, maybe a lotus. She sure doesn't seem like she belongs in a bakery in the middle of nowhere. It's ironic that she thinks Jo has it made, seeing as Jo feels exactly the same back home, like she doesn't fit, doesn't belong, and just wants to get away. This place seems dreamlike to Jo, somewhere she'd choose to stay awhile. The bubbling brook, the green grass. The boy with his funny toys. She reaches over and picks one up. It's a face carved into wood. The bottom has grooves all around, like a stand. "Did you make this?"

"Tom did. He gives them out to kids at the markets."

"Wow." Jo hands the toy back to Lukie. He grabs it and drops off the bench to follow Hattie, who's gone over to the rushing brook. She sinks into a crouch, staring into the water and humming. Lukie crouches next to her, a chubby little shadow.

Jo leans forward, asks in a low voice, "Why'd she say all that weird stuff?"

Amanda lifts an eyebrow. "Um, seriously?"

Jo shrugs assent, and Amanda gives an astonished little laugh. "Jesus. No wonder my mom's freaking out Maur left you the house."

The sound of a truck on the driveway interrupts them. Hattie looks up, dismayed. Jo hears doors slam, then Edie comes into view, sets across the yard with a young guy in tow. He's got long hair pulled back in a man-bun, a loose T-shirt with a screen-printed guitar on it. He's tan and lean and muscled and leaves Jo feeling like a shabby blob. Never mind that it's clear she's in the doghouse, big-time, given how Edie looks at her so sternly. He stays standing while Edie slides onto the bench next to Jo. Hattie approaches meekly, holding the doll like a shield.

"Hattie," Edie says sternly, "you know you're not to go anywhere without Tom."

Hattie nods.

"You won't do it again?"

Hattie shakes her head with equal fervor.

"It's my fault," Jo says. "I'm the one who said she could come."

Edie's bright blue eyes fix on her. "That may be, but Hattie knows better. Hattie, isn't there market this afternoon?"

"There's time. I won't be late."

"Mason should take you home, anyway."

Hattie shakes her head. "I want to stay with Jo."

Edie seems surprised by this, as if she hadn't thought it possible. Feeling vindicated, Jo says, "We rode bikes here, we can ride back."

"It's hot," Edie points out.

"We'll hydrate."

Edie sighs. "Well, go on with Mason for now, then. I need to talk to Jo."

Mason holds his hand out to Hattie, who reluctantly takes it and walks off with him. Jo hears him asking if she already had a pastry, to which Hattie replies no without missing a beat.

Edie gives a little jerk of the head to Amanda, indicating she should leave. Amanda rolls her eyes. She calls her son away from the brook, and they head up the yard.

"Well, then," Edie says. "I guess now you know not to take Hattie on outings."

Jo balls her fists under her thighs. "What's wrong with her, anyway?"

Edie lifts an eyebrow, peering down at her. "You don't know?"

"Why should I?"

"Because of your father."

"What's she got to do with him?"

"They have a lot in common."

Jo's heart races. "She said the same stuff my dad used to say, if that's what you mean."

"And?"

"And what? He couldn't go anywhere, either, till he got his meds. She should be seeing a doctor."

"Did doctors help your father?"

"Of course they did!"

"Did they?"

The cool questions unsettle Jo even more. She stares blindly down at her lap. There's no point to this conversation. *The whole town is crazy*, she thinks. She's starting to see why her mom hates it here.

"You look very much like him," Edie says suddenly. "Your hair, your nose, the shape of your mouth."

Jo glances at her sideways, detecting her change in tone.

"We were all sad when he left," Edie continues. "He was happy here. He worked hard. I remember him always with that big, big smile."

"I remember him like that, too," Jo mutters, uncomfortable but yearning now to hear more. "What was he like?"

"You mean when he was younger? He was funny. He was always making jokes. You couldn't be around him without smiling."

Jo thinks of the photo of him with Abigail, laughing together at the waterfall. "He was like that sometimes. I guess he changed."

"He shouldn't have left here."

"That's what Gammy always said, but I don't get why. I mean, he was married, he had a kid, of course he wanted to leave."

Edie seems taken aback. After a pause, she says, "Yes, I suppose it was natural."

"I mean, look at it." Jo gestures at the few buildings lining the road. "What was he supposed to do here? It's like Amanda. She wants to leave, and it makes sense. I don't mean in a bad way," she rushes on, detecting Edie's affront. "It's just, someone young, you want to go see the world, right?"

"Is that what you want to do?"

"Yes, it is. I've got it planned, actually. After high school, I'm going."

"So you'll sell for sure."

The blunt turn throws Jo off balance. "How did you know—?"

"Tom called," Edie explains.

"But why did he tell you?"

Edie wags her finger to silence her. "You sell, you sell to us, you hear? The house can't go to some flatlander come to live a dream of milking goats and sugaring."

Jo's cheeks heat up. "Like me, you mean?"

"You're Maur's granddaughter. You belong. But someone else? No. Absolutely not. Do you understand?"

Jo doesn't, not really. She's stuck on *You belong*. Edie said it grimly, like a sentence handed down by some judge, but for Jo it's appealing. She's never belonged anywhere, except maybe the first house with her mom and dad, long ago. But she belongs here: it's in the will, and confirmed by Edie, who seems to know what she's talking about, even if she's kind of harsh.

"I don't want to sell," Jo hears herself confessing. "It's Mom."

"It's your house. You can do what you want."

"Yeah, and then I'll get kicked out," Jo says. "That's what they'll do, you know."

"Then you can live here. You should anyway. It's your duty."

Jo wonders irritably if Edie and Gammy crafted that letter together. Edie's the one she's supposed to go to with questions, but she doesn't know what to ask, and anyway, she feels put off by the old woman's critical tone. "I guess maybe I could live here," she says, to stop Edie from going on about it. "I should go. I need to check on my mom."

"All right, then," Edie says. "You call if you need anything. My number's on the wall next to the phone."

"Thanks," Jo says, *but yeah, no thanks.* Edie makes Jo feel like she's done something wrong, like she might just whip out a ruler and rap her across the knuckles. She walks across the hot grass feeling Edie's eyes boring into her the whole way. It's a relief once she rounds the building. The tourists and van are gone. Mason and Hattie are sitting on the outside bench, Hattie devouring an éclair. She gives Jo a startled, guilty look, then licks a cream blob off her lip.

"We should head back," Jo tells Mason.

He stands up. He seems goofy and awkward, unsure of how to take his leave. It emboldens her. "Do you play?" She points at his shirt.

He looks down at it, startled. "Oh—yeah. Fiddle. I'm not that good."

"You're probably better than you think."

He smiles, revealing crooked, very white teeth. "I dunno."

"Well, thanks." Jo nods at Hattie.

"No problem." He raises a hand in awkward farewell, then ducks away around his truck and jumps in. There are stickers on the back: concerts, mountains, a moose.

"He seems nice," Jo says as they jiggle their bikes out of the rack.

"Jo and Mason sitting in a tree . . ." Hattie titters.

"Hattie!"

"K! I! S! S! I! N! G!"

"Oh my God!" Jo exclaims. "Stop!"

Hattie jumps onto her bike, singing over her shoulder,

"First comes love! Then comes marriage! Oh look!" she interrupts herself, pointing across the park. "I never get to go! Can we go? Can we?"

She pedals across the road before Jo can answer. She bops her bike right over the curb and races onto the gravel path. Jo has to work hard to catch up. Hattie goes straight to the playground fence and lets the bike fall in the grass. "Swing?" she invites.

"In a sec," Jo says, panting. She checks her phone to verify there's time to spare. "I want to look—" She points at the statue.

Hattie shrugs, grabs her doll from the basket, and runs over to the swing set.

Jo watches until Hattie's settled the doll in the infant swing and has built momentum on hers, then she heads back down the path to the statue. The plaque at the bottom reads:

JOSIAH LADD, HERO OF THE UNION

She backs away to look up. Her great-times-four-grandfather looks dashing in his uniform, fist on saber hilt, mustache swirled into points. He resembles Pops's ancestor, the one who had his leg sawed off; they pretty much all looked the same back then.

It's cool she's related to an actual statue in a town park, even if only by adoption. She pulls out her phone to show Ellie. Luckily there's service here. She positions herself so the statue's looming behind her, takes a selfie: check out my greatx4 grandfather.

She heads around the base to read the plaque on the other side, which describes how Josiah Ladd came here and built a farm and the town grew around it, then he went to war and came back a hero. Centered at the bottom of the plaque are the words:

From his sin he did not turn away

Jeez, Jo thinks. Maybe it was like his motto or something. Jo takes a pic and sends it.

OMG ur hanging with a statue

don't knock him he made this town

Jo sends a pic of the one road with its few buildings.

lol!

They carry on conversing as Jo makes her way around the park perimeter. She tells Ellie about Hattie's freak-out and sends a pic of Hattie on the swing in the distance. She says how everyone's mad at her and how Tom's all creepy and weird and might be a serial killer seeing as she found graves in the woods and he *said* they were animals but how can she be sure.

ur finally in your own horror movie, Ellie says, adding a series of ghost emojis.

totally, Jo agrees. he's sooooo weird there's something seriously wrong with him lol.

She feels a twinge of guilt for talking that way, but it can't really matter, Ellie will never meet them, anyway.

Then Ellie has to go, she's late for the skate park with Gabriella, can Jo believe it. She spams hearts, and Jo laughs, spamming four-leaf clovers and crossed fingers. They sign off with promises to talk again tomorrow at the same time. Jo checks for a reply from Diego. OK cool is all he wrote, with a pic of himself half-buried in sand. It's a reminder of how they've never talked much, just hung out that one time. Jo feels deflated and alone, and suddenly, horribly tired. She wishes now they'd gotten a ride with Mason.

Hattie is swinging high, kicking her legs out and leaning back. There's a good fifteen minutes before they have to leave, but Jo doesn't feel like joining in. *If you stand still in the woods*, Hattie's voice drifts into her mind. *You can hear them sing.* Her dad said the fairies sang to the children next to the flowing silver river, and there was ice cream and candy, and the animals could speak.

Jo heard something this morning. Not singing, really. But sort of. Maybe it was the fairies after all. Maybe she's turning into her dad. She should ask Hattie about it, she thinks bitterly, since apparently she has "a lot in common" with him, whatever that means.

Jo feels nauseated and hot. She swallows spit, looking around. There's a stone water fountain down the path. She heads there and drinks long and deep, splashes the cool water on her face and neck.

Just past the fountain, a low iron fence borders the town graveyard. It strikes her that Gammy must be buried there. The entrance is way on the other side, and seeing as Hattie's still swinging, Jo climbs over the fence and meanders through the oldest graves, reading the strange names and imagining their brief, harsh lives here without electricity or cars or anything. The usual arrays of tiny baby headstones poke out of the grass, illegible and sad. Life was so hard back then. Her great-times-four-grandfather, no matter how stoic he's made out to be by the statue, must have endured the same sufferings with his family in the Old House, huddled around the fire in winter.

In the center of the graveyard, she finds the Ladd family plot marked by a large, ornately carved monument, like a mausoleum except there's no door. The front is inscribed simply LADD. Rows of headstones stand like soldiers in attendance, the oldest dark, slate slabs closest to the monument. Jo spots Gammy's headstone right away, it's so new, the granite bright and polished. She approaches, feeling solemn. A vase stands against the stone, the cut flowers wilting in the heat. She wonders who put them there; maybe Edie. The inscription reads:

MAUREEN AMELIA LAVOIE
Steadfast & True
Mother to Beloved Lorenzo

The inscription fills Jo with sadness. When her dad died, Gammy wanted him brought here, but he'd left express wishes to be buried in the family plot in Newton, so as to be near Jo for all eternity, as her mom explained. When Jo grew distraught, feeling bad for Gammy, Abigail said, Just don't think about it.

It's hard not to, though. Especially here.

She snaps a photo, not for sending to Ellie but to keep for herself. Resolving to bring fresh flowers at some point, she carefully picks her way around the central monument, reading headstones, a mix of Lavoies and Ladds. They all lost babies. She comes around to the shaded back of the mausoleum, dark with moss. An obelisk stands against this wall, a cherub on top staring heavenward. It's so old its face has been almost completely eroded. The obelisk is a few feet taller than Jo. She stands on tiptoe to read the inscription on the cherub's base:

Cherished Ones Your Home Awaits

Under that she sees names engraved in a column, but there are no dates, not even last names. Edward is the most recent, about a foot from the top, then Erin, Jonas, Stephen, and a bunch more in two columns, the lowest buried under the lichen covering the stone. She bends over to work at the lichen with her fingernails. Gradually, the grooves become visible and she struggles to read the revealed names.

H, she makes out. And *T*.

Cold washes across her skin.

HATTIE.

She stares, her fingers scraping the last of the lichen. There's no doubt. That's the name. It can't be, though. It can't be the same Hattie. It's just random. A coincidence.

She stares at Hattie on the swing, her thin legs flailing kicks, going high, higher, then jumping off into the sand.

Jo's fingers are raw, but she kneels to dig at the thicker lichen lower down. More names appear, the engravings so faded some she can't read. *E . . . SP . . . TH* she thinks must be Elspeth. She saw that name on some of the graves; maybe it was common back in the day. And *AR . . . D* could be Armand. And *LO . . . NZO.* Alphonso. No, that doesn't fit—

LORENZO

Jo backs away, her knees scraping against the pebbly dirt. Everyone always called her dad Enzo, but his full name was Lorenzo.

Hattie and Lorenzo. One name could be random, but *two* of them?

None of it makes sense. Hattie's right there, alive as can be. And her dad was alive long after that name was engraved—it's got to have been there at least a hundred years.

She gets to her feet, her head thick with misgivings and confusion. She jogs back through the graves, steps over the fence into the park. She's so stupid, she thinks savagely, slamming the rusty bike into position and climbing on. What exactly was she thinking—that they were dead and came back to life?

She's already sick in the head, is the problem. She's showing symptoms, turning bit by bit into her father, just like she's always feared.

"Hattie, come on," she yells.

"Aren't you going to swing?"

Jo shakes her head, impatient with the girl's weird childishness. Hattie, disappointed, drags her feet getting to her bike. Jo watches without comment.

"What's wrong?" Hattie asks.

"You'll be late, you're taking so long," Jo snaps.

Hattie looks hurt, and Jo wants to say sorry but can't bring herself to, she's so fed up. She pedals hard, out ahead of Hattie, leaving the town and its graves and its stupid statue in a cloud of dust. She needs to remember she's here a week at most. She'll get through it and then go home and it'll all be over. She wishes she were in Wellfleet after all, taking those stupid tennis lessons and hanging with Diego, even if he's kind of dumb.

Anything would be better than here.

maur liked to say she had a long full life so she werent sad to die. she lived in canada when she were younger and she traveled. there are parts of this world you cant imagine she told me. parts made all of sand or all of ocean. people talk and you cant understand.

i didnt care for her stories. its enough to go one day to the next right here. all whats in this ground aint mine not anymore. the roots of things reach deeper than i can go. maur said look forward not back but if i close my eyes the colors start the reds and the hurting brightness and then the dark comes and if i wait like that staring with my eyes shut i can see.

what do you want with such a place maur said when here is where you are.

TWELVE

By the time they're pedaling up the endless driveway under the blaring sun, Jo's faint and nauseated. Hattie goes straight up to the greenhouse, barely saying bye, for which Jo can't blame her. She'll apologize later. She peels herself off the bike and lets it fall in the grass, stumbles up the porch steps into the kitchen. She drags the pitcher out of the fridge and drinks straight from the lip.

As her breathing settles, she notices how quiet the house is. Her mom must still be asleep. She drinks more, the cold water running down her chin. She's kind of hungry, so she opens the fridge again, stares at the contents. She could make a turkey sandwich. Or PB&J. A motion catches the corner of her eye. She looks down the hall through the sunroom to discover that actually, her mom is not in bed. She's outside, hunched over the Old House padlock.

"Mom?" Jo cries, barging out the screen door. "What are you doing?"

"Trying this key?" her mom replies irritably, meaning *duh*.

It's startling how bad she looks, pale, sticky, with bright pink circles in her cheeks. "You shouldn't be up."

"I hate lying around," Abigail retorts, her voice a thin rasp.

"Yeah, but you're sick," Jo points out.

Abigail bends over the padlock again, obstructed by her bulk, fumbling with her pregnant sausage fingers. The key slips home with a loud click.

"Mom, come on. You should go back to bed."

Abigail waves Jo off. She stares blearily at the padlock in her hands, gives the key a twist. The padlock drops open. "There we go," she says, dislodging the lock and tossing it into the grass. She points at the bar. "Get that off, would you."

Jo hesitates.

"Come on, Jo. Don't be silly."

But Jo can't move. *Sshhhh*, her daddy cautioned, tucking her to him as they went by. Little Jo-Jo wondered who might hear, since the house was old and empty. Both Gammy and her daddy said it was bad. It was a creepy, mossy ancient thing that hung over their days swimming in the pond and playing on the tire swing, always there, a shadow hulking over them.

Now, all is silent but for the hot buzzing in the meadow and the feel of the day's heat pressing down on her.

Her mom mutters a curse and attempts to lift the bar herself. She's not supposed to pick up anything heavy, and Jo, spurred by alarm, quickly steps in and takes over. It's harder than she expected to dislodge it. Finally, she pulls it off and props it against the wall. Her mom tries the door, but it's jammed, the wood swollen in the damp heat of summer. Jo leans in, using her weight to push hard. This time the door comes free, causing her to stumble.

Cool air wafts from inside, bringing stale smells of dirt and stone. The outside light illumines the layer of dust across the bare floor. Jo finds herself unable to go forward, fear trickling through her limbs, paralyzing her.

Her mom pushes past and steps inside. "My God," she waves a hand in front of her face. "It's a good thing we don't have asthma."

Gammy! Gaa-mmeeeeee!

The memory swirls up, so powerful that Jo sways, catches the doorjamb. She was standing here. She can see her sandals and bare legs, her hand on the door like it is now. It was sunny. *Gaaaaa-mmmmeeeeee!* she shouted, her shrill voice echoing in the shadowy room.

The door was open. She'd seen it and walked right in, looking for Gammy.

Who swooped out of nowhere and lifted her right off her feet. *Be quiet, girl!* she hissed, carrying her back out into the sunlight. *You don't want them to hear!*

Gammy was really angry—or no, she was frightened. Jo sees her distraught expression, feels her tight grip. Jo-Jo started crying, she was so startled. She'd done something terribly wrong and now Gammy was upset.

Jo tries to focus on now, on the present. The low ceiling and uneven stone slabs recall any one of the usual, boring colonial structures she's visited back home. But she can't help it, she's afraid, deep down in her belly, sick and tremulous.

You don't want them to hear.

"Wait, Mom," she says.

Abigail watches as Jo hunts around in the weeds till she finds a big enough rock, jams the door open with it. "So we don't get stuck," she says in response to her mom's amused arched eyebrow.

"Well," Abigail says, her voice ringing hollow in the dim, low-ceilinged space, "nothing here to see. I guess it wouldn't need to be torn down, though, would it?"

"No," Jo says.

"It could be a guesthouse," Abigail muses. "It's a shame to keep it closed up. It's a piece of history."

Abigail could care less about history. It sounds like something she's rehearsing for the real estate agent. Jo watches her mom obliviously go around opening all the shutters until every corner's exposed. There is nothing here. No well, no danger. The two adjoining rooms, probably once bedrooms, are just as bare.

"I wonder what the fuss was all about," her mom sighs. She leans in the doorway, looking like hell. "God, I have to go back to bed. You're going to have to take care of things today, all right? I just can't."

Jo responds to this with her best death glare, but her mom ignores it, instead listing everything Jo's supposed to do. Make a fire and burn all the folders, because what on earth will they do with them. Find big garbage bags and leave some in each room. Start a shopping list if she can't find any of the aforementioned bags. Make chicken soup from scratch, as it's the best thing for a cold.

"Are you kidding me?" Jo exclaims. "It's freaking a hundred degrees, and besides, I don't know how to make soup!"

"Shush. I'll tell you how."

Well, that's news. Her mom hates cooking. Someone comes in three times a week to prepare meals. The fridge and freezer at home are always stacked with labeled containers, but now here she is, croaking out a recipe like she's Betty Crocker. Jo's even supposed to gather vegetables from the garden. Dig up potatoes? She has no clue how to do that. They only have potted tomatoes and sometimes peas back in Newton. Her mom can't be bothered to cook or garden, but here she is listing what to harvest as if she does it every day. She lived here for a while way back when; maybe that's how she knows stuff like how to find potatoes.

It's just one more piece of her life with her father that she buried and hid from Jo. The personal chef and frozen meals are a lie, just like everything else.

"Fine," Jo snaps. "I'll do it all. Just go to bed already."

Her mom bestows one of her wounded, martyred looks. "I would help if I could."

"Sure, whatever." Jo folds her arms, exuding boredom.

Her mom delivers a pronounced sigh, then shuffles out the door, groaning her way off the stone step and across the yard.

Jo feels bad, but not that much. It's good her mom's gone. She shouldn't be here, in this place.

She shouldn't be here: that's something else Gammy said. Was it the same day?

She yearns to dash outside, lock everything up again. But the sun's shining, and all is silent. The door's propped safely open. *Nothing will happen*, she insists to herself.

She circles the front room, looking for anything to explain her weird memory. There's a giant hearth with a single iron pot on a coal rack. Against the wall is a bench, the only piece of furniture. There's nothing hanging on the cracked plaster walls darkened from time, no sign that Josiah Ladd and his wife and three kids ever lived here. Everything must have been taken out when the new house was built. Jo runs her fingers across empty, dusty shelves, opens cupboards that turn out to be bare. It makes no sense. Why should this vacant, boring place be dangerous? And where had Gammy come from that day? She'd been inside, Jo's sure of it. She wanders around once again, touching cracks in the wall, searching for a hidden door.

She becomes aware of a cool breeze on her feet. She's near the hearth, so maybe it's from the chimney. She crouches down, feeling at the floor. Cold seeps from between the slabs. There must be a cellar, she deduces, though why air would actually blow from it, she can't say. If there is a well after all, then maybe air could come up from there. If it's dry, and there's a cave at the bottom, with more caves leading to the outside—what does she know about wells and caves? It seems plausible, though.

She hunts around and finds what she overlooked: the cupboard floor has a wooden trapdoor with an iron ring for a handle. She runs her hands along the edges, feeling the cold, then lifts the door a little to peek. Stone steps lead into complete darkness. Her heart speeds up, hurting her chest. She slowly pulls the trapdoor all the way open till it drops back against the shelves with a thud.

She digs out her phone and switches on the flashlight.

The steps lead down to an earth floor. She doesn't want to go in. She wants to slam that door shut and leave. But then she'll just have to come back, she reasons. There's no way she'll be able to just forget this.

The trapdoor will stay open. The front door is open. It's daytime. There's probably nothing down there, just the supposed well, and she's hardly going to fall in.

She goes down one step at a time on her butt, shining the light this way and that. The cold deepens, damp and heavy feeling. On the last step, she climbs to her feet to shine the light all around the space.

The floor is earth and gravel. Some wooden barrels stand against one wall, empty shelves above them. Toward the back, the floor looks dug up. *Maybe this is the well*, she thinks confusedly, though it doesn't jibe with the image she had of a tidy round brick structure.

There isn't anything else here. It's just an old root cellar, damp, unpleasant, and empty. Maybe Gammy hadn't wanted her falling into the cellar. Maybe Jo misremembered the warning.

She steps forward with caution, aware of the dark pressing all around. There's something off, something not right.

It's the breeze. Cold wafting about her ankles, as if coming from somewhere deeper. And this upheaval of stone and earth is definitely not a well. It's more like the detritus from an earthquake, with a huge stone slab forced up and lodged in place by scree. The breeze seeps from a narrow opening beneath the slab, no more than five or six inches wide.

She's been here before.

The knowing floats to the surface, clear and indisputable. She can't remember. But she knows.

Trembling, she lowers herself to her knees, creeps closer to the scree. She reaches out, touches the cold stone. Her hand runs across something sharp: a jagged piece of iron rebar. Next to it, more iron junk, strewn among the stones. The breeze wafts across her face, her lips. Dizziness causes her to teeter, and she gasps, propped on her elbows. The cool air smells rottingly sweet, like flowers and wet grass.

Like her dreams.

You likely fell in the grass that night, Dr. Coletti told her.

That's how he explained the almost suffocating smells of earth and damp when she'd wake. His theory sounded stupid then, and even more so now.

It was this place. I was here.

She leans a little closer, breathing in the strange air wafting from the darkness, mingled with the cloying, earthy damp of the cellar. She lifts her phone, tilts the light into the crack: gravel and dirt and rocks disappear into pitch black.

There is something there.

She reaches hesitantly into the darkness until her fingers touch the thing, which is oddly rigid. She tugs and there's a faint snap, and then it comes free in her hand.

She edges away, shaken. After a moment, she directs the light onto the object in her hand.

She can't make out what it is. There's a long bit like a straw, the part that broke, and attached to this are the frayed remains of something like cloth, or some kind of plant. Transparent, veined. Like a web, but with different patterns.

She reaches back in, groping for more of the thing. She tugs till it comes free, a much larger piece, about two feet long. The cloth part hangs limp, riven with tears and holes, and yet when she rubs it between her fingers, it doesn't disintegrate. It's strong, more like embroidery thread. It doesn't resemble anything she's ever seen. It was part of something even larger, that much she can tell.

She maneuvers onto her knees, wincing at the gravel digging into her skin, then clambers to her feet. Her toe strikes something hard, and she whimpers at the bright, sharp pain. The cone of light swings, searching for the obstacle.

It's a manacle, connected to a chain that snakes away through the gravel to the stone wall, where it's soldered to an iron ring.

Jo stares at this bizarre object. Its presence is inexplicable and terrifying.

No one would hear you scream.

She hurries to the stairs and climbs hand over foot, tumbles into the main room. Her legs give out and she sits heavily on the stone floor.

Her rushed escape has wrecked her find. Bits of the black netting drift to the floor. Understanding comes to her at last, like a bit of memory floating past and pricking her awake. It's part of a wing. The complex pattern fits together with pictures she's seen in biology class of cicadas, grasshoppers. The hard, almost plastic quality to the edge, it's because it's cartilage.

Except this wing, if she extrapolates from the bit she has, would be much bigger.

"What did you do?" a voice cries.

Shock sends Jo fumbling backward, trying to get up. Hattie stands frozen in the sunny doorway, Tom just behind. Her face stretches into a mask of panic. "You weren't supposed to touch it!"

Jo looks where she's pointing, the shredded bit of wing falling from her opened hand.

"Why?" she whispers, fear rising inside her, growing from somewhere as deep and dark as the opening itself.

"Because now they'll come," Hattie says, and bursts into tears.

THIRTEEN

Tom stands with his long ropy arms hanging and his head bent. He bears no expression, staring into the blackness of the cellar as if listening or waiting for something.

"She broke the ward," he announces at last. "Door's open."

Jo gets slowly to her feet, the strange words muddling inside her head. *Ward* is from storybooks and fairy tales. *Door* could mean the trapdoor. But he means a different one, she knows. The one down below, where she found the raggedy bits of wing now scattered across the stone floor.

"Did you move the iron?" Hattie asks. She sounds frantic.

"I—I don't think so. I don't know."

Hattie wipes her teary face with her forearm, then she clambers down the steps into the cellar. Tom stands aside, staring after her.

There is a door to another world, her daddy incanted in his storytelling voice. That was always the beginning, the words themselves a door to the magic closeness with him, to tales about fairies and children playing and singing and eating as much ice cream as they wanted. She used to imagine herself dancing into that world in a pretty dress, like the girl in Oz.

He never said it was that gash in the rocks, filled with blackness and cold.

Her mind isn't working right. What she's thinking is impossible. It has to be.

Hattie comes back up the steps. "It's all there," she says.

Jo feels dumbly relieved, as if she did something right. Tom nods, rubbing his jaw, then he nudges the trapdoor with his boot. For a moment it stands vertical, then it drops. Jo shrinks in anticipation of the bang, but instead the door lands on his other waiting boot. He releases the door with barely a thud. Hattie at once steps onto it and paces back and forth, making sure it's fully closed. Tom watches her. When she's finished, she looks at him with a pinched, scared expression. "It should've lasted longer."

"She went poking around," Tom says, as if Jo isn't right there.

His remote, indifferent demeanor is somehow worse than Hattie's panic. "I'm sorry," Jo whispers. They look at her, so she blurts, by way of an excuse, "We had to come in—we have to get the house ready to show!"

She shouldn't have said that. Of course she shouldn't have. Tom's face hardens. His gaze travels the tattered, dark wing pieces strewn across the floor, his mouth twisted and bitter.

"That may be," he says. "Door's still open till it gets closed."

"What does that mean?"

He ignores her, prods Hattie toward the outside. "We've got market to get to."

Jo stumbles behind them. She almost falls, her body weak as jelly. Outside in the hot sun, Tom slams the door and bars it and claps the padlock shut. "Won't make a difference but a small delay," he says, turning around and handing her the key. "Your mama should leave."

The words don't register for a long, hot, sunbaked minute. Jo takes in his brown, angled face, the thinness of his lips. His lashes are unusually long and dark. "Why?"

"They'll sniff her out like ants to sugar."

"Who will?"

Tom mutters annoyance. Hattie looks at him, then says, "The little ones."

A weakness plummets through Jo's body, like she might faint.

You have to hide, Jo-Jo.

Her mouth is so dry, she can barely speak. "Who are they?"

Hattie furrows her brow. She sneaks a glance at Tom, but he's staring off at the gardens, likely worrying about the market. "You still don't know?"

As if she's supposed to.

Hush, Jo-Jo, or the little ones will find you.

Jo can't believe she's asking this. She forces the words out in a stammer. "Are you talking about—fairies?"

"Yes, that's right," Hattie says with obvious relief. "Not the old ones, the little ones. They're the children the fairies give wings to so they change. They come here when the door opens. You'll need to put out the candy." She counts on her fingers: "A bowl at the kitchen door, a bowl at the sunroom door, and one on the inside, and then at the front, which isn't really the front 'cause we don't use it."

Jo looks at her in confusion. "Candy?"

"So they leave the house alone. They make awful messes. You really don't know anything?"

Jo's head feels thick, heavy with anxiety. "No."

"Your dad never told you?"

Jo hesitates. "He told me stories."

Hattie looks perplexed. "And?"

"It was make-believe. Bedtime stories, that kind of thing."

"It wasn't make-believe," Hattie says. "There are children get turned into little ones. If the door's open, they come. They steal others to take back."

"Those were delusions," Jo argues, though it sounds weak, pathetic even as she says it.

Tom is fed up. "Little'uns are real and they'll come, could already be here. The market won't wait. Come, Hattie."

Jo grabs his arm. "But what about my mom? What did you mean?"

He stares at her hand until she lets go, embarrassed. He says, "They'll want to get close with a baby on the way."

"But will they hurt her?" Jo's voice rises, panicked.

"Not my business what they do or don't. We can't be late."

"But—"

He turns on his heel and strides off. Hattie casts an apologetic look before following him at a trot.

Jo stands there, the sun baking her in place. Then she forces herself to walk to the sunroom, and she latches the door, because now that she's alone and now that all is silent but for the birds and the rustling leaves, she feels afraid.

She makes her way to the wicker love seat near the door going into the house. A path to escape. Her eyes fix on the Old House with its dark walls and opaque windows and weeds growing up all around. She opens her sweaty hand. The key has dug pits into her skin, she's been gripping it so tightly. An urge to check the padlock sweeps over her. But it doesn't really matter. It makes no difference. She understands now. The lock and bar aren't meant to keep anything in; they're for keeping people out.

A small delay.

She can't fathom what that means. What sort of creature might find a barred, padlocked, fortresslike door merely a delay? He said they might already be out. Her skin prickles with fear. There's nothing here. The room is silent and empty but for her, sitting rigidly on the edge of the cushion.

The fairies her dad told her about were magical creatures that could make themselves any size they chose, and turn invisible, too. They were golden, or green, or many colors, and they had splendid wings that could snap open in a heartbeat, so huge they blotted out the sun. The fairies played with the children, swimming in the river and eating ice cream and candy, and no one ever had to go to the dentist. Jo-Jo had loved that part. Sometimes they made other fairies, he'd called them little ones, and she'd imagined littler fairies. He never said they were made from the children themselves. Or did he? In her head, they were all the same. They snuck through and Jo-Jo had to be careful, because even if it was fun over there in the fairy world, did Jo-Jo really want to be stolen away from her daddy? No, she did not.

Hush, Jo-Jo, or they'll hear!

It was a game until they came here, and then it became frightening because her daddy was so distraught. The little ones were creeping into this world through the dark gash in the earth, down in the silence of the cellar. That's why they fled this place. That's what he was scared of when he hid her at the seaside motel.

She blindly makes her way to the kitchen, scrubs her face at the sink, drinks the cold water with deep gulps.

Get out! Gammy hollered.

Jo freezes, her surroundings obliterated by the violence of remembering. The night roiled with terror. Her daddy ran toward her, mouth open, crying hoarsely, *Jo-Jo! Jo-Jo, run!*

He was too late.

He was too late.

The odor of grass and river and earth fills her mouth, then blackness: Nothing. Gone.

She leans over the sink, gasping.

Your nightmares are your father's delusions playing out in your subconscious, Dr. Coletti chides from his armchair, somewhere far back in her mind.

He was so wrong. They were never nightmares. They were memories.

She was in her room. In bed. She remembers now. The moonlight across the bare floor. The darkness beyond.

Something else was in the room.

Get out! Get out! Gammy hollered. Then her daddy was there calling her name. But he was too late.

It touched her.

There's nothing else after that. Just the odor gagging her throat, and the profound sensation of falling, falling, far away through a vast empty space.

She breathes over the stained porcelain sink, watching the water swirl down the drain. Listening.

She suddenly wonders if her mom's awake. She's desperate to be with her. Abigail will know what to do. She always does.

She hurries down the hall, sliding into near paralysis when she glimpses the Old House through the window. Her breaths fill the silent air as she climbs the steps, fighting the urge to look back over her shoulder. She edges the bedroom door open ever so slightly.

Her mom's passed out on the bed, mouth wide open, the fan blowing across her balloon form. The sight of her sinks Jo's heart. There's no way she can tell her mom what's going on.

She'll think Jo's crazy, just like everyone thought her dad was. Jo can't tell her anything, not one bit of it.

As quietly as possible, she closes the door again and backs away.

She digs the candy bags out of the garbage and piles them on the table. She finds four big bowls and cuts slits in the bags, pours them out. They're children, that must be the reason for the candy. Children living in a fairyland with fairy wings. Flitting here unseen, maybe already in the house.

Her hands are shaking. She mixes the candy in batches. Kids want variety, after all. Five sorts in each bowl is how it ends up. Fairy children probably can't figure out the candy's expired, or maybe it's just Gammy as usual unwilling to throw away food despite the date, and the little ones better make do like the rest of the household.

She carries every bowl to the designated doorways, sets it in the middle of every step so it can't be missed. The action brings some comfort, as if she's taking charge, as if she's got this under control. The bowls fit in with the iron junk, which must also serve to ward them off. She imagines Gammy out there adding a piece here, a piece there, over the years. It's heartening. Gammy knew what she was doing, clearly, and all Jo has to do is the same.

She sets the last bowl down at the wide-open front door, the one next to the TV room. The weedy stone steps lead into a riotous expanse of daisies and uncut grass. The laundry hangs in a pretty row across the line. The sun pours across the green, and wind blows through the beeches at the edge of the yard, shivering their pretty leaves so they sparkle. The wind is picking up, she notes. There are storms on the way, the heat will break soon. She looks down at her feet, planted solidly on the worn wood floor. They're striped with flip-flop tan marks. She never paints her nails; maybe she should. She should go for a swim, actually. Or a hike, then a swim.

Because everything's normal, and this can't be happening, not really.

Wait, her daddy whispered.

They were at the edge of the forest, they'd just visited the sugar shack. She remembered this earlier, when she was out there. It's more vivid now.

Can you hear? he asked, gripping her arm so it hurt, and she understood he was worried. Jo-Jo craned her neck, staring up at the patches of blue between the swaying trees.

Let's go, her daddy ordered. He pulled her arm, forcing her into a run.

What's wrong? she cried, and he turned as he ran, finger pressed to his lips in warning.

It's all coming back in bits and pieces, but reordered, placed in a new frame.

The frame in which her father wasn't delusional after all. The frame in which all the stories were true.

They just can't be. They can't.

Except they are.

Jo stands at the kitchen screen door, watching Tom and Hattie in the distance. They're loading the truck bed. The clock ticks. Water trickles inside the fridge, then it makes a mechanical thunk and starts a loud hum. Soon they'll be gone, and she'll be here alone.

The notion of this is a steady, sawing terror at the back of her throat, choking her.

She spies a basket on the front porch and picks it up. The heat pounds into her as she sets out across the yard. Sweat pours down her sides. She's in a tank top and jean shorts and it's still too much. She should go swim in the pond. She can't believe her mom wants her to make soup in this heat. Sure, in her condition, it's the only thing that might help, but does it really? It sounds like an old wives' tale.

Then again, here, old wives' tales are real.

The truck's parked under the oak tree, and they're loading large plastic bins onto the bed. Tom ignores her, but Hattie stops to see what she wants.

Jo holds up the basket. "I need to get stuff for my mom's soup," she says.

Hattie looks at Tom inquiringly.

"Hurry up," Tom says.

Jo names what Abigail asked for: onions, garlic, potatoes, carrots, celery. Hattie beckons Jo to follow and weaves her way through the tidy vegetable rows. Celery is first. Then Hattie grabs a sprig of greens, wedges a trowel into the earth, and pulls.

One carrot after another comes up, some bunched together, different sizes. Hattie shakes the earth off and hands them to Jo, who puts them in her basket.

"You want to try?"

Jo hesitates, then kneels and pulls at some greens.

"Dig around it a bit," Hattie instructs.

Jo pulls again, and the carrot comes up. She stares at it in astonishment.

Hattie gives her a quizzical look, and Jo feels herself flush. "I never get to do stuff like this."

"We do it every day," Hattie remarks. "Garlic's this way."

Jo follows, the basket heavy on her arm, aware now of the hot smells of earth and greens and her sticky, sweaty skin. It must be hard doing this every day, nonstop, but Hattie's got the energy of a bird, hopping this way and that. *Like a fairy.*

Her mouth dries up. Her chest hurts. "Hattie? Wait a sec."

The girl turns, her stringy hair hanging about her gaunt, sunburned cheeks.

"I just—I can't deal with all this. None of it is really true. Is it?"

Hattie scrunches up her brows. "It's outsiders don't believe. You should be different."

"Why?"

"You're the Lavoie."

"Why does everyone keep saying that?"

"Because you are. Plus, Tom said you got taken once. Onions are over there."

Jo follows in numb silence. *Taken.* She can't fathom how Tom would know anything about her. Maybe Gammy told him. Her mind rushes and tumbles backward to the night, her father yelling. Her eyes swim and the world starts to go dark. She bends forward to stop herself from fainting.

Get out! Gammy screamed.

Hattie crouches next to her. "Are you OK?"

"I don't know." Jo feels ill, and she lurches alarmingly trying to sit upright. She takes a deep breath. "I—I've been remembering stuff, I think."

Hattie nods sympathetically. "Sometimes bits and pieces come back."

"Why didn't anyone tell me?"

"Edie said not to. She said it's better you come around your own way, and if you didn't, she'd figure out what to do next."

Edie tried to prod her, Jo realizes, saying all that stuff about her dad. "You said I was taken—?"

"They didn't take-take you," Hattie amends. "They only tried."

Gammy and her daddy yelling, the night, the moon. Gammy must have been swinging the rake to fend them off. "I don't remember."

"That's how it is. They make you sleep, and when you wake up, you're over there."

"They took you, too," Jo says, understanding at last.

"Yeah, then they sent me back." Her voice sounds small. "The ones they don't want, they send back."

"I'm sorry," Jo says. Hattie seems so dejected. "It's not all that bad, though, is it—to be back?"

Hattie curves her shoulders inward, shrugging. Of course it's bad, Jo realizes. She can't go anywhere, can't talk to anyone. She has to say she can't remember if anyone asks.

Cold washes across her skin. Jo thinks back to the graveyard, the ancient cherub obelisk engraved with names. "Hattie—was my dad like you? Did he get sent back?"

Hattie nods.

So that's why Hattie's and her dad's names were there together. It's a monument to the stolen kids, hidden away in the shadows of the Ladd mausoleum. "But they've taken so many—how many come back?"

"I don't know," Hattie says, her voice pinched. "Not a lot."

"How does it happen—how did Maur find you?"

"I was in the Old House, I don't know how long. It was dark. Then she showed up. I was scared."

Jo loses what to say for a moment, imagining the girl in the dark, frightened and alone. And her dad, long ago, just a boy, then the tall old lady showing up in her huge boots. "She took care of you."

Hattie nods tearily. "She was teaching me reading and all. I miss her."

She kneels and plunges her thumb into the earth at the base of some long, spindly greens sticking straight out. Gammy taught her this, too, just as she taught Enzo, and however many others. Jo wonders where they are now; if they left, like her dad, or if they died here. Hattie gouges the earth, working swiftly and in silence, and then she pulls out the plant at last and points at the white bulbs. "Onions," she says with a note of triumph. "They're green but you can use them in the soup anyway. You can use the green part, too."

"Thanks," Jo says. "I wouldn't have known how to do all this."

"Sure." Hattie vigorously rubs her palms to shed the soil. "There's just no potatoes yet. But you can make a soup without those. Rinse everything off in the sink," she points at the shed. "I have to go."

Jo doesn't want to be left alone. "Do you have lots of markets?"

"Every week all summer. The next one's tomorrow morning all the way in New Hampshire. We'll leave super early."

"Wow. That's a lot of work. Do you like them?"

"I like them a lot." Hattie breaks out in a big smile. "It's when I get to go places."

Tom is at the wheel, the driver's door open, staring at Hattie without calling.

"Is he mad at me?" Jo asks.

"Yes," Hattie says with disarming honesty.

"But I didn't know, I swear."

"It's not that. It's because you're gonna sell. I have to go."

She runs off before Jo can answer. Jo stares after her, the laden basket dragging at her arms. Hattie dashes around the truck, and Jo glimpses her getting in on the other side and bouncing onto the seat. The doors slam. The truck rolls down the dirt road, kicking up a cloud of dust. She can't believe they've taken off like this, as if it's any old day.

She forces herself to trudge back to the shed as Hattie directed. She empties the vegetables into one of the slop sinks, sets the sprayer going. She looks around. There's a wheelbarrow propped against the wall. Spools of wire, some stakes. A pair of sandals sitting on top of a wooden box. There's a door at the far end, and she opens it. It's a walk-in fridge, kept cool with an air conditioner. The metal racks have a few bins on them, empty but for dried-up leaves and stalks, leftovers from previous loads. She wishes she could close herself in there, it's so nice and cool.

She watches the earth swirling down the drain. The cold water on her hands and arms is such a relief. She rolls the vegetables around. There's the noise of the water hitting the sink and the heavy vegetables thunking. There's the smell of the wetness and the earth. That it's all true is shocking amid all this realness, in the heat, in the noise of the crickets in the meadow and the truck speeding away and her mom dozing in sweaty sickness, the fan blowing hot air around the room.

Like ants to sugar.

She rolls the vegetables around faster, dumping them into the basket once they're clean. She heads back, the basket dripping and heavy. Loco lifts his sleepy head, at his post under the maple. His tail thumps a few times, but even though she whistles and calls, he doesn't follow her into the house.

Her mom's still sleeping, the fan blowing wisps of hair up with every pass. Jo gets to work in the kitchen. After she's chopped everything and set the chicken to defrost in a pot under a trickle of water, she peeks in again on Abigail. This time, she finds her lying on her side, awake, glazed over, and miserable. She's pallid and sweaty, a high pink still in her cheeks. She looks like she's been crying.

"It's so hard being here," she whispers.

No kidding, Jo thinks. "You're really sick."

"It's not that." She unfolds her hands. Inside them is the crumpled photo of herself and Enzo at the waterfall.

So that's where it went. Abigail is staring so sadly at the picture that Jo feels increasingly awkward and tense. Her mom never acts like this. It has to be the fever.

"He was strong," Abigail whispers. "He knew everything. I loved that about him. Any question I asked, he knew. I could ask about a tree and he knew. I could ask about the teeniest stone and he knew."

"Mom, it's OK," Jo says. *Stop*, she thinks, *just stop*.

"It was my fault," her mom continues, as if Jo isn't even there. "Just being here, I see now," she makes a weak wave at the room. "He was in his element here, king of the world. I took him away. She was right. I ruined him," she finishes, her voice cracking, holding back sobs. "And then, seeing him like that—it was like a bear in a circus—my God, what they did to him in those hospitals—"

Jo reaches out and shakes her mom's arm hard, startling her to silence. "It wasn't your fault, OK?"

Abigail stares blearily, confused, the room laden with the strangeness of Jo's sudden outburst. "How do you know?"

A storm of words fills Jo's head: *Because he wasn't actually delusional. All the stupid doctors and medications spun him upside down and inside out. If he'd stayed here, he would've been OK.*

That's what Gammy always meant: Jo gets it now.

She can't say all that, of course, so she says, "I just don't think it was."

Abigail turns her face away. "That's nice of you to say, but he was different here. You wouldn't know."

The words cut deep. Of course she wouldn't know. Jo's never been able to talk to her mom about him. He's a topic that's always been shut down for good, like a closed criminal case. But her mom can just bring him up out of the blue and get all emotional and then tell Jo she knows nothing.

"He actually did get happy again, you know."

Abigail shifts, her attention drawn. "What do you mean?"

"You'd just drop me off and you wouldn't even speak to him. But he was happy. He had a job and he lived with Sue."

"That woman," Abigail huffs.

"She took care of him. They were always laughing."

This, Abigail registers. She looks at Jo, waiting for more.

"He had a garden with a little maze kind of path behind her house. He grew herbs. He was happy," Jo repeats, because it's true, and she wants her mom to hear it and be hurt by it.

Instead, the strain in Abigail's body seems to melt. A tear rolls out of her eye and plops onto the pillow. "I'm glad," she whispers.

A chasm opens in Jo's heart. The love her dad had for her mom seeps in, a fiery pain. *Jo-Jo*, he chided when she grumbled about her mom being so awful. *Abby is still my Abby.*

Her mom had loved him, too, once. They'd laughed by the waterfall in cutoff shorts, they'd driven around in a truck on dirt roads. And they made Jo.

Outside somewhere, Loco starts barking.

"I should go downstairs," Abigail whispers. "It's so hot up here."

An image comes to Jo of her mom moving about the rooms, a swollen, helpless target. "That's not a good idea."

"But—"

"I saw mice in the dayroom. And the TV room gets the afternoon sun. And the sunroom will be the same, and there's no couch."

Abigail gazes at her with half-lidded eyes. "You don't want me downstairs."

"That's right. I don't. I'll have to help you all around the house and to the bathroom," Jo improvises. "Here it's right there, and it's yours. What if you need to throw up?"

Abigail nods assent, worn down by this barrage. Whatever suspicions she has are too exhausting to explore, and she closes her eyes once again.

Jo is just letting out a sigh of relief when there's a crash from downstairs, something falling over. Her mom's eyes fly open. Jo hurries to the doorway, listens.

Silence.

"Damn cats," Abigail mutters. "One was in here earlier."

Jo stares hard through the open door at the landing, where there is no motion and no sound. Her mom's words take several seconds to sink in.

"There couldn't be," she says. "The door was closed."

"Oh, it was here," Abigail insists, settling back into the pillow, eyes closed. "Freaking thing was on my chest. I must've been sleeping. I couldn't even move, I was so asleep. It was prodding me the way they do."

She gestures at the giant mound of her belly. Jo stares with mounting horror. She crosses the room slowly. "It was *on* you?"

Abigail's eyes flutter open. "What's the matter?"

"The cat couldn't have been in here, Mom."

"Are you saying I imagined it?" Abigail raises her hand to brush her forehead. "My fever must be so high. My God."

"We should take your temp," Jo says automatically, staring at the tears in her mom's nightie she hadn't noticed before. She bends a little closer, glimpses the taut white skin through the tear, and a razor line of red, like a paper cut.

"It scratched you," she says.

"It did?" Abigail lifts her head, aghast. "I didn't feel it."

Jo backs away, looking around. *They were in here. It has to be them.* A panicked image pops up of stuffing the crack between the door and the floor with towels. But that's for fire, not fairies.

And doors don't stop them, anyway. How did they get in? Through the sliver of space between the door and the stone slab. Maybe through the window. But if they're big enough to make that scratch, then how do they fit through a crack?

They can be big or small, Hattie said in the café. Her dad told her that part, too: the fairies could shrink, like Alice did in Wonderland. Jo stares in consternation at the narrow space under the door. She says, "Let's move you downstairs after all."

"Oh, God," Abigail moans. "I don't think I can walk."

"I can keep an eye on you better downstairs," Jo insists.

Abigail lets herself be pulled to a sitting position. "What was that noise, anyway? Did you go see?"

"I've been here the whole time," Jo says.

"Oh," Abigail says vaguely. "Get the thermometer, will you."

Jo helps her across the room, ducks into the bathroom to grab her mom's necessaries. They make their way down the stairs. The umbrella stand is knocked over, the canes fanned out across the floor. Sunlight pours in through the screen door. Birds whistle outside, and there's the hot buzzing of crickets hidden in the tall grass.

"Maybe it was the wind," Abigail remarks.

Jo can't respond, her voice wadded up tight in her throat. The bowl of candy sits on the brick stair outside. It's been ransacked, candy scattered everywhere, wrappers tossed in the grass. The candy was supposed to placate them. You'd think all the Lavoies who came before might have come up with something more effective, something that bought a little more time. And what about the iron? All the fuss about not moving it, and they still got in the house.

She grips her mom's arm, guiding her slowly down the hallway. The house is pervaded by strangeness, echoing with memories of her time here with her father. She dashed around corners, tinkling laughter. She sat at the kitchen table eating Pop-Tarts, her fingers red and sticky. She rocked on the hobbyhorse and Gammy scolded her because it was an antique. Night came and Gammy yelled. She felt the stubbly grass prick her soles, and the trees bent in the wind.

Run! her daddy hollered.

There's nothing more. The worn pine floor is restored beneath the slow march of their feet. The curtains hang still in the hot afternoon air.

FOURTEEN

The truck engine and tires crunching gravel wake Jo from a doze in the TV room. She switches off the TV, which is now on some show about forensics. It's already six thirty, past dinnertime. Her mom's asleep in the recliner, head tilted to one side, mouth wide open.

Jo shouldn't leave her alone, but she has to see Tom and Hattie. She hurries through the house, darting out the kitchen and down the steps. The truck is parked up at the shed, a dust cloud still hanging in the air. The sky has darkened on the horizon, and the trees bend in wind gusts in the distance.

"They were here!" she shouts, running up the slope.

Tom turns to her, holding the folded canopy tent under one arm like it weighs nothing, his face blank and unreadable. Hattie pauses with a bin in her arms.

"They went to my mom," Jo tells them, frantic. "What do I do?"

Tom shrugs. "Told you she should leave."

"How am I supposed to make her leave?" Jo cries.

"Ain't my concern."

He trudges toward the shed, and Hattie says cautiously, "I don't think they'll hurt her."

She sounds like she's trying to be comforting. Jo stares at her blankly, her head fogged up. What's she supposed to do? Hattie drags another bin off the truck bed. Jo imagines herself stepping up to help, but then recalls her mom in the recliner, lying there defenseless. She turns on her heel and runs back to the house.

She bursts into the TV room. Her mom hasn't moved.

She sinks onto the edge of the couch, listening.

Waiting.

A little while later, Jo doesn't know how long, she hears the screen door slam and light footsteps signaling Hattie's in the house. Her mom's awake now, complaining how if she's sick one more day, she's going to break something.

"I have to go talk to Hattie. Call me if you need anything."

Abigail nods, knuckling her eyes and groaning.

Jo finds Hattie in the kitchen, which is unpleasantly humid and hot from the soup simmering on the stove. She's counting bills with her face screwed up in concentration, the doll lying at her elbow. The leather tool pouch is still sitting in the middle of the table, and Jo wonders if she should ask about it, but Hattie's so intensely focused.

"Is that the money from the market?" Jo asks once she's done counting.

"Two hundred thirty-three dollars and sixty-five cents." Hattie looks crestfallen. "It was mostly tourists today. They walk around and don't buy nothing. They think the market's cute, but for us it's our living."

"What do you usually make?"

"Four hundred, five hundred." Hattie carefully stacks the bills and squares them off. Abigail has that amount for change in her purse, Jo thinks, and here Hattie's treating it like treasure.

"Sorry," Jo says.

"It's OK."

Jo follows her into the hallway. Abigail's huge mess covers the desk and floor. Hattie stares in dismay. "Why is everything out?"

"Mom was looking for something," Jo lies. "I'll put it away again."

Hattie places her doll amid the detritus, then crouches under the desk to drag out a small fireproof safe. She spins the combination to open the lid. Inside are manila folders and papers and a tin box. Hattie lifts out the box and opens it to reveal a rubber-banded wad of bills with a note stuck on top. Tongue curled over her upper lip, Hattie laboriously makes the calculation and changes the total.

"There's seven hundred eighty-six dollars in here now,"

Hattie announces. "Can you put it in the account? Maur used to take it to deposit. There's only supposed to be two hundred in here for sundries and emergencies."

Jo doubts she can make deposits, but she agrees because Hattie needs her to so very much, she looks so worried about the money being the wrong amount.

"We told Edie. She'll warn everyone," Hattie says.

It takes a moment for Jo to comprehend. She wonders who that includes. Lola, for sure. This will seal her opinion of Jo once and for all. "Was she mad at me?"

"A bit."

Jo had hoped for *No*. "So everyone knows about this?"

Hattie nods, fusses with folding the wad of bills into the money box.

"Like *everyone*? People in other towns, too?"

"No, just here. Here is where they are."

The fairies, she means. "So—it doesn't happen anywhere else?"

"This is where they live," Hattie says with a touch of impatience, as if Jo's being obtuse. "They have to stay close. They can't go far."

"Why?"

"Because they change back if they stay too long, and they don't want that."

Before her dad brought her here for that doomed visit, he'd sneak around the house in Newton with Jo, looking for messes.

Maybe he didn't know the little ones couldn't go far, or maybe he'd gotten confused. A plug of grief blocks Jo's throat. He'd tried so hard.

"I gotta get back," Hattie says. "I gotta help Tom."

"Wait a sec," Jo says quickly. "Do you know anything else? Like why they're here to begin with?"

Hattie pulls the doll off the table and wraps it under one arm, ready to leave. "It was Josiah Ladd brought two fairies here in a box, all the way from England."

"A box?"

"They can get very small. They could fit in there."

Jo stares down at the tin box. She wonders with a chill if it's *the* box. So much for the legend of him arriving with just the clothes on his back. "Why did he have them?"

"Maur said he meant to make money showing them in carnivals and such. But they didn't do well. They were sickly from being prisoners. Maur always said it was mean what he did to them. It was a sin."

"A sin—like the sin they wrote about on the statue?" Hattie looks bewildered, so Jo waves this off. "Never mind, go on."

"Maur said eventually he felt badly about what he did and let them go. They went and made a fairy world inside this one. But they were still mad, and they took one of Josiah's kids to get revenge. Maur said she would have done it too, if someone had captured her and dragged her half across the world. But then they took more kids from around the area, and Josiah got in trouble with everyone for bringing it all about to begin with.

So he figured out ways to keep them away."

"You mean like the iron stuff everywhere."

"Yes. It worked on the first fairies, but the kids they stole and sent back through, the little ones, iron doesn't work on them the same way. He tried spells, and special stones or something. Maur said those ways didn't work so much, and they were 'labor-intensive.'" Hattie enunciates the last in careful syllables, getting the term right. "He tried filling the hole with iron, but the little ones just pushed it out of the way. If they touch iron just a bit, it can't really hurt them, not unless they're already weak from being here."

"But there's still iron down there, and all over the place."

"To make sure the two first fairies don't ever get through," Hattie explains. "They hate this world. They hate this house. If they came back, it'd be really bad. If they make it through the door, then at least maybe they can't get inside the house. Maur said they'll never quit trying. You can't ever move any of the iron."

Jo flashes to her toe stubbing the iron weight, how it moved a tiny bit. "I won't, I promise."

"It was Maur's granddad who figured out about the wings, for stopping the little ones. He was the first Lavoie here. He only spoke French. Maur spoke French, too," Hattie adds, sounding proud.

"What about the wings?" Jo asks, thinking of the shredded pieces falling from her fingers, the jagged, dark space.

"One time it just happened he killed one. He left it at the

door. It kept them from coming back, except for a long time there was the rot that carried over to this house. So the next time, he cut off the wings, and it worked. The wings is where all their magic is, that's what Tom says. So after that, the custom changed. You block the door with the wings and bury the little one out in the woods."

The clearing, Jo realizes, where she saw the stacked logs for a fence, the dried-up flowers scattered across the grass. *Creatures*: that was what Tom said, and Jo had assumed goats, chickens.

"You can hear them out there," Hattie says. "They get drawn to the graves, and they sing and play there in their world, on the other side of this one."

Jo's breath catches. The sounds she heard—they'd been right there, next to her. "How many are there? I mean, it's been going on for so long."

"I dunno. Before the door could get closed, they took kids whenever they wanted. Maur said no one from outside took notice because back then babies died all the time anyway."

Jo thinks back to the rows of tiny, dark headstones. So many gone, and then the others, their names engraved in secret, hidden from view. That grim record wouldn't have even started until the first child was returned.

"The wings work good," Hattie continues. "Maur said they can even go four or five years, but you have to keep an eye out all the time in case they fall apart. Maur called it a gift when they last long. She didn't like the killing. She said it wasn't the little ones' fault they do what they do, but she had to close the door. Now you have to do it, because you're the Lavoie."

"What do you mean?"

"It's the Lavoie that does it," Hattie repeats. "It's your work."

Necessary work. Jo thinks back to her interpretations of driving a tractor or caring for animals. If only. "I can't do that," she shakes her head.

"But you already got the tools out."

Hattie points toward the kitchen, and Jo understands: the leather pouch from under the sink. The iron chain, the shining blades—her stomach tightens, her skin goes clammy at the images racing in her head. "I just found those by mistake. I can't, Hattie. No way."

"Then who's gonna do it?"

The simple question stalls Jo for an awful moment. "I don't know—just don't worry about it, OK?"

Hattie's obviously got no confidence in this. Jo can't blame her. She says, "So they send the little ones here to take kids because they're still mad. They'll just do that over and over, forever?"

"Yeah. And the ones they don't want, they send back."

Jo fills with pity for the narrow, bony frame and limp hair hanging around her sad face. "They shouldn't have, you know. You're a great kid."

Hattie's eyes flutter side to side, listening.

"I'm glad you're here. We lucked out. They made a mistake."

"That's what Maur said. But I still miss there."

"What was it like?"

"We played all day, and there was singing. And we could have ice cream anytime."

Jo knew what Hattie's answer would be, but still, to hear the things her father said in his stories, all these years later, makes her unutterably sad. He supposedly didn't remember his past, but he'd shared all of it with Jo, in the form of stories. Again and again he told the stories, every night. "My dad missed it, too."

"It was nice," Hattie says, her voice tiny. "They didn't mean no harm."

Jo hesitates, then says, "But they did do harm. They stole you."

"I know," Hattie whispers, drawing the doll tighter to her chest. Its eyes click, stubby arms splayed. "I can't remember nothing, though. I was really little."

"That's the doll you had when they took you," Jo says, understanding dawning.

"It's in the story. I can only read bits of it so far. I still have to learn my spelling."

"The story?"

Hattie's fingers scramble at the manila folder in the safe, seeking purchase. She pulls it out and thrusts it at Jo. "These are the kids come back."

Jo receives the folder into her hands. The title on the tab is written in faded ink cursive: *The Cherished.*

She feels a chill. *Cherished ones your home awaits.* Gammy called Hattie cherished in her letter. Jo thought it was just an adjective.

The papers inside the folder are delicate, old, a mix of yellowed newspaper clippings and inky, shiny printouts, like the ones Jo had to use for a research paper last year. *Microfiche*, the word resurfaces. She sifts through, her head a high hum, knowing in her body what she might find but unable to form the thought clearly in her mind. "Boy Stolen!" reads one headline. Another, "Two-Year-Old Girl Vanished While Mother Weeps." This one is Hattie, Jo realizes. Hattie McDougal. Her parents lived in Newport and had come to the area for a country weekend. Their baby girl was taken from right under their noses at the playground, when they turned away for no more than a moment. She had her doll and was in a white dress.

The date at the top reads *1902*. Jo looks up at Hattie. "It's over a hundred years ago," she says, bewildered.

Hattie regards her above the cracked porcelain doll head. "Maur said time passes different over there."

Jo lowers her blurred vision to the papers. The names on the obelisk, so old, eroded. *Cherished ones your home awaits.* Everyone in the town must know, for that thing to be standing right there in the middle of the graveyard.

She thumbs through the papers more quickly, searching. "Baby Boy Missing," a headline reads from 1923. There's a photo of a toddler in a christening gown. She knows him at once: the cheeks, the big brown eyes, the shock of black curly hair. *Lorenzo Joseph Habib, aged 3*, the caption reads.

She skims the story that tells of his mother weeping inconsolably, the babe lost from a pram when she left it outside a shop. The father was a quarrier in Barre. Both were recent immigrants from Spain, he of Syrian origin, she Italian.

So he was part Arab. Jo imagines breaking this news to Nana.

"Is that your father?" Hattie leans closer.

"Yes," Jo says. Or tries to, her voice strangled and dry, because it's struck her that Hattie, once upon a time, might have known him. "Do you remember him? You were there at the same time."

Hattie shakes her head. "I don't know. Maybe. It's different there. It was like we were all the same. It wasn't like here where you have to know this person or that person and you know their names. It's OK," she adds after a moment. "Don't be sad."

"But—his poor parents—and yours—" Jo shakes her head in dismay. "I mean, maybe they had more kids, maybe he has a brother or sister or something—" The possibilities spin wildly, inchoate, overwhelming.

Hattie taps her arm, looking stern. "Now is now. That's what Maur told me when I got sad."

Now is now, Jo thinks confusedly. She looks around. The space leaps back at her in stark relief. The musty hall, the desk, the worn wooden floor. Her mom in the TV room, helpless and alone, the giant mound of her belly exposed, the child within squirming. Jo has seen Baby Charles's fist, a foot, pressing out against the skin sheath like something from some gross horror movie.

She sets the papers down. Her hands are sweaty, she wipes them on her shorts. "I don't get what they want with my mom if all they want is kids. The baby's not even born."

Hattie shrugs her own ignorance. "Me neither, but Tom said she should go."

"How does he know?"

"He just knows."

"Did he come back, too?"

Hattie's eyes flicker sideways, and Jo senses the girl concealing something. "Hattie, you have to tell me the truth, you understand?"

Hattie clamps her lips. Color drains from her face. Then she whips around and tears off down the hall, her bare feet slapping the wood floor. She's out the sunroom door in a heartbeat, the screen smacking the frame hard.

Jo stares after her in astonishment. She can't believe she was starting to count on Hattie, who's just a little kid who freaks out at the smallest thing. Jo would run her down, but she has to check on her mom. She shoves the folder back in the safe along with the tin box, which might have once contained a pair of fairies and now contains equally impossible truths. She notices some papers, official-looking documents. She slides them out. The top one's a birth certificate for Hattie, she realizes in astonishment. Hattie McDougal, born just thirteen years ago here in Laddston. And with that, legal forms confirming Hattie's adoption by Gammy, signed by none other than Nathanael Fletcher, Esq.

There are so many people involved in these deceptions. The birth certificate is totally real: it has a seal and everything, signed by the town clerk. And Nate Fletcher, he's a lawyer, but he's lying in these documents, even though he could get disbarred.

Then again, there's not much risk, because who would ever check? Laddston is barely a dot on the map. Her dad probably had the same fake papers, as did all the returned kids—*the Cherished*, she amends. It's not like there's a steady stream of them, just one every once in a while. Hattie must be the most recent.

Jo replaces the papers and closes the safe. She hesitates a moment, then snaps the combination lock shut. She can get the code from Hattie at some point, but for now, it better stay locked, just in case her mom goes poking around again.

She goes back to the TV room to find the recliner empty. "Mom!" she screams. "*Mom!*"

"Upstairs."

Her mom's voice is barely a croak. Jo bounds up the stairs two at a time, bursts into the room.

Abigail is examining herself in the ancient mirror hung over the dresser. "Oh, there you are," she says. "I decided to get up for a bit. The fever broke."

She looks waxen and sounds hoarse, but she's upright and

dressed in one of her maternity sundresses that looks like a tent.

"What's the matter with you now?" Abigail frowns. "You look upset."

"Nothing."

Abigail snaps open a fan with a geisha on it and flaps it near her face. "Look at this thing. Maur has the strangest things lying around."

"I think she traveled," Jo says faintly. "I saw pictures."

"Really, Jo, what's wrong?"

Jo feels sick with nerves, anticipating her mom's inevitable reaction, but she has to try. "I feel like there's something off about this place."

Abigail shoots her a sharp look, eyes narrowed. She closes the fan. "What do you mean?"

Jo's mouth opens and nothing comes out.

Abigail steps closer. "What do you mean?"

Her mom smells of soap and sweat. Jo wishes she could just bury herself into a hug, the way she did sometimes when she was little. "It just feels off. Tom, he's so weird."

"What are you talking about? Did he do something?"

"Oh my God, no, Mom—I don't mean that! I mean they're just so weird, is all," she repeats lamely, grasping for something to say that will resonate. "Maybe I'm just homesick."

Her mom looks nonplussed, mouth open, then her expression turns to suspicion. "I knew you shouldn't have come here."

Great: now her mom thinks she's losing it. "Mom, I'm *fine*. I just haven't met such creepy people before, is all."

"They're not *that* creepy," Abigail says, turning the tables. "You just haven't lived anywhere else than Newton. You're too sheltered."

That's rich, coming from her. "Never mind, OK? I was just freaking out a bit."

"Oh, Jo, honey," Abigail sighs. "It'll be fine. Let's go downstairs. It's too hot here." She squeezes past Jo, turning her bloated body to the side. She grasps the banister rail and starts down, bobbing side to side like a penguin on her swollen feet.

Jo sags into the wall, staring blindly after her. She becomes aware of the breeze, the curtains. The sun is lower in the sky, but this side of the house is still a furnace. She shudders, pressed against the wall. *Daddy*, she begs, *tell me what to do*.

But all she hears is the steady tick of the fan turning this way and that.

FIFTEEN

The rain starts at dusk, accompanied by huge rolls of thunder. Lightning cracks the sky. The laundry is gone; Hattie must have taken it down.

Abigail wants to eat in the sunroom because it has a ceiling fan, and it's hard enough eating a hot soup in this weather to begin with. Jo trails her without protest, because what can she say: *Mom, that's too close to the fairy door?*

"You'd think they'd stop by," Abigail remarks, miffed. "I mean, you saw them, right?"

Jo says yes, but that they're probably tired from the market and all.

"So that's it, then." Abigail blows on her spoonful of soup, takes a cautious sip. "Wow, honey. Not bad. You picked the vegetables all by yourself?"

"It was mostly Hattie."

She describes how she did get some carrots, and how smoothly they came up and how they were all in a bunch, just like that. Abigail is amused. "Your father and I went out every day. It's a ton of work. And I was pregnant. I was doing farmers markets: Can you imagine?"

Jo can't. Her mom stares out the screen at the scrubby yard and the meadow beyond. The rain is loud on the roof, blowing sideways in sheets now. She sighs. "It was a different era."

Not really, Jo realizes. Her mom was pregnant then, too. The only difference is Gammy managed to get her out of here. *We should leave, Mom.* The words crowd inside Jo's mouth. There's no way to say it, no way to explain why.

Abigail examines her. "What's wrong now?"

Jo shakes her head, shrugs.

"You're always so sullen," Abigail complains. "This whole teen phase is killing me."

They eat in silence. A motion catches Jo's attention. It's the cat stalking the periphery of the room with that singular focus on invisible prey. Jo stares hard, trying to see what's there. *You can't see them,* her daddy waved his finger in her face, *not unless they want to be seen. Do you ever think you see something in the corner of your eye?*

Yes, Jo-Jo said. *It was the mouse!*

Her mom had brought in pest control with their horrible traps and poisons, making Jo-Jo cry.

Not the mouse, her daddy corrected. *If you ever see something, and it's not a mouse, it could be one of them.*

Are they little like mice?

They can make themselves little, or make themselves bi-i-i-g!

210

Her daddy drew out the word and reached for the ceiling to describe the fairies' awesome size.

Jo's been catching swift motions in the corner of her eye. It could be them; it could be mice. It could be she's so jumpy, she's seeing things. The cat's up on its ratty window seat, staring out at the yard. There's nothing there.

"Why aren't you eating?" Abigail says. "Don't tell me you're starting with that vegan business again."

"It's not a 'business.' I'm just . . . I'm not hungry right now."

"Is this some kind of diet?"

"I'm just really stressed out, OK?"

"I don't know what you have to be stressed out about," Abigail rebukes. "Is it not being able to use your phone?"

The arch little joke, criticism nestled within like a poisonous pearl. Normally, Jo would push back her chair and stomp off, but her anger dissipates as swiftly as it rose. Her mom is clueless, totally helpless, still living in the normal world of just hours ago. It doesn't matter what she says: Jo can't leave her alone. She bends over the bowl, forces herself to take a bite, then another.

She does the dishes a while later, her gaze constantly turning to the dark walls of the Old House. The rain's let up for the moment. In the distance, she sees the meadow and the crab apple trees darkening against the sky. She can just make out Tom sitting on a stump, puffing on a cigarette. It makes Jo uneasy that Gammy's letter said he doesn't belong here. Edie said Jo does, and her pleasure at that now feels embarrassing. This place is much more a part of him. He looks like a thing grown from this earth, a living gnarl of bone and flesh born from dirt and rock. His teeth crooked like a jumble of stones, and those gray eyes. His big hands haul things—stumps, logs—as if they have no weight at all. He chopped down the tree he's sitting on, and pounded and baked the bread she eats in the morning, and slit the necks of the chickens in the freezer. Everything in this place has been touched by his hand, at one time or another. Sitting on his stump to stare across the meadow, he looks like the overseer of this land. Way more than she could ever be, tripping over roots the way she does and gasping at the dog eating coyote poop. How could she ever belong here, truly?

Her mom is in the hallway office, back to poking through files, muttering disapproval. Jo hangs up the towel. It's gotten gross, so she opens up the pantry to find a clean one. She discovers the rice bin overturned, grains scattered everywhere. Cans lie in disarray on the shelves. A bag of flour has exploded on the floor, a trail of footprints visible. Jo stares down, thinking *mice*, thinking *squirrels*. But the prints are too long for squirrels. They're elongated, with toes. They could be from a raccoon, Jo supposes hopefully. There are handprints, too. The fingers long and thin, the palms smaller than her own.

They are naughty and clumsy in this world, her daddy told her. *You will always know if they've been here because of the mess.*

Jo backs into the doorframe. It might be here. Hiding, watching her.

If you see one, he warned, *you have to run!*

Her heart pounds so hard it hurts. She presses against the wall to keep upright.

"Jo!" her mom cries. "Come see this!"

Jo forces herself to move, her whole body a tremulous blob she can barely keep together. She closes the pantry door, goes through the kitchen, following the sound of her mom's voice.

Her mom is back in the screened room standing under the lamp, her tent-dress unbuttoned. She turns her stricken gaze to Jo as she approaches.

"Look," she whispers.

The razor-thin scratch on her belly is swollen and red, the edges crimped and bunched, turning outward, pink and fleshy and gross, peeling away from the dark, swollen middle.

It looks jarringly, sickeningly familiar.

Cross-legged on the floor inside the tent. Her dad gently unrolled the bandage, and she whimpered, looked away.

Not a rake, Jo realizes, feeling at the two long, ridged scars down her arm. *It was one of them, when they tried to take me.*

"It's infected," Abigail says with disgust. "This can't be good. My God, what if it spreads to the baby?"

Her dad soaked the wounds with alcohol, making Jo squeal. She dreads the notion of doing the same to her mom. She holds her by the elbow, helping her down the hallway to the kitchen. "Should I drive you to the hospital?"

"Maybe," Abigail says, giving Jo a lurch of hope, but then she veers toward the table and sits down. "I really don't want to go. Not yet. It's just a scratch. Get me my first-aid bag, would you?"

Jo hesitates, glancing at the pantry door. All is silent. *You can't see them, not unless they want to be seen.*

"Mom, listen—"

"What?"

"If you see anything, just yell, OK?"

"See what?"

"Just stay here," Jo says. "That way I can hear you."

"For heaven's sake, Jo, it's a scratch, not a mortal wound."

Jo runs, takes the stairs two at a time. She searches frantically in the bathroom, then the bedroom, then her mom's suitcase. There it is, the pristine first-aid kit with the red cross on the front. She hurries back down, dashes to the kitchen.

"My God, Jo. What is wrong with you?"

"Nothing. I'm worried, is all," Jo says, unzipping the bag and opening it flat on the table.

"Well, I don't think there's any need." Her mom withdraws the alcohol swabs and some antibiotic cream.

She'll do it herself, Jo realizes with relief. "You look like you still have a fever."

Her mom touches her forehead, nodding. "That's from the cold."

"How do you know?" Jo argues.

"I'll be OK, Jo. Frankly, I'm surprised you're so concerned."

That rankles, even though Jo isn't worried for the reasons

her mom thinks. "Of course I am," she says, offended. "I mean, he's my brother, right?"

Abigail arches an eyebrow. "I thought he was 'the amoebert,'" she air-quotes.

Jo's mouth drops open in shock, then embarrassment floods in, turning her face hot.

"I don't live under a rock," Abigail points out. "You think I wouldn't find out?"

"How did you?"

"Your phone." She fesses this up without even a hint of shame, swabbing away at the cut.

"You spied on my *phone*?"

"It's what modern moms have to do." Abigail tosses the alcohol swab onto the table, her own anger spiking in response to Jo's. "You think I don't worry? You think I don't wonder, Is she taking drugs, is she having sex, is she safe?"

"*Sex*?" Jo exclaims. "I don't even have a boyfriend!"

"Well, good. Keep it that way."

"You have no right. No *right*!"

"I have every right. And I'm glad you think of Baby Charles as your brother. This amoebert thing, really!" She gives her head a dismissive shake. "It's childish, Jo. I'd expect more from you."

Jo just sits there like a lump, too distraught to come up with a reply. Her mom spreads the antibiotic salve on her cut. She's so expert at sending out her poisonous darts, then acting as if nothing's happened. If Jo says anything, she'll act all surprised and ask why Jo's bent out of shape. It's beyond ironic: she gets mad at Nana for how Nana treats her, then she goes and does the exact same thing to Jo. There's no use bringing it up.

And what does it matter, now, anyway? She stares blindly at her mom's hands as they reseal the tube and tuck everything back into the first-aid bag. Her mom will have a scar the same as Jo's, but she'll never know it, which is upsetting in a way Jo can't define. Jo reaches out and crumples the alcohol swab, stuffs it back into its torn wrapper. Her mom peers down at the great, smooth mound of her belly. Her hand strokes a smooth, gentle circle. Jo wonders if she acted the same when she was pregnant with Jo, all dreamy and reverent. Probably not. After all, Jo was a mistake, whereas Baby Charles was planned and has a nursery that's already decorated and perfect.

And then, in this pocket of quiet, Jo glimpses on the distended taut skin, out of her mom's sight, three more scratches.

Jo freezes, the wrapper clenched in her fist. Her mom obliviously buttons up her robe. She looks exhausted and pale. Her ignorance of the new injuries leaves Jo sick, her throat tight and hurting.

"I'm sorry I check your phone," her mom says suddenly. "There's just so much to be afraid of nowadays. My God, when I think of all you could get into."

"I haven't gotten into anything," Jo says, strangling on her own voice. "You should trust me more."

"I understand why you're so mad about the baby. I really do."

"I'm not mad," Jo lies automatically.

"But it will work out, won't it? You won't hate him?"

Abigail actually sounds emotional, and Jo squirms with discomfort. "Of course I won't hate him, Mom."

"I know, I just—"

"You're sick, Mom," Jo interrupts. "You're not yourself. Let's just go watch some TV, OK?"

Abigail seems relieved by this idea. They head down the hallway, Jo glancing all around as they go, eyes peeled, listening. *Maybe they've left*, she thinks with a touch of optimism; then she's struck by what that means for everyone in town and beyond. They're in danger and it's all her fault. She's the one who went down beneath the Old House. She's the one who opened the door.

And she's the one who's supposed to close it. They'll all be expecting it, she realizes sinkingly, just like Hattie does. Expecting her to kill one of them down there in the cellar, as if she has any clue how to kill anything, let alone that. She stifles a sudden, horrified laugh. It's crazy. It's totally, utterly crazy, and tomorrow morning, no matter what it takes, she'll convince her mom they need to leave.

SIXTEEN

The night is filled with soft scratching noises, creaks, rustling. Jo lies in tormented wakefulness, the lamp on next to her bed. She creeps to her mom's room so many times she loses count. Her mom snores, one arm thrown behind her head, mouth open. She's always been able to sleep anywhere, anytime, as if there's not one worry in her head. It's unfathomable to Jo.

The rain picks up again, tapping the windows. Jo sits on the edge of her bed, straining to hear anything unusual. She spies the canvas satchel stored next to the dresser. She hasn't taken out her sewing even once, she realizes. There's been no time or space to spread it out the way she likes to, mull over what to do next.

She brings the satchel over to the spare bed, empties out the bags of material and sewing stuff, sets it all aside. She stares at the objects at the bottom, then takes them out, too. They are heavy and cold. They must mean something. They must *do* something, else why would her dad have carried them around?

Jo drags her bedding down the hall and into her mom's room. She lays the chain on the floor the way her dad did. The house is slammed by wind gusts and driving rain. Maybe it's too wet for the little ones to go anywhere. She puffs her pillows, curls up with the bell tucked close. The floor still feels hard, even through the blankets. She drifts in and out of a light doze, her body stiff and sore.

Jo is in a dark, oppressive space, curled up and sinking farther and farther away. *Jo-Jo!* her daddy yells. *Jo-Jo!* She yearns to answer, but she can't open her mouth. Her body's tightly curled up, caught in a net. His voice is a faint pinprick through the clotted, opaque thickness enveloping her. The rich scents of grass and wet, fecund earth fill her nostrils, making her ever more sleepy. *Jo-Jo!* her daddy cries, more frantic.

"Jo! Jo!"

Jo screams, her limbs a scrambling tangle in the sheet. Her eyes fly open, searching, terrified.

She's on the floor. In her mom's room. The light's on.

She rolls off the blanket and clambers upright, her eyes crusty with sleep, her limbs weak and wobbly. "Mom?" she croaks, stumbling into the lamp's glare.

"I felt something," Abigail says frantically. "There was something here. Did you see anything?" Then she frowns, confused. "Were you sleeping on the floor?"

There's a dark stain across her mom's nightgown, the material dangling in shreds. Abigail follows her gaze. "What's going on?" she whispers, hands hovering over her belly in dismay.

Jo wills herself to go closer. She bends to look, rubbing her eyes hard to clear the sleep-fog. The first cut is bigger, and it's bleeding. There are several more slashes crisscrossing her mom's belly.

"It hurts," Abigail says, hysteria edging in. "Why is this happening?"

"We have to get out of here," Jo says. "Come on, we have to go. Now."

"What's that?" Abigail seizes Jo's arm. "Did you see? Over there."

There's nothing where Abigail's pointing. Just the bureau with its ornately carved mirror and rows of dusty knickknacks. But the small carpet in front is bunched and out of place. A hairbrush lies on the floor.

"Come *on*!" Jo pulls on her mom's arm.

"Didn't you see?"

"You can't see them unless they let you!" Jo snaps. "Mom, we have to go!"

"Who's them? What are you talking about?"

"The little ones, Mom! Fairies! OK?"

Abigail stares at her, mouth open. "Jesus Christ Almighty," she whispers, dropping her head back, eyes fixed on the ceiling. "This isn't happening. It just isn't."

"It *is* happening, Mom!"

"I can't take it! I just can't, Jo!"

Jo blinks, a glint in her eye blinding her. The thinnest sliver of green, a flash of gold. Her breath hurts in her chest, caught tight like a fist. She scans the room, eyes peeled, burning. There's nothing. Not that she can see.

Then a vase tips and crashes to the floor. Abigail lets out a cry. Jo grabs her arm, pulls her off the bed. Abigail whimpers, "I can't," and stumbles into the wall, clutching her belly. "It hurts."

Jo maneuvers her into the corner. They can't possibly go through walls, she reasons, pressing back against her quivering mom, shielding her. She peers across the room. Something clatters to the floor—her mom's jewelry box, the contents exploded out.

"Get out!" Jo screams at the room. The words from long ago rise up and hurl out of her like missiles. "Get out! Get *out*!"

"What is it?" Abigail cries.

Jo spies the chain, lunges for it. The metal clacks against the wood floor. She returns to her mother, out of breath. She can't see the bell, lost inside the bedding on the floor.

"You listen to me, Josephine! You tell me what's going on right now!"

"It's the little ones," Jo says, her voice harder than she knew it could be. "They're here."

"Don't be ridiculous."

"I'm not."

Abigail's breaths heave against Jo's back. She pushes uselessly, weakly. "It can't be."

Jo sees something: a sinuous shape, inching across the bedsheet. She clutches her mom's arm, silencing her.

The sheet crumples, drags across the bed. Jo glimpses a hand, clawlike, shimmering, and she gasps, gripping her mom's arm tighter. She feels her mom's ragged, warm breath against her neck. The sheet slides, rustling. And then in an instant, the whole creature shimmers into view, hunched spine and scaled body, its eyes golden orbs staring right at them. The luminescence reminds Jo of dragonflies in sunlight, the veined wings so delicate, except these wings are tremendous, unfolding up to the ceiling.

"Oh my God," Abigail whimpers. "Oh my God, oh my God."

A rustling sound cracks the air, the wings fluttering as if in response. The fairy's eyes stare hungrily, pinning them in place. Its face could be human but resembles more an insect, elongated and perfect. Jo's mouth goes dry. She feels ill. She wants to draw closer, touch the shining, smooth skin beneath those giant eyes. There is a sadness in them, so profound and so full of yearning. It drains her utterly. She wants to fold herself inward and sleep.

They can make you helpless just by looking at you, her daddy said, widening his eyes and bending in so that Jo-Jo screeched in mock terror.

"Don't look," she whispers, jerking on her mom's arm. She

blinks furiously at the floor.

The fairy hisses. It drags its nails across the sheet, ribboning the material. Abigail sobs. Jo feels her trying to shrink away, but there's nowhere to go. The fairy edges off the bed to the floor, its eyes fixed on them.

"Get out!" Jo screams, and hurls the chain through the air. It flies right by and thunks onto the bed, then cascades off the edge, clatters in a heap on the floor.

Jo looks around frantically, spots a paddle against the wall next to them, *1904* painted on it, some commemorative knick-knack. She grabs it and brandishes it at the fairy. "Get out! Get OUT!"

The fairy shrinks a little, eyes narrowed, then inches closer, its gaze fixed on Abigail.

Jo leaps forward, smashes the paddle down hard.

There's a shriek, then a gust of wind slams Jo back across the floor. She scrambles toward her mom, who cowers in the corner, arms folded over her belly. In the whirling wind, Jo hears a sharp snapping sound. For an instant, the fairy reappears in the air above her upturned face, but tiny now, like a bird. Their eyes meet, and Jo glimpses the malevolence in the creature's gaze. A blur, and Jo gasps, pain slicing her cheek: it struck her. She swings her hand at the tiny thing and misses. All at once, the curtains billow outward. Rain whips into the room, wetting Jo's face.

The curtains flutter back down, then go still, drenched. Thunder explodes in the sky, shuddering through the walls.

Jo clambers to her knees. She checks on her mom, who is white and stiff, her face etched in a tight grimace, eyes roving the empty room.

"You saw it," Jo says.

Abigail doesn't answer. Her face is drained of all color, eyes searching the ceiling.

"Mom, it's gone."

Abigail's gaze swings to Jo. "It hurt you."

Jo reaches up to her cheek, where her mom is looking. Her fingers come away red. The moment she sees that, the cut starts to smart awfully.

"Oh Jesus . . ." Her mom crumples, turning her face to the wall. "It was real. It was real all along."

The rawness in her voice paralyzes Jo. She doesn't know how to handle her mother in this state, all emotional, wrecked. She says, "You're bleeding a lot. We have to go to the hospital."

Abigail awkwardly adjusts her position to look down. Her whole front is soaked. At the sight, her mouth crumples in dismay. Tears roll down her cheeks. "What if the baby—oh my God—"

Jo tugs on her arm. "Can you walk?"

Abigail nods into her hand.

There is a silence during which they fumble and grunt working together to get Abigail to her feet. They pause in the bathroom to tape gauze over the cuts. Jo has to do it because Abigail almost faints and plops onto the toilet gasping. The cuts are vicious and deep. She imagines the claws sinking into her mom's skin in the silence of the bedroom while she lay sprawled in stupid sleep on the floor. Terror rakes her bones, weakening her so she can barely help her mom stand.

"I can't believe it," her mom says. "I can't. Oh my God, Enzo."

Jo focuses on easing her mom down the stairs. She can't absorb her mom's ramblings. She just can't. Nor the swell of sorrow in her chest at the knowledge that if only her mom had believed him, he could have stayed. They could have taught him how to be in the world safely. They could have stayed together.

Something thuds upstairs. They freeze, staring up.

"Do you think it's back?" her mom whispers.

They listen. Silence.

Jo pulls on her elbow, and they creep as swiftly as possible along the hallway dimly lit by the ancient chandelier, Jo glancing back fearfully at the dark corners. Her mom is wheezing a bit, wobbling, her hand out to the wall for support.

"Jo, it really hurts," Abigail manages between pants. "The baby."

The amoebert. The giant mound of her mom's belly suddenly floods Jo with panic. She's seen every one of the ultrasounds because Abigail hangs them on the fridge and makes everyone look. In the last one you can see Baby Charles sucking his thumb. For the baby shower, Jo got him a teether with a bunch of different-colored rings and a hippo. It's sitting in the crib, waiting for him.

Jo doesn't want him to be hurt. She doesn't want him to die.

They will *not* take him—she won't let them.

"Keep going," she urges. "We're almost there."

She settles her mom in the car and makes sure all the doors are locked, then runs up to the cottage. She's soaked through by the time she gets there. The front door stands wide open despite the rain, and through the screen she sees Hattie and Tom at a wooden table. They're playing checkers. The scene is shockingly peaceful and ordinary. She pauses outside, trying to collect herself. Tom plays with studied concentration, his giant hand hovering over the pieces before making his deliberate, slow moves. One, two, he jumps, the wooden piece clacking in the silence. Hattie gasps as if she hadn't seen it coming. He responds with a slow, wide smile, and then he catches sight of Jo.

He abruptly pushes back his chair and stands. She says in a rush, "We're going to the hospital!"

"What's wrong?" Hattie snatches up her doll and folds it into her arms.

Jo's words fall over one another. "They were in the room. She's got more scratches. There's a lot of blood."

At the last, her voice catches in a sob. They just stand there, and then they exchange a look.

"What is it?" Jo begs, thinking, *They know doctors can't help. They know she's going to die.*

Instead, Hattie says, "You can't leave. Not now."

This takes a moment to sink in. "I have to. My mom—"

"Tom can take her."

Tom Pierson taking her mom to the hospital—it's beyond absurd. "No way. It has to be me."

"But the leggsy—"

"The what?"

"The leggsy. Maur left *you* the house. *You're* the one supposed to close the door."

Legacy: the nonsense word translates in her mind. "I—I can't do it," Jo protests. "I told you I can't."

Tom shifts in place, drawing their attention. Time seems to slow to a stop, consumed by the black hole of his silence.

"What?" Jo demands.

"Maur left you the house," he repeats Hattie's words. "It's work meant for you."

Necessary work, the letter said. *Hard work.* Jo flashes to the moment she smashed the paddle through the air. The explosion of wings, her body flung aside, sliding across the floor.

"I can't," she shakes her head. "I never even asked for the house, OK?"

"That don't change it's yours."

Jo looks to Hattie for help, but the girl's frozen in her typical, wide-eyed stare, her mouth dropped open, knuckles white, clutching her doll.

"This is crazy!" Jo blurts. She puts up her hand as if to stop them, though they're motionless. "I'm going now. I'm taking my mom to the hospital, OK?"

227

She backs away, then turns and runs.

"What's their problem?" Abigail pants as Jo turns on the engine.

Jo looks where she's looking. Tom and Hattie have followed, come to a stop at the edge of the driveway. The headlights illuminate them in the slanted rain: Tom's hatchet glower, eyes narrowed. Hattie scared and clinging to his hand, the doll held tight.

"They said I'm not supposed to go." Jo grips the steering wheel hard. *From his sin, he did not turn away.* "They said Gammy left me the house, so I'm the one who has to stop the fairies."

Abigail's eyes shine in the dark. She's breathing slowly, deliberately, and now she looks angry. "Bullshit," she says between breaths. "Go."

That's the mom she knows: not the whimpering, frightened one. Her hands trembling, Jo puts the car in reverse, spins around, then guns out the drive for good measure. In the rearview, she sees Tom and Hattie still standing there, watching.

maur said life is a force it beats down on you and alls you can do is make do. she wouldve never come back from her travels but it was obligation. she had to. she were the only one left.

i said i wished shed stayed traveling then id not be stuck here. she had no care about that. everyones got burdens she said. it dont matter how they came to be only how theyre carried.

SEVENTEEN

The machines beep, reminding Jo of when she visited her dad, when he was dying. All hospital rooms are the same: colorless walls, acrid medicinal odors mingled with soap and warm, soft foods, the steady humming of machines, the anxious disordered yearning for something to happen, something to change.

"I feel like it's here," Abigail repeats, her voice thin and cracked. She struggles to sit up. She shakes her head, feeling at the back of her neck, running her fingers through her hair.

"It's not, Mom," Jo says tiredly. "You need to quit this."

She shudders. "It's like ants in my hair and down my back."

"You're just stressed."

"God, I want to get out of here," Abigail snaps, dropping back onto her pillow. Her eyes rove the ceiling, her jaw clenched.

The silence between them resumes, punctuated by the steady whirs and beeps.

Robert will be here within an hour. He's called three times

since he got on the road, saying how he told Abigail not to take this trip and look what happened.

The doctors patched up the injuries, but they aren't buying Abigail's story about cats, though they ran the obligatory toxoplasmosis test. They asked if she self-harmed, which made Abigail furious, doing nothing to help her case. The on-call OB has recommended a mental health eval. They're going to be stuck here for ages, at least till Abigail's OB back home can be reached to put an end to this charade, as Abigail calls it.

It's going on five in the morning. Jo's been listening to muffled screaming from another room for way too long. Her head aches. She lays her head back and closes her eyes, trying to shut out the awful noise.

What feels like a second later, she starts awake. Her body's stiff and hurting from falling asleep crookedly in the chair. She blinks crust from her eyes, registering the time on the clock: almost an hour has passed. Abigail's sitting upright, pulling hard on the blanket to get it out from under the mattress. All this fuss is what woke Jo. Her pillows are on the floor.

"Mom, jeez, what's wrong?"

"I felt something."

She sounds frightened. Jo jumps up, tidies the blanket, and restores the pillows to their proper place. "Mom, stop. If that shrink shows up and sees you like this, he'll never believe you!"

Abigail covers her face with her hands. Jo teeters next to her, exhausted and helpless. The machines beep.

"He told me what happened," Abigail whispers. "He *told* me."

"What are you talking about?"

She lowers her hands, looking away, unable to meet Jo's eyes. "He said Maureen saved you from them. He said you were sleeping and you'd never remember. What was I supposed to think? It sounded insane."

"When did he say that?"

"It was after he got out. Mom and Pop were *so* angry. They couldn't believe I let him see you. But I did. I thought he'd be OK with the new medication. But he just wasn't. I know what you're thinking." Abigail gives a sharp, pained laugh. "I should have stuck it out, right?"

Jo has thought that all these years, but suddenly, she's not so sure. "I guess."

"You have no idea how long I did. It started when you were *born*, Jo."

"What do you mean?"

Abigail sinks back into the pillow, sighing. "He always acted so—strange. It was too much. He hovered over you constantly. He wouldn't let you sleep alone. You know how when I finally got him to agree you should sleep in your own crib—"

"He slept beside me on the floor," Jo completes the old family story.

"But I never told anyone the rest of it. Right from the start, he was going on about how you were in danger, how he had to protect you from 'the little ones,' he called them. I wasn't allowed to take you anywhere on my own"—Abigail's tone turns bitter—"because I wouldn't know what to do if they showed up. Which is *the* most extreme example of a man thinking only *he* can take care of a problem, right?"

Jo cracks a reluctant smile. Her mom can always whip out a sarcastic joke, no matter how devastating the situation.

"I thought he was going crazy, Jo. It was so awful. I actually hid it from Mom and Pop. I thought maybe it was some kind of male postpartum, you know?"

Jo nods, though she doesn't, not really.

"I got him into therapy, and he got medications. They seemed to calm him down. I knew he told you stories about fairies, but I thought he'd found a way to—to compartmentalize, or whatever. Like he knew what was real, and what wasn't. It was OK like that, for a while."

"But you had separate bedrooms," Jo says, recalling her mom's room, pristine in shades of white and gray, the door closed against intrusion.

Abigail gives a wan smile. "Because he was such a slob. Don't you remember the state of the house?"

She does. Her dad left dishes piled up, tossed his dirty socks on the couch. Abigail yelled at him, her voice shrill, and her dad sat there bemused, saying what do messes matter.

"You thought he was the fun one," Abigail accuses, reading Jo's mind. "I begged him to find work, do something with his time. But he'd just spend his days carving, or baking chocolaty things for you, and putting the house into such a mess. All I did was clean up after him!"

"Yeah," Jo concedes. "I guess it was pretty bad."

"And then, Vermont," her mom sighs. "I was already at the end of my rope, and after that . . ." Her voice trails away, and she shakes her head sadly. "After the divorce, after everything was all sorted out, I let him see you now and then. He seemed better, he really did. And then out of the blue, it started up again. All of a sudden, he's saying he needs me to understand. He's saying he had to take you far away to protect you, in case the little ones came after you. Those damned *things*, all over again! He said, and I'll never forget this, because it was so insane, he said, 'They don't like to give up on one they've touched.'"

Jo reaches involuntarily for her left arm, closes her hand around the scars. Her mom doesn't notice, staring off into her memory.

"I remember it so clearly. We were supposed to go to the park for a few hours. We were in the foyer. You were in your blue coat, the one with the penguin buttons."

"I remember that coat."

"I told him I needed to get something. I took your hand and brought you upstairs. Then I called the police. I told them I was scared he was going to kidnap you again. And I *was* scared, Jo. I mean—*fairies*! He was still sick—that's all I could think, that he was still sick and he was going to do something stupid."

Abigail gazes up at Jo, silently begging her to understand. Jo says, "Go on."

"So, I put the TV on loud. I went down and told him not to yell or he'd scare you. When they came he just went. His eyes were so big and sad. That was the last time he was in our house." Abigail sucks in a deep, shuddering breath. "Before they took him, he said it was his fault. He said he shouldn't have brought you back to the house at all, but it was only for a few days, and he thought if you just kept quiet—" Abigail's voice cracks. "It just made no sense, Jo."

She squeezes shut her eyes, stifling tears. Jo waits.

"So that's it," Abigail says at last. "I never for a second thought it was all true. How would I? How on earth would I? Do you know what went through my head? This business of you being touched? I was out of my mind!"

Jo retreats to the chair and sinks down, seeing her little self on the floor staring up at the TV while her dad was led away, silent so as not to scare her.

Her mom, meanwhile, was scared out of her mind.

Jo's always believed her mom never gave her dad enough of a chance, but in reality, she lived with so much for so long, She tried to get him help. Even after the divorce, she let him come visit. Jo can only imagine how pissed Nana and Pops must have been, and even so, her mom still tried. That was worth something. And now, realizing he'd told the truth all along . . .

"I didn't know," Jo says. "I'm sorry, Mom."

Her mom doesn't answer, so Jo looks up.

It takes a long, horrible moment for Jo to register the reason for her mom's stretched-wide mouth, the terror on her face.

The shimmering green, clawlike hand, the stuttering wings. The fairy's crouched on her mom's belly, the size of a hamster. The wings flare the instant it realizes Jo has seen, and the tiny face twists in a grimace. The wings click rapidly, a threat.

They don't like to give up on one they've touched.

Jo almost screams, and in that instant she buttons up her voice, aware through the torrent of her thoughts that screaming from this room will not do her mom any good.

"Get out!" she hisses, uselessly.

The fairy goes still. It looks nervous, which is odd, but it empowers Jo to get up and approach in a crouch, hands out, weaponless.

The fairy snaps to, whipping up and to the side. Its motions seem panicked, clumsy. It goes backward, smashes bedside table items into the air—paper cup, a metal tray, the open toiletry bag, scattering its contents across the linoleum floor. It bumps the wall, spins, then floats confusedly. The fear on its features is unmistakable now. It must be utterly disoriented here in this weird, antiseptic space. Jo almost pities it, except for her mom cowering in the pillows, bunching the blankets over her belly for protection.

Jo lunges around the bed, banging her shin on the metal frame. The fairy darts up and away, plastered for a moment to the ceiling, then it swoops across the room to Jo's chair, where it crouches, wings clicking.

They all go still. The machines hum and beep.

Abigail whispers, "It looks scared."

"I know," Jo says, her eyes fixed on the creature. The fairy's size keeps shifting, shrinking as if to disappear, but it can't. Its tiny, pointy face gapes, eyes darting frantically around the room. For a second, Jo glimpses something familiar, human in its features. The child it once was. *Does it even know?*

Suddenly, it flees upward, smashing into the blinds. The window behind is closed. Stunned, it drops to the floor with a thump.

Jo edges around the bed, closing in. The fairy hisses weakly, wings stiff and tall.

"Open the window," Abigail says.

"I need to get there first," Jo retorts out of the corner of her mouth.

She inches forward, hands out placatingly. The fairy pants, staring up as Jo takes a wide berth around it to the window, pulls up the blinds. The view shocks her, it's so ordinary: asphalt parking lot, green grass. It's raining lightly.

"Oh my God," Abigail hisses. "Robert's here!"

Jo registers the sound of his voice in the hallway. She pulls at the window. It's locked. Frantic, she searches for a latch, a lever, anything.

The door opens. She glimpses Robert in his weekend kha-kis and a button-down, an apparition from another universe.

She whirls around. The fairy panics, darting back and forth

along the wall. Jo blocks it with her shoe, shepherds it under the chair. It scuttles out of sight, the tips of its wings dragging on the linoleum.

"Darling, what on earth happened?" Robert sinks onto the bed, wraps Abigail into his arms. She murmurs she's all right, nothing to worry about, staring wide-eyed at Jo over his shoulder. Jo takes this opportunity to turn around and search for the window lock, which she discovers lower down on the side. She shoves the window wide open. There's a beat, then all at once, wind rushes through her hair as the fairy swoops past, trailing its earthy scent. She blinks at the dot, then it's gone. Rain blows onto her face.

"That's not permitted," someone says sternly.

A nurse briskly strides past to close everything up again. Jo meets Abigail's eyes over Robert's shoulder and gives a nod.

"I was feeling nauseated," Jo tells the nurse.

"Why don't you take a walk outside, then."

The nurse briefly inspects Abigail's chart, then catches sight of the mess on the floor. Jo tells her not to worry, they'll clean up, it was an accident. She departs, closing the door behind her. Robert strokes Abigail's hair, kissing her forehead, while Jo picks everything up and returns it to the bedside table. Robert doesn't question Abigail's excuse that she got frustrated, knocked things over. He thinks she's upset because of the cuts and worried for the baby, when it's so much more than that. Abigail seems to be getting some comfort out of him, though.

She's got her cheek pressed to his, eyes closed, arms wrapped around his neck. She keeps saying how glad she is that he's here. She sounds like she means it.

Maybe she actually does love him. It's a new, unsettling idea. Jo's relieved when they disentangle, she feels so embarrassed watching this display.

Robert releases Abigail back onto the pillows. Her hands rest on her chest, covered by his. "I can't wait for you to get me out of here," she says.

"Well, you're not going back to that house, I can tell you that," he promises. "My God, what if it was rats?"

"We're definitely not going back," Abigail affirms. She casts a quick look at Jo. In that look is hidden their secret, all they are keeping from him.

"We'll head straight home when we're done here," Robert says. "I'll get someone to take care of things."

"You can't do that," Jo interrupts.

Abigail shoots her a warning glance. Jo responds with an *Are you crazy?* look of her own.

"Your mother doesn't need attitude right now," Robert says sternly. "And what on earth happened to your face? Was it the same—?"

He looks suddenly confused. Jo can't blame him. "It's nothing," she says. "I ran into a tree branch."

"She's fine," Abigail interrupts further questions, "but Jo, let's just talk later, OK?"

Jo gets up from the chair. She can't bear to be in this room.

Everything feels all wrong with no way to convey why, not to her mom, not in front of Robert, and maybe not at all.

"I'll be back," she says, her voice dried up and hoarse.

"Josephine!" her mom calls, but Jo keeps going, closing the door behind her.

The nurses at reception barely look up. An orderly ambles by pushing a cart. Jo heads down the hallway as if she knows what she's doing. She wanders through the main part of the hospital until she finds herself outside the cafeteria. No one's in there. The breakfast smells leave Jo queasy. In the sitting area there's a vending machine and a TV with cartoons on mute. She digs coins out of her pocket. She can't decide. The machine hums. The white walls and gray floor make her woozy. Finally, she chooses pretzels. The bag drops with a thunk and she reaches in to get it. The pretzels dry out her mouth, like eating sawdust.

She finds a bathroom down the hall, drinks from the sink faucet, and rinses her face. She looks like hell in the fluorescent light, the life sucked out of her eyes, the cut on her cheek nasty and red.

She touches the cut lightly with her fingertip, remembering the clicking, rushing sound of wings, the glancing light in the fairy's slitted, furious eyes. The one here looked so distressed. Did it find its way back to the hole beneath the Old House, skitter into that slit of cold darkness, away to its own world? Or is it still out, looking for a child to steal? She should never have let it go. She should have captured it, taken it back to the door. Or killed it.

Her hands shake, turning together under the water. She's dehydrated, exhausted. She leans over and drinks again, grimacing at the chemical taste. She's gotten used to the pure water at the house, straight from the well.

Fall down the well, Gammy threatened, *and no one'd hear you scream!*

Anything to keep little Jo-Jo out of the Old House. No wonder they'd shushed her all the time, fingers pressed to their lips. It had been so frustrating, and of course she took every opportunity to shout and giggle, all the louder when they reprimanded her. The fairies must have heard through to their world, the way Jo heard them out in the woods. It was her noise, probably, that gave them the courage to bust through the ward.

Her dad must have really missed Gammy and his home to take that risk, especially when it depended on little Jo-Jo obeying the rules. Jo could never follow rules. Abigail even took her to a specialist once, because she was so stubborn and willful, but it turned out she didn't have some kind of disorder, it was just who she was.

Anxiety bubbles up, acid and painful. She still doesn't follow rules. She entered the Old House when it should have stayed locked. She opened the door, and now the window like an idiot, and children everywhere are in danger.

She can't remember the moment she was taken, only her belly-deep fear and the grown-ups yelling so awfully. Even with

Gammy and her dad there, Jo was still almost lost. Other children don't stand a chance, they get taken without anyone ever seeing a thing. They just vanish, like the old newspaper articles described.

She wonders what's happening back at the house. The image of Tom and Hattie is seared into her head, the two of them standing in the rain, lit up by the headlights, their expectations of Josephine Lavoie in ruins. You're the one supposed to close the door, Hattie said, so surprised, like she never imagined Jo could do otherwise. Even Tom seemed baffled she was leaving.

She had no choice, Jo reminds herself. She flashes to the awful gouges in her mom's belly. There was so much blood. Her baby brother might have been hurt, even killed. She'd had to get her mom out of there.

Gammy used those same words in her letter: *no choice*. She'd meant something different, though. For sure, she didn't imagine Jo sitting safely in a hospital far away, leaving Tom and Hattie to cope on their own.

What they must think of her and how they're managing, all of it leaves Jo's head feeling clogged and numb. There's nothing she can do: she's stuck here. She makes her way back to the waiting area and sinks onto one of the hard plastic seats. Out of habit, she pulls out her phone and switches it on. At least there's Wi-Fi. She longs to text Ellie, but it's too early, and even so, what would she say? *Hey, Ellie, guess what? Fairies are real. And also, they're scary as shit.*

She'll tell her eventually—or maybe she shouldn't, she

doesn't know yet. Regardless, she can't do it in a text. She scrolls through friends' Instagram posts, trying to distract herself, but the more she looks, the more agitated she becomes. Everything her friends are up to is utterly meaningless compared to what's going on here. Her infatuation with Diego seems so stupid now. He keeps posting selfies showing his tan chest with its sprinkle of hairs, the ocean crashing in the background. He still hasn't asked her about the inheritance and Vermont. She abruptly switches off the phone, leans her head back against the wall.

An older couple enters the waiting area. They hold each other in unsteady passage across the room and sit down, leaving a wide gap between themselves and Jo. The woman cries into her hands, and the man rubs her back. Jo casts them a sympathetic look. She feels she should leave, but there's nowhere to go. She hunches down in the seat, wishing she could disappear, staring blankly at her phone. The woman babbles through snot and tears about someone who didn't deserve this, and how they didn't deserve it, and what have they done for things to be this way. Jo eyes them through her hair. The husband looks disheveled and helpless. After a few minutes, he gets up and heads across the room, and Jo realizes he's getting the remote. That's one way of handling things. He switches channels and puts the volume up.

"Let's see if it's on the news," he says, which silences his wife. She stares up at the screen as if seeking salvation.

Jo shifts in her seat, unable to leave, uncomfortable about staying. The anchor cycles through the morning's stories. One of them is indeed theirs, Jo can tell from how they react: a drug shooting downtown, a young man in critical condition. They stare up at the screen, slack-jawed and gray. It must be their son, Jo decides. She feels so bad for them. The segment ends and they slump in defeat, as if the story promised some hope that is now gone. Commercials drone on. Jo hopes their son makes it. They seem ordinary and nice, just regular people who didn't deserve this, like the woman said. They've got wispy gray hair and sagging skin and shapeless clothes. They look like they don't have much money. She hopes they won't need to pay for a lawyer.

The news comes back on, and the woman exclaims, "Not again."

Jo looks up. It takes several moments for the oddly familiar scene to register: it's Edie's shop in Laddston. Two state police SUVs are parked outside, people milling around. The camera cuts back to the reporter with her bright face and perfect hair, and Jo finally hears what she's saying: "... *similar coyote attack happened some years ago, in this same area. I spoke with Edie Collier—she owns the Country Store—and she said it's well marked that there's no camping here, but people come anyway.*"

The scene cuts to this earlier interview with Edie, inside the shop. Jo freezes, staring up. "*They like to come, as there's a pleasant spot near the river right up over thataways,*" Edie says, "*and it may be they didn't know it wasn't allowed. It's a tragedy all the way around.*"

"*How many are in the search party?*"

The camera pans around the packed shop and to the

245

window, showing more people outside. Mostly men in orange hunting jackets and rifles.

"Oh, the whole town's pitching in. We're just so cut up that this happened."

"It's been hours since her parents first realized she was gone. What are the chances of finding her alive?"

Edie's expression tightens, and her mouth draws flat. *"We just have to hope, is all we can do."*

Jo's throat constricts at the cruel charade Edie's forced to play, the little fairy probably long gone with its prize. The scene switches back to the reporter in present time outside, the parking lot empty. *"The search party just headed out again. If she was taken by a coyote, or some other animal, the remains may never be found, but state troopers assured me that the search will continue till nightfall. Back to you—"*

Jo stares blindly at the anchor, who segues to the next story about a traffic accident on 91. The coyote story seems wildly implausible, but it must be how things have always been handled.

"That town is cursed," the woman says.

"It sure is."

Jo peeks at them. She doesn't want to intrude, but on the other hand, they're already talking about it. She asks, "What do you mean?"

They start, as if registering her presence for the first time.

"Sorry," Jo mumbles.

"It's all right, hon," the woman says, hand on her chest. She sighs. "All the way back when I was a kid, I heard stories about that place. Little children going missing and never getting found. Remember, Harry?"

"Sure do." He rubs his scraggly jaw, looking upward in recollection. "There was one little guy, his picture in the paper. It hit me hard, I was his age, seven years old."

"There were more. I don't remember them, but there were more. It's been a while now, though."

"Uh-huh," Harry agrees. "It's been a while."

"It was coyotes?" Jo presses.

"Oh, no, hon," the woman replies. "They had someone in custody a while, remember, Harry? Some poor fellow passing through, turned out it wasn't him. There were so many stories in the papers, all sorts of theories and investigations. Every time something happened, it'd all flare up again. It's been a while. Last I heard of something out of Laddston, it was, oh, fifteen years at least? Twenty? Oh, Lord, how time passes by."

Jo nods, barely able to process her words. For so long, Gammy kept the little ones from stealing a child from this world. Jo undid that in a single day. *Maybe there's time*, she thinks frantically. *Maybe the fairy hasn't gone through yet. Maybe Tom went to the door.*

But it happened at night. It's been ages. Edie said they had to hope, but it was obvious she had none.

"Personally, I say it's a serial killer," Harry announces. "He's laid in wait and now he's back at it. You from around here?"

It takes a moment for Jo to track the shift in topic. "Oh— we're just visiting."

"What a way to spend your visit," his wife says sympathetically. "Who's in here?"

"My mom. She's pregnant. She, um, she thought she was in labor."

"Oh, dear, hon, that's no good. I hope she feels better soon."

"I hope your son does, too," Jo offers, her inadequate words strangling on themselves.

They fade away from her, their interest slipping back to their own sorrows. They sag closer together, gazing at the floor as if remembering why they in turn are in this awful place. Jo gets up as quietly as possible, passing them a small nod that goes unnoticed. She tiptoes away down the hall. The nurse's station at the emergency area seems so calm with everyone bent over paperwork, in contrast with the discordant beeping filling the air. Jo feels suffocated, hot with nerves. Edie's wizened, exhausted face won't leave her head. *The whole town's pitching in.* The whole town takes part in mitigating Josiah Ladd's original sin, from faking birth certificates to wasting a day on a coyote that doesn't exist.

The whole town except for Jo, who's safely tucked away here, out of the picture.

In her letter, Gammy said there was no one else to leave the house to. Jo took that as a kind of insult, except now she understands: no one else should have to take care of that house, no matter what Edie said about selling to them if need be. It's her job, not anyone else's. *Work meant for you* is what Tom called it. And while all those people are out there trudging through mud and rain, she's been eating pretzels and scrolling her phone. That old guy from Edie's shop, Amos, he's probably telling everyone he knew all along she'd suck as the Lavoie.

She wouldn't exactly blame him.

She raps on her mom's door a few times in warning, then walks in. Robert looks up, startled, then mimes she must be quiet, jabbing his finger at the bed. Abigail is asleep despite the recent racket; but that's her mom, always able to pass out no matter what.

"I have to wake her up," Jo hisses.

He looks shocked.

"I have to," she repeats, rounding the other side of the bed in case he tries to stop her.

"No, you don't!" He clambers awkwardly out of the low chair. "She needs rest, Jo!"

"It's important! Mom. *Mom.*"

Abigail stirs, her eyes fluttering open.

"We need to talk." Jo glances meaningfully in Robert's direction. He's just standing there, open-mouthed at her brazenness.

"Is there another one?" Abigail cries, scrambling to sit up.

"No! It's not that."

"What do you mean, 'another one'?" Robert asks.

Abigail meets Jo's eyes, then turns to Robert. "We need a minute. Please," she insists over his protest. "It's important. Why don't you see if you can find some food?"

"The cafeteria's open," Jo says helpfully.

He looks from one to the other, then tosses his hands up in defeat. "Fine. I could use some breakfast," he mutters. He bends to kiss Abigail's forehead. "What do you want, Jo, a bagel?"

"I'm OK. Thanks."

"He's so worried," Abigail sighs when the door closes. "I don't know what to tell him. What's the matter, then?"

"I just saw the news."

"And?"

"A kid disappeared in Laddston. There's no way it's a coyote like they were saying."

Abigail looks at her suspiciously. "And—?"

"I have to go back."

"No, you do *not*. It's not safe, Jo."

"I have to. I'm the Lavoie. I'm supposed to stop the fairies."

Abigail lets out a laugh. "No, you aren't, absolutely not! How would you do it, even if you wanted to?"

"I don't know for sure," Jo hedges. "Necessary work," she attempts a joke. "Down and dirty."

"Don't," Abigail says sharply. "This isn't funny."

"I know, Mom."

"Those *things*—it's just too dangerous!"

"Gammy did it. I can, too."

"But you're already hurt."

Abigail looks increasingly distraught. On impulse, Jo reaches out and places her hand on her mom's belly. She feels motion within, and it sucks the breath out of her chest to think how close things came. "He's OK, right?"

Abigail nods, teary-eyed. "He's OK."

"Mom, if they take another kid, it'll be my fault."

"It's not your fault."

"It is. I'm the one who has to fix things, that's what Hattie said."

"That girl," Abigail scoffs, but weakly.

"Gammy said it in the letter, too. That's what she meant about having no choice. I can't just leave everyone to deal with it. It's my house. I have to go, Mom."

"God, Jo."

Abigail's hands rest protectively on her giant tummy. She looks like she doesn't have anything left in her to argue. Jo feels bad, but she can't back down. "Nothing'll happen to me," she promises. "Look at Gammy. She was OK."

"Huh. If you call that OK." Abigail squeezes shut her eyes, taking a deep breath. She's considering it; Jo can sense her weakening. Then all at once, her eyes fly open. "If you go—and I mean *if*—how will you even get there?"

Jo hadn't thought of that. She's not supposed to drive alone. She could call Tom, but—no way. "It's Saturday," she says. "There's, like, zero traffic. It's not like Newton here," she rushes on, seeing Abigail forming her protest. "Mom, what else can I do? I have to go!"

"Robert will never let you drive off on your own!"

"So don't tell him till I'm gone. I'll just duck out. You can make something up later."

"Jesus, Jo," Abigail says miserably.

"Mom, I'm doing this, OK?"

They both hear Robert greeting the nurses in the hallway. Their eyes meet. Abigail gives a small shake of her head. "Please don't," she whispers. "It's not safe, Jo. It's just not safe."

Jo presses her hands together in a silent apology as the door swings open. Robert enters with a laden tray. "I got you a bagel," he tells Jo, unloading items onto the side table. "They didn't have cinnamon-raisin, so I got sesame."

"Thanks," Jo says, realizing she's ravenous. Watching him unpack the paper bag onto the bedside table, she feels bad. Robert's annoying, but he does take care of her and her mom. "Steady and stable" was how her mom described him way back when, trying to sell the marriage to Jo. He was nothing like her dad, who had such a big, smiling face, an explosion of unbrushed curls. Her dad never looked at Jo without grinning. *You are the joy of my life!* he cried, twirling her around by the arms till they both fell to the grass. Everything was so different with him. Always exciting, unpredictable, and definitely dramatic.

And for her mom, so frightening. For the first time, watching Robert fuss with the food and arrange the plastic cutlery and napkins, Jo can kind of understand why her mom thought boring looked pretty good.

Abigail pulls herself upright with heaving side-to-side motions and unfolds a napkin across her chest. Jo holds her wrapped bagel and the cream cheese packets, waiting, until finally Abigail notices.

They stare at each other for a moment. *I have to*, Jo mouths.

Abigail looks ashen, miserable. She shakes a ketchup packet at Robert. "Can you open this stupid thing?"

He tears the packet open and hands it back to her.

"I'm gonna eat in the waiting room," Jo says casually.

"Oh, you don't have to do that," Robert says, startled.

"It's OK. I like it there." She's surprised by how guilty she feels lying to him. Her mom looks stricken, but Jo can't help that now. "This way, you guys can have some time alone and all. So, uh, I'll see you later."

She looks back to see her mom clutching her egg sandwich halfway to her mouth, staring after her. "Please, Jo. Be careful," Abigail calls just as the door swings shut.

Outside, the rain dribbles down her face. Thunder booms in the distance. At least the heat wave is broken. She hurries to the car, gets in, and buckles up. The asphalt yawns ahead, rows of parked cars, the road beyond. Someone gets out of a car and jogs toward the building, head bent. She thinks of her mom tucked in the bed, looking so worried. Robert laying out the plastic cutlery, his usually perfect hair a ruffled mess. The scene seems so ordinary, and already so far away.

She turns the key and the engine rumbles to life. The rain falls harder, pouring down the windshield, drumming the car. She inches out of the parking lot, the blinker ticking loudly though no one's around. It feels so strange to be driving this car—the one her parents drove around as young newlyweds with a baby in the back, the one her dad drove when he brought her here all those years ago. His hands held this same steering wheel, he went up this same highway. Jo imagines herself in the back, staring out the window at the wide, green world racing by. Her dad used to sing in the car: ditties and made-up nonsense poems. They echo in her head as she picks up speed, long-ago bits of sound, soothing and familiar, as if he's there next to her, guiding her home.

the yearning for home dont ever go. its a field
overplanted till the grounds got nothing left to
give and nothing can grow there no more. maur
said thats no done deal. a field lies fallow it
comes back and alls you do is wait in patience
and the time comes around again.

im not a field i told her. time don't come
around for me.

she said it will and everyone and everything is
part of this earth even me. she said i should
count myself lucky for so much chance at this
beautiful life.

EIGHTEEN

The rain's let up by the time she gets to Laddston. Two state police vehicles are still parked at Edie's market, and she can see lights on inside. She hunches close to the wheel, hoping to slip through town unseen, but up ahead, Lola and Amanda, her son riding her hip, are practically in the middle of the street next to a parked car. It's impossible for Jo to just roll on by. Sure enough, Lola catches sight of her, stops midspeech, her mouth an O of surprise.

Jo reluctantly brakes and rolls down the window. "Hi," she calls.

Lola opens her hands in confusion. "Where've you been? Do you even know what's going on?"

"Yes—I'm sorry. I was at the hospital with my mom."

"I'm getting out of here," Amanda snaps, interrupting whatever Lola was going to say. Lukie sobs, and she covers his mouth with her hand, shushing him. She holds Lukie close, trying to maneuver a suitcase around to the back of the car.

The suitcase flips sideways off its wheels, and Amanda curses, struggling to drag it back upright. Her mom steps forward and helps shift it into position.

"This is stupid, Amanda!" she says. "How long d'you think you can stay with Ben?"

"It doesn't matter!" Amanda retorts. "We can't stay here!"

Lukie lets out a wail, shattering the silence of the empty road. Amanda drops the suitcase and crushes him to her, pressing his face into her neck, muffling the sound.

So the little ones don't hear. Jo's breath stops, she peers through the windshield. The street glistens in the gray light, leading off into the mist. The sidewalks are empty. Amanda rocks from side to side, desperate to silence the boy's cries. Something collapses in Lola's face. She gently moves them out of the way, then pops open the trunk and heaves the suitcase in.

She catches Jo watching. "Are you going to the house or what?"

She's not angry, Jo understands. She's scared and stressed, her daughter's leaving, the baby's crying, and Jo's just sitting there. She slams on the gas, guns it out of town and up the hill.

The house isn't as far as it seemed when they first arrived, which feels like weeks ago. She pulls up to the garage and switches off the engine, gets out. The air is muggy and warm. The house looks drained and abandoned in the gray light, the sun a faint misty orb through the clouds. She sees Hattie and Tom on the porch, side by side on the wicker couch, watching her. She lifts her hand in greeting. Hattie holds up her doll. Tom bends back down over his lap, busy with something. The gravel crunches under Jo's flip-flops, then turns to muddy grass that squelches over her toes. She climbs the creaking stairs, pulls at the screen door. It's stuck again. She yanks it hard and it pops open.

"You came back," Hattie says.

"I heard what happened."

"Can't get to market today," Tom says, accusation in his tone. He's whittling, the shavings flying off onto the porch floor. "This one's been in and out the cellar all morning doing your work."

"I set the fires but I didn't do it right," Hattie says. She looks miserable, the doll in a stranglehold against her chest. "They took a baby girl."

"I—I came back to do like you said. I can try and stop it."

Tom looks up. "Too late. That baby's gone."

Jo feared as much, but the words still cut hard. "I'm sorry."

Hattie holds her doll up, hiding her face. "I tried to stay down there, but I couldn't. I was scared."

"Not your work," Tom says, his knife moving in even strokes.

"Hattie, I'm so sorry. I'll go now."

"It was a little Canadian girl taken," Hattie says, as if she hasn't heard. "They aren't supposed to camp around here, but they do anyway, and now look what's happened."

Hattie falls silent, draws her knees up, curling tight. Tom blows on the piece of wood. It's a car, like the one Lukie had.

He weighs it in his palm, staring down at it, then sets to carving again. His knife scores the wood with steady strokes, making a small scratching sound.

Maybe she'll be sent back, Jo almost says, but what comfort is that? Hattie is malnourished, illiterate, unable to go anywhere without supervision. The magnitude is only just sinking in: How old was this baby girl, what did she look like, what was her name? Jo should have been here, like Tom said. Now her parents will never see their girl again, and yet she's right here, just on the other side of this world. Her voice might drift across to them one day in the woods, singing fairy dirges. They'll die never knowing—

She can't think about that now. She just can't. She doesn't even know if she could've saved that girl. All she can do is focus on closing the door so it doesn't happen again.

She forces herself to move. At the kitchen doorway, she discovers the table overturned, chairs scattered. A bowl stands upside down on the floor. "What happened here?"

Hattie says, "Little ones went all over and messed things up."

"It's messes that delight," Tom adds.

The strange words hang in the air.

Jo asks, "What do you mean?"

"All stays the same over there. Here, it changes."

"How do you know?"

Hattie looks at her with her wide green eyes, then turns to Tom. He shrugs. Hattie, as if given a directive, turns to Jo and says, "Tom was a fairy, but now he's just Tom."

Jo digs her fingernails into the door frame. "What do you mean?"

"He took you," Hattie says. "Maur got so mad she kept him."

Jo stares at the shining knife whittling steadily away. "I don't understand."

Tom pauses his work to look up. "She shackled me down cellar. I fought her"—he holds up his left hand with its two gnarled finger stumps—"but iron saps us. Not the pieces lying around, but touching us."

Us, Jo thinks. He sounds so bitter.

"The iron took my strength, and she took my wings. It was a crime what she did, keeping me alive. She never said sorry. She said a person ought to pay for such crimes as I committed. I said I was no person. She said I once was and now am again."

He speaks in a monotone, as if reciting something. Jo has the unsettling image of him in his cabin or the greenhouse, muttering this litany to himself over and over, for years. Hattie cuddles up to him sympathetically. She's probably heard all this before.

He took you. Jo claws backward in her memory, seeking him, but finds only the stifling, dank dark of her nightmares. He must have looked like the fairies she's seen: scaled and swift, insectoid but with humanity flitting in their features. When he carried her he would have been smaller, faster, with wings snapping the air. He changed back once he was trapped here, but something of the fairy remains in his disjointed ways, the flat animal stare.

Understanding arrives, shocking her. Her arm. She touches the scars, as if discovering them for the first time. "It was you."

His eyes follow, and he nods. "I tried to keep you. I was too weak."

He goes back to his whittling, heedless of her reaction. She can barely make sense of what she's feeling. Something about how they're the same, in a way. Both there that night, both maimed. He got the worst of it, though. He was alive when Gammy cut his wings off. Was he awake—did he feel it? The scars up his arms and the hacked-off fingers—Gammy probably used that machete. The notion is sickening. Except he's fine now, she reminds herself. Relatively speaking. He blows on the wood again, sending a cloud of sawdust into the air. Jo wonders what he feels when he sees them, the little ones. He knows their comings and goings. He knows the baby's long gone, as if he's still connected to the fairy world. Except he's not. He makes toys for kids and hands them out for free. It must be a sort of penance. All those little toys, made in his scarred hands.

It dawns on her that his name must be on the obelisk, too. He's one of the Cherished, even if he didn't come back quite the same way. "Do you know who you were?"

He shakes his head without looking up.

"Maur never found his story," Hattie explains. "He was probably from the town, from way long ago. There are old names carved down at the bottom of the stone. Since Maur never knew which one he was, she just picked Tom."

"Thomas," he corrects. "Tom for short."

Hattie rolls her eyes.

"Wouldn't there be some kind of record? Something in a newspaper?"

"Not if it was from way back," Hattie says. "And if a Laddston kid goes missing, they never tell the newspapers or the police anyway, because they already know what happened. It stays secret, just for people here."

Hattie leans on Tom's arm, watching him work. *Secret.* Hattie herself a secret, and Tom even more so. When they're at a market far away from here, bagging vegetables and counting change, no one has any clue. An image keeps flickering in Jo's head of herself curled inside a scaled, dank embrace, limp and helpless. It can't be a memory, but it feels like one, acute, clear. All these years she's woken from nightmares, the taste of something forgotten on her tongue. And here's her answer, this strange man who's not a man, this damaged, awkward girl croodling up to him like his child.

"Hattie, do you know what I'm supposed to do at the door?"

"You wait there."

"And?"

"You have to get the tools. They're still in there somewhere."

Jo goes into the kitchen, picking her way through the mess. She finds the pouch under an overturned drawer, cutlery scattered everywhere. She picks it up. The weight of its awful contents drags at her arms. She doesn't know how to use these things. In the night, she threw the chain and it fell uselessly to the floor.

"Hattie," she calls, in the same moment wondering if it's Tom she should be asking, but she's interrupted by the telephone ringing.

"I'll get it!" Hattie cries, dashing by before Jo can even move. Answering the phone is clearly Hattie's prized job. Jo hopes she isn't too disappointed; it's probably Abigail calling to check in. Hattie darts around obstacles—an overturned chair, a scatter of tins—and grabs the phone off the wall, yells, "Hello!"

Jo stands with the pouch in her arms but does not have to wait very long, as Hattie suddenly drops the receiver. It crashes into the wall, then bounces this way and that on the coiled cord. Hattie gazes at her, stricken, her face drained of color.

"What? What's wrong?"

"Lukie!" Hattie cries. "They took Lukie!"

NINETEEN

"But I just saw them—she was leaving, she had a suitcase!"

"She put him on the sidewalk to open the car 'cause the door always gets stuck—she's coming here!" Hattie's voice spirals into a wail. "What if you already missed it? What if Lukie's already gone?"

Tom's come in amid the racket, and he lays his hand on Hattie's head. "He's not gone yet. It'll stay a while. They can't help but want to stay."

He clutches the half-whittled car in his hand, clumsily patting Hattie's hair, worry all over his face. He knows Lukie, of course. He gave him a whole set of those toys. This show of feeling unsettles Jo—what else goes on inside that strange skull of his? Does he remember her? Does he feel bad at all?

The noise of an engine in the wrong gear roars up the driveway. They rush out onto the steps, look on in shock as a car careens around the bend. There's a terrible metal crash as the car clips the Subaru's bumper, spins, and stops.

Amanda tumbles out. She's lost all coordination. She stumbles and flails across the lawn. Her mouth is slack, wide open. An awful sound emerges from her, a keening wail. Jo stares in horror at this shambling zombie. She'd never have imagined Amanda so undone.

"They took Lukie," she says, the words weak puffs, barely audible. She points, then follows her own direction, half running. Almost at once she slips in the mud and drops to her knees. Her labored panting carries across to them as she scrambles to her feet, keeps going.

The door, Jo understands. Amanda thinks she can intercept the fairy. Jo flashes to the moment she swung the paddle in Gammy's room, the sharp rake of claws across her face. Amanda's no match, not in this state.

"Amanda, no!" Jo cries out, leaping down the stairs.

There's a blur of motion, and to her shock, Tom runs past. He catches up to Amanda in a few strides, grabs her by the arms, and pins her in place. She convulses, drawing her knees up and shuddering. "I want him back," she sobs. "I want my baby boy. Please. Please."

"Jo'll get him back," Tom tells her.

"She CAN'T!" Amanda screams, twisting in his unyielding grip. "Only Maur could, and Maur's dead! Oh my God!" she gasps. "He's gone. I can't—please—"

Jo's chest feels crushed, so painful she can't breathe. She's never seen anything so horrible. Even being with her father in the hospital wasn't like this. The grief she felt then was huge, but it was normal. It was contained, the way he was, tucked into the tight sheets in a clean bed, in an orderly room with schedules and plans. This is wildly different. She sees the little boy's chubby arm driving the wooden car back and forth on the picnic table. He had brown hair that was really thick and curly, and Amanda kept pushing it out of his eyes. Then Edie came and was mad at her, and Amanda led Lukie away in the grass. It was just yesterday.

"Where's my baby?" Amanda begs. Her body jolts, drawing tighter into itself. "Please. *Please.*"

This last broken plea unlocks Jo's paralyzed legs. She backs away, then turns and runs into the house, careening down the hallway and grabbing the banister railing to swing around onto the steps. She runs up two at a time, aware of her ragged, panicked breathing. What she's doing is stupid, but she can't help it, she just can't, and besides, Tom said the fairy was still out. Tom, the fairy, a fact whose horror hasn't yet sunk in, but that doesn't matter right now. She bursts into the bedroom. Her mom's stuff is strewn everywhere, drawers upside down, the suitcase upended. The bedspread's dragged across the floor, a curtain is down. The little ones must have spun through here, looking for the baby. Maybe not so stupid she retrieves the paddle after all, she thinks, picking it up with a surge of relief. She feels stronger with it. She's used it once, she can do it again.

She gets tripped up in the tangled bedsheets on the floor, raps her ankle on something hard. It's her dad's bell, lying on its side. *Daddy.* He carried it everywhere, he must've had a good reason. She wrestles it out of the sheet, and the room fills with melodious deep clangs. She grabs the clapper, and the last gong abruptly stops.

She sees the Old House walls through the window, dark and wet in the haze. She grips the paddle hard and runs back the way she came. She almost knocks Hattie over in the downstairs corridor.

"She won't stop," Hattie cries, rocking with the doll over her head. "I wish she'd stop."

She means Amanda, who is emitting hitching, pitiful cries. It sounds like she's on the porch now; Tom must have taken her there. Hattie rocks, the doll wrapped around her face, stuffing drifting to the floor. Jo meant to sew it up, show Hattie how to make a little dress for it. That plan seems irretrievably distant.

"Hattie," Jo says, then more sternly, "Hattie!"

The doll slides from her face.

"Do you know how I do it?"

Hattie gulps, trying to speak.

"Focus!" Jo snaps. "Gammy must've told you things! Tell me what you know!"

"If one comes and it's got no baby, you have to let it through. It's just trying to get home. You have to watch. They get real small."

"What else?"

"Wait for the one with Lukie. It'll be really tired 'cause they stay out as long as they can, all the way till they're weak. If they stay here past time, they change back, and they don't want that. It'll try to go home and you have to stop it. Smash it, kick it," Hattie splutters, "Just get Lukie back!"

The last comes out in a scream, the girl's face twisted with rage. Behind her, Tom appears in the doorway. He moves into the corridor, places his hands on Hattie's shoulders. She crumples at his touch, whirls around, and presses her face into his chest, sobbing. He loops his arms around her, drawing her close. Whatever emotions Jo glimpsed earlier are walled up again behind his inscrutable stare.

"Get it in the shackle," he says, "then drape it with the chain. It can't fight no more then."

Jo swallows. "And after that?"

"Kill it whichever way suits you. Then close the door. Best get going now."

He bends over Hattie, stroking her back. Jo slips by, holding the bell close to her chest. *Whichever way suits me?* she thinks as she gathers up the pouch in the kitchen. As if she's got an array of choices. As if she's tried out a whole bunch of ways of killing things, and now she just has to pick one.

Axe, machete, iron stake, chain. The list hits a near hysterical pitch in her head as she maneuvers down the narrow hallway. The paddle hits some of the pictures on the wall and knocks them askew, then she almost drops the pouch, all while clumsily trying to hang on to the bell. She steps outside with her awkward burden and is immediately aware of the rumble of idling car engines. It sounds like three or four trucks out front. Whoever's here includes Edie and Lola, hovering at the corner of the house, staring at her.

She stares back in confusion. They stay rooted to their spot, as if behind an invisible barrier. The yard does look forbidding in the hazy light, the Old House looming darkly above the dead grass patches, the open door a black hole. Loco sits on the stoop, the noise of his panting carrying across the still air.

Lola holds out her hands imploringly. "Please," she cries, her voice low. "Please get him back."

It's unnerving to see Lola transformed into someone so helpless. Edie solves Jo's problem of how to respond by making a stern little motion: *Get going.*

Jo tries to manifest confidence she doesn't have. She strides across the yard, conscious of the paddle, which seems so dumb now, but at least she's got the pouch and bell, and they must know what all that's for. She pauses in the doorway so as to look back, a habitual polite gesture, but in that instant, she realizes it might undo her resolve. There's no looking back. No going back.

I'm the Lavoie, she thinks, and steps inside. The stone floor is scattered with candy wrappers and bits of garbage, smashed glass. The air reeks of urine, and she steps forward gingerly, becoming aware of the dark stains on the floor. *They must've peed in the house, too*, she thinks in dismay.

There's a jarring disconnect between this wreckage and what her dad described in his stories. Sunlight and ice cream, really? Hattie spoke that way, too, but the way they smell, the rancid mess they've made, it doesn't make sense. From what she's seen of them, she can't imagine them laughing and playing tag, either. And if they do live like that, then why is Hattie so sickly looking? If it's all so lovely over there, why is Hattie so tormented, so hurt seeming?

She stands over the open trapdoor, wrinkling her eyes at the acrid, chemical wisps of smoke pushed along by the breeze from below. The smoke lifts into the room, slows into a floating cloud in the muggy air. She creeps down the stairs using her phone flashlight, switching it off once she sees how well lit the cellar is. This is what Hattie meant by the fires: a row of burners like the ones Nana uses to cook fondue at Christmas. They're placed in uneven rows in front of the door, lodged on the piles of scree, and scattered below like land mines. The flames, fed by the fuel gel, can't be extinguished by the breeze.

Jo approaches, acutely aware of the dark gap of the door, the cool breeze wafting around her ankles and dispersing the smoke now that she's closer. She sets the pouch, bell, and paddle on the floor. She can see how the little one that took the campers' baby got through: they can shrink so small, and every so often gaps appear in the flames, holes of black where a fairy might dart through safely. Jo can see why Gammy called this labor-intensive. The fires are only a deterrent, they won't ever suffice on their own.

There's some iron junk littered here and there: a bell without a clapper, parts of tools. The little ones must have pushed these pieces aside climbing through. There isn't that much out of place; Hattie was probably staying on top of this till she got too scared to come back down. Jo goes around on her hands and knees, gathering up the iron. She wedges the pieces behind the flames as best she can, as close to the opening as possible, hurrying. The fairy that has Lukie could be here right now, sneaking by, invisible. It comes to her that if the fairy shrinks to its smallest size, then Lukie will be no bigger than a bean. She can't count on seeing him: she's going to have to spot the fairy itself.

She chooses a good vantage point and sits down, back to the wall. From here she can see every part of the room, and she's only about a foot from the closest flame. Next to her is a bucket with a click lighter, burner fluid, and more pots. It looks mundane, like a party pack for a cookout. She wonders where it was stashed; she thinks she might have seen it in the pantry.

She keeps her eyes peeled, examining the whole room, motions startling her constantly. But there's nothing here. It's cold and damp, and she's tired, hungry, and thirsty. The smoke stings her eyes. She's sinking in a dream of suffocating darkness. What is she doing in this place? It's insane. And yet it's not. It's real as can be. Amanda's shrill weeping echoes in her head, mingled with the stark vision of her mom's terrified look from the hospital bed, her hand reaching out for help.

She wonders how her mom's doing. She'll completely freak out when Jo finally explains the work Gammy referred to in the letter.

If you get to tell her.

Gammy had a limp and a mangled ear, and who knows what other scars hidden by her clothes. Jo's face is already cut and she's barely done anything. She should ask Hattie, or maybe Edie would know better, if there are any stories in the family lore about a Lavoie losing the fight. Maybe there are one or two out in the woods, rotting next to the fairies.

Not me, she resolves. *No way.*

Time passes with agonizing slowness. Some of the fires are burning out. She creeps along on her knees, replacing the tins with new ones, lighting them with the clicker. This is her job every year on Christmas Eve, from when she was little, helping out with the catering. She arranges the tins a little closer to the opening. The flames dip and flatten in the breeze. She checks her phone: an hour's gone by. She settles on the floor again, then changes her mind and stands up. Her butt bones hurt. Everything hurts. The paddle drags at her sweating, stiff hands, so she lays it in the dirt near the opening. She gets onto her knees, then resignedly sits down again. She'll be here a while. She'd better find a way to get comfortable.

It's my leggsy after all.

She giggles.

"Legacy, my ass," she tells the empty room. It's her mom's favorite exclamation. She misses her mom. She even misses Robert. She wonders if they're still in the hospital, or on their way here, frantic with worry. That'd be something, them finding her in the cellar guarding a row of fondue burners. Although her mom wouldn't risk coming back here, no way, so it'd just be Robert. She pictures him standing here in his nice khakis and loafers, baffled. It would be so totally crazy.

She kind of has to pee, which poses a dilemma. You'd think that after generations, some Lavoie along the way might have installed a toilet down here. Maybe the supply bucket doubles as a port-a-potty.

It strikes her that Gammy probably sat right here where she is now, the same fires burning. It's eerie, like Gammy's ghost is with her, outlining the form of her body with a pale glow. Gammy spent a whole lifetime doing this, and Jo's been here only an hour. It makes sense now that Gammy never had kids. How could she, in this place? She had only one job, one duty, and it excluded everything else.

Necessary work. Hard work.

So will this be her fate as the Lavoie—no living abroad, no kids of her own? Not that she wants any; world overpopulation, after all. But can she really bear to be stuck here forever?

Maybe she can outsource, she muses. It's Robert's favorite concept. Outsource it! he exclaims whenever Abigail complains about the labor of keeping up her rose garden, or painting the shed, or any one of her projects she takes on with such fervor. He doesn't get that Abigail needs to do all this stuff or she might turn all her energy to murdering him. That's how Jo used to see it, anyway. Things seem different now, after the hospital.

She can't outsource, regardless. She can hardly hire some

random outsider, and no one in the town should have to do this work. They already do everything else: lie to the police, forge documents, lose their children. She truly gets it now. This part of it is up to the Lavoie.

She's never felt like a Lavoie. Her dad was adopted, after all. He wasn't really anything, was how she grew up thinking, maybe because of Nana and Pops's undisguised concerns about his heritage. It feels like a shallow way to see things, now. Even if her dad was adopted, he was Gammy's son, a hundred percent. He's everywhere in this house, in the pictures, in the stories. And there's Gammy's gravestone: *Mother to beloved Lorenzo.*

Gammy didn't leave the house to just anyone—she left it to her granddaughter. Jo is the Lavoie, and all of it is for her to tend: the house, the land, this gash in the rock leading into darkness.

Loco barks. He barks and barks, the noise reverberating through the dark. The fires flicker and flatten. Jo crouches with the paddle held tight. She's boiling with fear, every part of her body so taut it might explode. The barking stops. She stares around the room, her eyeballs drying out, hurting.

There.

Near-invisible motion to her left. It was trying to sneak by. She glimpses the shining green of wing, the scuttle of legs.

She smashes the paddle into the dirt. "Get back!"

The fairy pops into view, exposed by her rage. It's as small as it can get, a wide-eyed mouse, the wings sticking out and stiff with shock. The tiny face is twisted in a snarl, but it's afraid, Jo can feel it sure as if it spoke.

"Open your hands," she says.

There is a pause. Then the creature slowly unfurls its claw-like hands, reaching out toward her. There is no child. Lukie isn't there. Its wings tuck close to its body. It shudders, glancing at the fires. It's stayed out as long as it possibly can, and now it just wants to go back home. The one that's got Lukie won't be far behind.

Jo reaches out, feeling like a giant in a story, her arm's so big and pale in the flickering light, dwarfing the shrunken fairy. She nudges a tin out of the way with her finger, creating a gap. The fairy hesitates. Its wings tuck hard and close to its body, and it seems to be trying to shrink even more, but it fails. It looks petrified. Jo nudges the tin a little farther. "Go on," she says.

It creeps forward, flattening itself, and slips like a cock-roach through a slit between the rocks.

Jo pushes the fire back in place. Her whole body melts, weakens with exhaustion. She wishes she could tumble into sleep right here on the floor.

She waits and waits. Her phone clocks her time down here in the dark, breathing in the chemical fires and the wisps of air from the fairy world. She thinks about how no one ever knew where her father came from, except it turns out he came from here. He couldn't remember, the story went, not one thing, not one detail other than his name. Who remembers nothing? Someone scarred by something so wrong, so hideous, that he should never be trusted, and sure enough, look what happened.

But it wasn't actually like that. He did remember. He dwelled out of time in another world, dashing through forests screaming with laughter, gorging on sweets, and falling unconscious in mossy groves.

If it was really like that. She doubts it more and more.

Why did they send him back? she wonders. Why not keep him, or Hattie? How do they choose? They made Tom into a fairy, but not her dad. It makes no sense. Maybe it's not supposed to. Maybe that's how the old fairies hurt the children, how they get their revenge, through this random selection process. Hattie surely is hurting, even after all this time.

Jo crouches close, moving some of the tins to reach over the scree, float her hand over the dark opening. The coolness washes over her splayed fingers, bringing its faint, weedy lake scents. *Grass and trees and rivers and the children play and laugh and eat sweets and no one ever has to see the dentist.* A pretty scene that enchanted her, and in fact, it must have been an enchantment, it can't really be like that. Tom said everything's the same there. That doesn't sound like the vibrant landscape her dad described. Look at Hattie with her yellowed teeth and stunted, scrawny frame.

Her father overcame whatever happened there, growing big and strong, so maybe Hattie will, too. Jo hopes so.

The way he told the stories, she wonders if he ever really

grasped what was done to him, what he lost. *Lorenzo Joseph Habib.* The bright round baby eyes in the photo haunt her. She imagines his parents—her grandparents—searching for him day after day till hope gave out. They died not ever knowing what happened to him. Maybe they had other children and she has relatives somewhere, maybe even near Laddston. She could look them up, she realizes. If they had another son, that would be her uncle—but he'd have to be dead by now. Maybe he had kids. They'd be her cousins, except they'd be so much older than her, old enough to have kids of their own. She imagines finding them, spying on them. Her dad being adopted has always affected her awfully, especially in her mom's family with all that history going back to the Civil War, whereas her own story goes back one generation, then nothing. But maybe she does have family. Maybe they look like her.

Not that she could ever actually introduce herself. What on earth would she say?

The mystery of what lies beyond the darkness nags at her. She's always felt edgy, uncomfortable, no matter where she is. She thought it was because she couldn't get along with her mom, or because she hated Robert, or because of how she looks so different from everyone else. Maybe all that was true, but there was also this: the thick, warm coil wrapping her into sleep, the journey's beginning, enveloped in the scent of another world. Maybe, when the fairy touched her—*it was Tom*, she thinks jarringly—she was infected with that world, like a disease that stays in the bloodstream, so she's never felt at home anywhere since. Because of that briefest contact, she comes, in essence, from the same place her dad came from. A dreamworld, an unworld, a world of not-ever-here.

Why are you so sullen, Josephine? her mom always complains. Why do you sulk so much? Why can't you be happy?

This is why.

The world that touched her warped her life, as it did her dad's, and Hattie's, and Tom's. She chafes no matter where she is, at home, at school, wherever. Every step, her feet feel wrong, out of place. It makes sense now. Look at all this. Of course she doesn't fit in anywhere.

Except for here, in Gammy's house, she thinks suddenly.

Here, she belongs.

It's the same for Tom and Hattie. They might not fit out in the world anymore, but they fit here, at Gammy's. They can never, ever leave. It doesn't matter what Robert or her mom says, Jo's never selling this house. She feels a wave of sadness for her father, who belonged here most of all and innocently left, transported by love.

Josiah Ladd may have heroically faced his sin, but it will never be fully righted. It's still harming everyone to this day. Look at Gammy, stuck here her whole life after all her travels. Look at her dad, and Hattie, and even Tom. The old fairies will never stop exacting their revenge, they'll go on forever. That's just how it is. There's no prettifying it, no ribbon to tie up on an ending. And someone has to be here to work against them. She'll need to have kids after all. Or find someone to be the next Lavoie, one day far in the future.

She edges back to her place against the wall. She could pass out, she's so tired. She wishes she had cold water, or food, anything to keep her awake.

Barking erupts again. The sound crashes down the steps into the dark cave of the cellar. Jo jerks upright, scrambles to her hands and knees. She can picture Loco with his front paws lifting off the ground with every bark. She struggles getting to her feet, weak from sitting so long.

A smell seeps into her nostrils, of moss and earth and wet fecundity. She blinks, dazed with fear. It won't want to be seen. It has to be here, though, the smell is so stifling.

The paddle—! She doesn't have it, she realizes frantically. She gropes around, trying to keep watch on the staircase, the far wall, the corners.

A flicker catches her eye. Green, shimmering, then gone.

It's a few feet away, to her right.

"Get back!" she croaks, her voice dried up from disuse.

The figure vanishes, but not before she glimpses the hunched shape of it, the spindly legs.

They stare at each other through the fire-smoke and flicker. Its eyes glow gold and green, luminescent as a beetle's shining carapace. Its breaths come short and sharp, the dark-haired toddler nestled in its scaled arms. Lukie's thumb is halfway in his slack mouth, eyes closed. He seems to barely be breathing. Jo panics he might be dead. Her eyes feel scraped raw from watching his chest, till it moves, so slightly it could be an illusion.

The fairy shifts, makes a rasping sound. Its long fingers tighten around the child. It's full size, she suspects to intimidate her. But like Hattie said, she can see it's tired, deeply so. It sways, sagging, and there's desperation in its expression, transparent in the way of a child unable to conceal the truth.

"You can't keep him," Jo says. "You have to let him go."

Spit drools from the gaping mouth, sucking air.

She wonders if it knows. That it has to die.

You have no choice.

This was what Gammy meant: not all of Jo's stupid notions earlier. Clammy illness washes over her skin, through her skull. Rancid wetness fills her mouth.

"Let him go," Jo repeats, her words a bubble. She spits in the dirt. "You have no choice."

She searches its face for the child it once was. It looks ancient, the skin tight across bone, glimmering gold and green. The smell of it fills her nostrils, thick, muddy. It makes her head swim.

"Do you remember what you were?" she asks, to fill the silence, to mark time.

The creature stares.

"You were like him," she points at Lukie. "You got taken. Your parents probably cried every day for years. You want to do that to his mom?"

There is a flicker in its eyes, a shifting of weight. Then it grimaces, hissing. The teeth are hideous yellowed crumbles with dark gaps.

"They really should let you all go to the dentist," Jo says.

Sss-ssssss-ssssssssssss.

The wings click, staccato anger. All at once, the fairy makes a break for it.

Jo throws out her arms, yelling, "No!"

It recoils, hunches backward, spitting.

"You can't keep this up," Jo says. "You have to let him go. If you let him go, maybe I can do the same for you."

The wings click. Jo understands from its narrow, enraged stare that it doesn't believe her.

"Trust me," she says, sickened by how easy it is to lie, but there's no other way. "We can discuss it. Just let him go."

She's only half-aware when it happens, adrift on the edge of hallucinations, her body leaden with exhaustion. Through the haze she hears a thump. She blinks in surprise. It's Lukie, lying in the dirt. He looks dead.

How I must have been. Then her dad scooped her up, ran for the car.

The fairy's eyes flick greedily from her to the door. It edges closer, shrinking.

It thinks she might let it through. The manacle is just there, within reach. The fairy's tired and weak. It creeps closer, wings dragging in the dirt, its mouth hanging open.

Lukie sleeps on his side, one chubby arm out, knees tucked to his chest.

Her hands are sweaty fists, nails gouging her palms. She reaches for the manacle. The fairy bares its teeth, but the hiss ends in a gurgle. Spit dribbles from its mouth. Its roving eyes settle on the space behind Jo, gateway to freedom. It claws at the dirt, trying to drag itself forward. The flames dance, spitting smoke trails.

A sound emerges from the fairy's chest, a throaty cry. It launches forward, smacking the tins aside. Its wings lift with a shuddering rattle.

For an instant, Jo's world lurches with bright panic and relief: it's over, it's escaping, and there's nothing she can do.

Then reality: the creature has barely moved. Its mighty effort carried it forward only some inches; it knocked only one of the tins out of the way, and the flame's burning in the dirt now, close to the fairy's stricken face. It can't even refold its wings. They're splayed out across the floor.

It tried so hard. It probably believed it would make it. The flame terrorizes it, but it can't move.

Jo crawls closer. She moves the flaming tin away.

Their eyes meet.

"I'm sorry," Jo whispers.

The fairy's mouth draws back in a snarl. Foul, dripping teeth, golden eyes slitted with hate.

Its right leg is closest, scrawny and muscular, splayed out on the earthen floor. Jo reaches out cautiously. The fairy bunches and tenses at her touch, then attacks. Her shoulder explodes with pain, and she blindly swings back with the paddle, making contact. She hears a groan, the shushing and clicking of wings. The wing brushes her arm. She scuttles back, lands heavily on her butt.

Her shoulder throbs awfully. She blinks, unable to see clearly. Her fingers come away from her eyes covered in blood. It must have scraped her head, too. The fairy is completely done in now, the manacle chain draped across its leg, the iron sapping its strength. It can do nothing but stare, leaching distress and rage, spit pooling in the dirt. She drags the manacle into place. The fairy's skin is hard, much colder than Jo imagined. The scent she knows so intimately fills her nose and mouth, seeping into her whole body. She clamps the manacle shut and turns the key. The fairy emits a croaking cry, too weak to even wail. Jo wipes at the tears now blinding her. She imagines unlocking the manacle, shoving the fairy through the opening. It would be the right thing to do. This is terrible, a crime, a cruelty so low and so evil she feels physically ill. But there is also Lukie slack in the dirt with that glazed-over stare like something dead, and his mom waiting up in the house.

You have no choice.

"I'm sorry," she whispers.

The fairy gazes through the row of flames at the pitch-black slit in the scree, its mouth drawn, teeth bared. It claws at the dirt, a soft scratching in the dead cellar air.

She unwraps the leather pouch. The tools clank against one another, causing the fairy to start, turn its desperate stare to the pouch's contents. Jo feels tears pressing behind her eyes, filling her throat. She doggedly lifts the chain and lays it across the spindly, chilly legs. The fairy emits a whimper that ends in a sigh. Jo forces herself not to look up, just keeps unlooping the chain, draping it up the body in a snake shape. There is no resistance, only the ragged breathing that starts to slow as she works. The last of the chain lands near its throat. It looks like a corpse buried in an iron grave. Its eyes drift shut, one hand still extended toward home.

"I'm sorry," Jo whispers again, but the fairy doesn't move or show any sign it heard.

Jo struggles to pick up the chubby lump of a kid with his dangling arms and legs. He weighs a ton. She manages to hoist him into her arms. She backs away clumsily, gouging the dirt with her heels. At the steps she adjusts him so he lies in her arms more comfortably. She looks back at the fairy one last time. Then she goes up the steps, holding Lukie tight.

TWENTY

Gray light and warm drizzle on her skin. She blinks up at the vast sky, astonishing after the close, dank darkness of the last several hours. Her legs plod with leaden slowness, her whole body weighted by the boy in her arms. She stares down at his peaceful face. He's so much smaller than Jo was when she was taken, and she barely remembers it. He won't remember anything at all. But still, he might have dreams. At least Amanda will understand and won't stick him with a Dr. Coletti.

She sets across the yard, and the screen door flies open. Amanda comes out running. Within moments, Jo feels the boy slide from her arms, the heat of his body evaporating from her skin.

Amanda rocks him close, crying into his hair, mumbling, "My baby, my baby," over and over again. Lola takes shape in Jo's bleary gaze, and Edie behind her, and Mason. Hattie squirms in to get a closer look, standing on tiptoe.

"We heard Loco," Edie says, "so we were waiting."

That makes sense, but the closeness of all these people unnerves her. She wishes she'd had a few more minutes alone with Lukie, which isn't fair to his mom, of course, she knows that. But it's because it happened to her, too. She wanted to see herself. She wanted to remember. She can hardly see him now, folded up in Amanda's arms and surrounded by others. A glimpse of his hair, the white skin of his fat foot.

"Thank you," Amanda sobs into his hair.

"You're welcome," Jo replies automatically, then realizes how dumb that sounds.

No one seems to notice. Amanda's saying they have to go, she can't be here a second longer. Lola embraces her, propping her up, and they make their way around the house. Jo notes how the driveway is jammed with cars and trucks parked every which way. There's Mason's truck, and another one that must be Edie's.

Edie says, "Is the door closed?"

For a second, Jo doesn't know what she means. Then she says, "I wanted to get Lukie out right away."

"It's chained?"

Jo nods.

"You can leave it for a spell. Tom said it's the last one."

"But what if more come through?"

"They won't. Not when they see."

Of course, Jo realizes. The door will be closed soon, and they could get trapped here.

Edie turns to Mason. "Take Hattie back and watch some TV."

He tugs on Hattie's shoulders till she complies, turning with her bare feet dragging. She looks more miserable than ever, clutching her doll close. They go through the sunroom and disappear into the house.

"I thought she'd be happy," Jo says.

"She's seeing a mama find her baby, when she was never found, and her mama's gone and dead for a hundred years."

Jo feels her heart cracking open.

"Come inside," Edie says. "You're looking faint."

Jo lets herself be led into the house. She stops at the bathroom to pee and wash up. She examines her shoulder in the mirror, gashed and crusted with dried blood. It starts throbbing now that she's seeing it, a steady beat of nauseating pain. Her head hurts, too. She fingers her scalp, finds scabbing blood. Not as bad as the shoulder. She waits a moment, thinking she might throw up. The wave passes. She makes her way to the kitchen, which has been restored to order. It's strange to think people were tidying up the house while she was in the cellar. She sinks down at the table. Edie's in the pantry. There is the noise of rooting around, clunks and slams. She comes out and unloads first-aid stuff onto the table. She gets a glass of water, and Jo drinks, gulping down all of it.

Edie washes her shoulder with alcohol, which stings awfully. "Hold still," she orders. Jo clenches her teeth. "You're a strong girl," she praises. "I'm sure you gave as good as you got."

Jo flashes back to the blind swipe with the paddle. It was a backhand. Nana would be proud, all the tennis lessons finally coming to bear. But she hasn't had lessons in anything else. She doesn't know how to do the rest of it.

Jo closes her eyes, but the tears seep out nevertheless.

"Look at me," Edie tells her.

Jo obeys. Edie's eyes are hard blue chips in her wizened face.

"There's a piece of rebar with Maur's tools."

Jo nods.

"How she did it is one thrust below the sternum, straight up to the heart. You understand?" Edie demands.

Jo doesn't want to nod, but she does.

"Don't be thinking you can keep it like Tom."

Jo has, in fact, been thinking that. A secret, hidden idea she herself hadn't faced yet, and yet somehow, Edie sussed it out. "Why not?"

Edie sits back, her knuckles rapping the table lightly as she speaks, as if to keep Jo's attention. "Maur had to hold Tom down there for over a month. First in iron, then in ropes so the damn thing would wake up and she could talk to it. But it didn't matter what she said. When she finally let him go, he tried to kill her—twice." Edie jabs two fingers in the air in front of Jo's face. "She ended up in the hospital. It took well over a year for him to settle down. Then another few to teach him to speak and mind his manners!"

"But he's OK now," Jo says.

"He turned out OK," Edie concedes. "But you don't know what might happen with this one. There's Hattie to think of. You want her hurt?"

Jo shakes her head.

"So put the notion out of your mind. Your mother called, by the way. I said you were just fine, and so you are."

Jo recalls her mom with the sheets bunched up over her belly, terrorized. It feels so long ago. "There was a little one at the hospital."

Edie perks up at this. "So far?"

"I think it came with her, in her hair or something."

"What happened?"

Jo hesitates, wishing she hadn't mentioned it. "I let it out the window."

"Huh."

A silence forms around Edie's disapproval. Then she says, "Well, you can't let this one out the window."

Jo sets her jaw, staring down at her bobbing legs. Edie's right. She knows she is. But still.

"You listen to me," Edie says. "After Tom, Maur didn't take any chances. She always regretted it, if you want the truth. She should've sent Enzo packing what with you being there, too, but she couldn't bear to. She'd missed him so, and she wanted time with you. I suppose she thought she could manage. But of course, a child so close to the door, even the fires couldn't stop them coming."

Ain't no place for a child! Gammy hollered, spanking her. How hard she'd tried, barring the door, keeping Jo under watch at all times. The dog in her room, barking warning.

"Why did he bring me? He knew it was dangerous."

"I suppose he just wanted Maur to meet you at last. He'd visited before, and then he turned up with you, just like that, out of the blue. She'd hurt her ankle, and he had a notion he'd help out."

Gammy was on crutches, Jo suddenly recalls. She lurched next to Jo all around the meadow, teaching her the names of flowers. Her dad carried buckets back and forth: she can see him trudging in the sun, the buckets swinging.

"It was her fault, you see, for being so weak, letting you stay when she shouldn't. That's why she got taken by such a rage, why she did what she did. But she regretted it, you hear me? The door's opened twice since Tom, and she did what she had to do, the proper way, as it should be. Do you understand?"

There's a hardening ball of hurt in Jo's chest that she can't bear any longer. "So I just murder it, is that it?"

"It's the only way."

"It was a *kid* once," Jo says. "Could *you* kill it?"

Edie stiffens, her hand drawing into a fist on the table. "Every one of us in this town pays."

"Yeah, how?"

"My girl was taken when she was two. I was nineteen. It's how I came to be Maur's friend."

Her words take a long, awful moment to sink in.

"Every child that comes back, I dream it's her, and it never is. They come so rarely. I have to make my peace I'll probably never see her again. But maybe she's been given wings. Every one that Maur killed, I felt it in my own heart. Was it her? Is it over, or is she still there?"

Edie sighs, falling silent. Jo searches for what to say, but there's nothing adequate. After a moment, Edie says, "The service will be next week sometime. You should attend."

"Service?"

"For the girl now gone, Eloise."

She pronounces the name with a French accent. Jo repeats it in her mind: *Eh-lwaz*. She stares at the floor, stricken.

Edie says, "Maur failed, too, now and again. No one puts the blame on you. You should be there for the carving and the service. Everyone goes."

Everyone, as if Jo's part of the town now. She says, "I'll have to ask Mom."

"Well, then," Edie slowly pushes herself up to her feet. "I need to head back. I gotta make sandwiches for the search party, and last I heard the sheriff was on his way."

"Have you ever seen one?" Jo asks suddenly.

Edie stops, looks down at her. "I have not."

Jo picks over what she wants to say, licking her chapped lips. "If she was made a fairy—they're not kids anymore. I don't think they even know they once were. So if it was ever your daughter—it's not like—" Jo fumbles, losing her thread. "Though I guess she could still come back, too."

"She could." Edie gives her a small, sad smile.

She goes to the door, picks up her purse and car keys from

the chair next to it, then turns around. "You've done good, Josephine Lavoie. Maur did right to leave you the house."

With that, she clomps across the porch and down the steps in her rubber boots. Jo gets up to watch her climb into the truck, thinking how vast the difference is between her and Nana, the only other really old lady in Jo's life. She prefers this version of being old, she realizes. She wants to wear rubber boots and drive a truck, too.

When she can no longer hear the engine, the muggy, restful sounds of the yard gradually return to the fore. The chickens stuttering in the grass, birds singing up in the maple, the buzzing noise of crickets in the meadow. It's so incongruous, and yet also not so much. It's just how it is. She can hear the murmur of the TV from the other side of the house. She's glad Mason is with Hattie. It seems to be his role, since he took care of her in town, too. Everyone truly does have a part to play. How smoothly it all goes, if she thinks about it, for something so awful.

She wonders where Tom is now. Probably tucked away in the greenhouse among his plants. If he does have feelings after all, this can't be easy for him.

She steps back out into the yard. She's entirely alone now. The last of the morning haze is gone, and the sun's baking the scrappy yard brown. The air isn't as hot anymore; the storm took care of that. Still, there's sweat running down her sides, she feels hot and shaky. She pulls out her phone. It's going on eleven o'clock. She wonders if her mom's seen the shrink yet, if she'll call again soon. A drop of sweat plops onto the phone screen. She wipes it on her shorts, then tucks it back into her pocket. There's nothing she can do to delay any longer. It's a simple, numbing fact that propels her into motion. She crosses the yard, reenters the Old House, an act that feels almost normal now after so much fuss about keeping out.

At the trapdoor, she pauses on the top step to listen. There's no sound from below. She descends into the cellar, feeling her way one step at a time.

TWENTY-ONE

The fairy hasn't moved at all. The air is cold and silent. Jo stares at the chain snaking up the fairy's prone form. She can tell it's breathing by the slight motion of its chest, every so often.

She extinguishes the burners one by one. Some are already out. It gets too dark, so she switches on her phone flashlight, props the phone against the wall. She drops the burners by the handful into the bucket. The noise is deafening. The fairy doesn't show any sign it's heard. She carries the bucket across the room, sets it by the stairs. Returns to check for any burners she might have missed, though she knows there aren't any, but she can't bring herself to do what must be done, not yet.

Not yet.

She sinks down near the opening in the earth, as far from the fairy as possible. The cool breeze brushes her bare thigh. It's unsettling how Tom can be sure there aren't any more fairies out. What sense does he have, what does it feel like? Before him, there was no way the Lavoie could know if they'd all left. There must have been some that got locked out over the years, hovering near the house, unable to get back home. Maybe they're buried in the woods, too.

Her gaze wanders across the tools lying on the open leather pouch, then the manacled leg, the calf muscle ridged and sharp. The skin is greenish, faintly scaled. She wonders how long it would take for the fairy to change back. How long it took Tom. If Gammy waited next to him. If she cut the wings when he was like this, dead asleep. Did he stir, did he scream, or did he stay utterly still, like this one, buried unconscious by the chain?

And when he woke, what happened then?

She bends over her tucked-up knees, turning her face away. She stares into the darkness wedged between the rocks. After a moment, she reaches a little way in, tentatively floating her fingers in the drifting air. It's not really that cold, just kind of clammy. Earthy. The air breezes gently between her fingers as she reaches farther, feeling for the walls of the cave, but there's only emptiness.

All at once, she finds herself reeling with the urge to sleep, shockingly intense. Her eyes start to close, and she struggles to move, but it's as if she's being smothered under a heavy blanket. She blinks hard, fighting the urge to pass out.

Josephine.

A whisper, but not a whisper. A voice inside her head.

Josephine.

There's something touching her hand.

Like a vine, wrapping slowly. Tightening.

296

Fingers.

She tries to pull away, but the fingers squeeze tighter, hurting. She gasps at the pain searing her arm. The need to sleep crashes over her again, a dark, suffocating wave. She pulls as hard as she can, but to her horror, she's weakening. Her arm's getting drawn into the jagged opening, inch by inch. *It's pulling me in*, she realizes in shock. *It'll shrink me and pull me through!* She pushes against the scree with her other hand and scrambles her legs, desperate to find leverage. Then a motion in the darkness makes her freeze: a glint, a flickering.

An eye. Looking at her.

The malevolence swamps her with cold terror. This isn't like the other fairies she's seen. This is far worse.

It's one of them. The old ones.

They hate this world, Hattie's words echo in her mind. *They hate this house. If they came back . . .*

It knows her name.

How that can be is a frantic cascade: because she was almost taken, because they're fairies and they just know?

She cries out, her shoulder jammed hard against the stone. Her whole body feels like it's melting. She flails with her other hand, groping for something, anything. There's nothing she can do, she realizes with frozen, crystal horror. They'll take her, and there's nothing she can do. In a far-off corner of her mind, she wonders if they know her name because of what her dad said, that the fairies don't like to let go of one they touched. The thought is so far away. So very distant.

Her flailing hand raps into something, tweaking pain, momentarily rousing her. She can barely keep her eyes open, but she knows what it is: her dad's bell.

He said it was for protection. It must do something.

She struggles to grab onto it with her doughy, weak fingers.

"Josephine," the whisper leaches forth.

For a searing instant, Jo glimpses the tiny, ancient face framed with golden hair, the eyes wide, translucent green. It bares its teeth in what seems to be a smile, saliva dripping from silver lips.

"No!"

Her protest comes out a mere breath, barely audible. It takes all her strength to lift the bell at last. Just that small motion causes it to ring, the noise gigantic, reverberating off the cellar walls. At once, the crushing grip on her arm loosens. She shakes the bell again and again, and the fingers slide down her arm, all the way to her fingertips. The touch lingers for an instant, cold, soft.

And then the creature is gone, sucked back into the blackness like a wisp of smoke.

The sound takes ages to die away. Jo's heart beats madly, hurting her ribs. She edges back, holding her injured arm close to her chest. The fairy's grip left vicious red marks; she'll have a huge bruise there tomorrow. She stares at the blackness where it was, holding the bell tightly, ready.

All is silent. All is still.

It's gone.

It can't come through because of the iron, or it would have already. She's safe. Her breathing settles, realizing this. She should never have stuck her hand in there.

Live and learn, she thinks absurdly.

She becomes aware of the gaps between some of the iron pieces. There's no harm in shoring up, even if the barrier seems to be working on the old ones. She jams the bell into one spot, then casts about for any more iron she might have missed earlier. She finds two pieces flung against the back wall: a bolt with a rusted washer and a curved fragment, maybe part of a wagon wheel from way back. She fits them in, arranging the other pieces so they're closer together, all the while aware that this might be overkill, but she can't help herself, driven by irrational panic. It comes to her that she'll have to dislodge the iron all over again to put in the wings. She'll have to be careful reaching in; she'll need to keep the bell right next to her.

At last she crumples to a stop, hunched on her knees, the adrenaline rush leaving her sapped. She's done all she can. There's nothing there in the darkness and no sound at all. The old fairy is gone.

She can't delay any longer.

She has to be sure none of them can come through.

She has to close the door.

The pouch is lying open where she left it. She lays her hand on the rebar, closing her eyes for a moment, then she picks it up. It's heavy and cold. The fairy doesn't stir, driven into oblivion by the poisonous iron chain. She's grateful it isn't aware.

She kneels next to it, the rebar slippery in her sweating hands. The fairy looks so scrawny and small now, maybe four feet, if that. Its thick, glittery hair is fanned across the gravel, the wings open and flat, motionless. The chain snakes across the scaled, sunken belly, up across high-arching ribs, ending at the throat. Its breaths come deep and slow. Its eyes are closed.

If it stayed in this world, maybe it would look like Tom. Unless it's a girl. She can't tell.

She brings the rebar to the hollow beneath its ribs. The moment the iron makes contact, the skin flinches, a shudder ripples through the prone body. Jo freezes, but there is nothing more. A physical reaction. It isn't awake.

She sets her jaw. *There will come a time,* Gammy's words return, *when what must be done, must be done.* The letter has accompanied her all along, its meaning changing at every turn, and now she finally, truly understands it.

She pushes, leaning into the rebar. The wicked flat wedge slides right in, easy as sliding through butter. There is a blockage, resistance, and she pushes harder. The fairy utters the smallest squeak, then emits a breath, its mouth falling open.

She withdraws the rebar. Blood seeps out in a steady stream from the hole.

TWENTY-TWO

The blood darkening the earthen floor.

Everything is so still.

Silence. Light trickles down through the floorboards: she left the front door open. What does it matter? No one else is around. No one randomly comes to this farm. There's no farm-stand for a reason.

Through her daze she becomes aware, again, of the immobile, dark bulk of the thing before her. She draws her hands into her lap. Her knees grind into the gravelly dirt.

The cold breeze brushes her face, smelling of another world. A land of green moss and rivers, maybe, or something else. Grief seizes her, she can't suppress it. This creature, this being, is dead because of her, never to go home. Its arm still extended, reaching.

She curls over herself, balled up tight over her knees. The dead thing leaches its odors of blood and scaly otherworldliness, its lifeless wings spread across the floor. The stillness of it is so deep, and she herself is so racked and rocking and consumed, an opposite thing full to bursting, the other an unmoving lump, dead. For several moments the oppositeness bewilders her. She stares and stares, as if to will motion into the creature. She thinks she sees the tip of the wing lift slightly off the floor. She sees its chest rise and fall, breathing, breathing. Then the stillness clobbers her again, a huge wave of silence smashing into her, stilling her in turn. The nothingness of it. The deadness. The only breaths her own, ragged and harsh.

The wings have to be sawed off and stuffed into the hole. They have to be. They have to be.

She grips the machete hard. It's like cutting a chicken apart. Taking a leg off the carcass. Slice and pull. Blood seeps slowly down the green mottled skin into the gravel. The wing is surprisingly heavy. It will lighten with time, with age and rot. The cartilage will dry out and break down in the wafting breeze of its long-ago home, and the wings will disintegrate to threaded ghosts. And then the little ones will come again.

Not anytime soon, if she can help it. She moves a few of the iron pieces to create space for her work. The open gash fills her with urgency, even with the bell right there at her fingertips. She bends the wing till it cracks, forcing it into the space, tucking and pressing. There are still wisps of air seeping through. The second wing goes more quickly. She tucks and pushes, filling in every section until she can't feel any air at all. Then she sets the iron back into a jagged dark wall against the opening. The old fairy's whisper, *Josephine*, echoes in her head, filling her with sharp, bright panic. There are some small areas left she could still plug up, but it should be enough, she's used all the iron Gammy did, so it should work. Still, she checks again, and then again, for any sign of a breeze, passing her hand slowly back and forth across the barrier. She feels nothing.

She becomes aware, instead, of the metallic odor of blood hanging in the now still air, the dense, motionless heap of the creature behind her. She drags herself upright and, averting her eyes, makes her way to the stairs.

TWENTY-THREE

She comes outside, squinting as she adjusts to daylight. Hattie's sitting on the fountain building a tower of pebbles, her doll propped to watch. She looks up from her work. "Did you close the door?"

Jo nods, her throat a tight, dry knot.

One of the tractors is parked off to the right, a crumple of green tarp in the bucket. She sees Tom over at the edge of the meadow on his stump, smoking. He glances her way, then turns back to staring at the meadow. She wonders if she's supposed to bring the body out and wrap it, or if that's his job. She can't even begin to think about it now. She makes her way around the house to the rain barrels set high on concrete blocks, ignoring Hattie trailing behind her. She unhooks the hose and turns the spigot, runs the cool water over her slimy, bloody legs. Sobs catch in her chest, sharp as rocks. Hattie sidles around, staring at her with concern.

The roaring noise of an engine interrupts them. They both

freeze, staring toward the driveway. To Jo's horror, Robert's white Range Rover pulls up in a cloud, comes to an abrupt stop next to a truck. It's Mason's, so he's still here, Jo realizes distantly. Robert gets out. The door slams loudly in the hot quiet. Jo didn't think to slip away to the back of the house, she was so startled, and he catches sight of her almost immediately.

"What's happened to you?" he exclaims.

Jo has no clue what to say. She's still got blood on her hands and arms and maybe even her face. She goes back to washing, rubbing her skin vigorously under the freezing water.

"What's all that blood?" Robert demands with increasing concern. He approaches gingerly, circling the mud puddles formed by the splashing water. "Are you hurt?"

He sees Hattie and stares at her in bewilderment. Jo sees Hattie again through fresh eyes, so ragged and odd looking with that damn doll clutched in her bony hug.

Hattie says, "I taught her to kill a chicken. It got her upset."

"Jesus Christ!" Robert exclaims.

The lie is so smooth, so simple, that he doesn't question it for a second, which rankles because he should know that Jo would never be able to kill an animal.

She gulps at the recognition of all she's done instead. She bends her face, hiding from him, splashing water on her skin.

"Are you OK?" he asks.

He's genuinely worried. She nods, twisting the spigot closed. She reattaches the hose and wipes her eyes. "It wasn't fun," she says.

"Is this why you ran off like that, to kill chickens?"

Jo lowers her eyes meekly. "No. I'm sorry. I just—I needed to get back."

"Well, you're lucky you didn't get pulled over. Your mother said you've been very emotional."

Great. Thanks, Mom. She can't really complain, though, as he seems to have swallowed the excuse. "I'm sorry," she repeats. "Really."

"So this is it, then," he closes the topic, gazing up and across the building. "This is the famous house in Vermont. It needs a bit of work, doesn't it."

There is an awkward pause. He becomes aware of Hattie staring up at him. The doll eyes click.

"Is Mom OK?" Jo asks.

"She's getting released soon. She wants her things, but mainly wanted me to check on you."

"I'm fine," Jo says. "Really. How's Baby Charles?"

"All well," Robert says, shaking his head. "What a scare."

She leads him into the house as he explains what a headache it's all been, but it's over at last, and they'll be leaving this afternoon. They come into the kitchen, where Mason is standing at the stove waiting for the kettle to boil. He's in ripped cargo shorts and a loose tank. There's a snake tattoo wrapping his calf, and his feet are bare. Jo can only imagine Robert's impression.

She says, "This is my stepdad. This is Mason, and by the way, this is Hattie. I should've introduced you before."

"Mason," Robert repeats. Jo can almost see his brain running down the list, finding no Mason on it. "Are you one of the tenants?"

"Uh, no, I'm just—I live in Laddston."

"So, is *he* why you wanted to come back?"

"What? No!" Jo is aghast. Mason goes red and stares hard at the kettle, which isn't boiling yet. "Robert, seriously?"

"You worried us sick, you know, leaving like that. What, you think I don't worry about you?" he demands, reading her mind with that weird ability grown-ups have. "You may not appreciate it, but I do care, you know. You should call your mother, by the way. Where's her room? I need to pack her things."

"I'll show you," Hattie exclaims, and before Jo can protest—who knows what conversation will happen—she sets off, Robert in tow.

"Sorry," Jo mutters at Mason once they're gone.

"It's OK. He's your dad," he shrugs.

"Not really."

"Right, my bad. Still," he says, hesitating, "he seems OK. My dad left when I was five. Haven't seen him since."

Crap. "I'm sorry."

He tilts a small smile. "No worries."

"I should call," she points awkwardly at the phone.

He nods, turning back to the kettle as it starts its annoying whistle. She picks up the receiver gingerly, stares at the numbered buttons. She hasn't used an old-style phone before. It's nuts how heavy it is. She punches in her mom's cell number, then moves down the hall for some privacy. The coiled line stretches surprisingly far, so she keeps going, makes it all the way to the sunroom steps.

"Hello?" her mom asks loudly in her ear. "Hello?"

Jo holds the phone a few inches away. "It's me," she says. "Everything's OK."

"Thank God." Abigail exhales. "I've been so worried, I can't think straight. What happened?"

Jo's grip tightens on the receiver. *What happened*: the graveled floor wet with blood, the tangled hair and slack, fetid mouth.

"I closed the door," she says.

"What does that mean?"

"I—I killed one. Put its wings where they come through. Now they can't."

"Oh, Jo," her mom says softly.

There is a silence.

Then her mom asks, "Did it hurt you?"

The words bring awareness to the pain in her shoulder, the weak-kneed tiredness of her whole body. Jo sinks onto the step. "A little. I'm OK."

"You're sure?"

"Yes. I swear."

"And you're sure it's over?"

"Mom, stop. It's over. I swear."

Abigail lets out a big sigh. "You're so brave."

The words don't compute, not right away. Jo's not accustomed to praise from her mom.

"Honey? Jo?"

"I'm here. Sorry. I'm tired. Is Baby Charles OK?"

"Everything's completely fine, you don't have to worry. Edie called."

"She did? Why?"

"To convince me to let you stay longer. Robert's *not* happy about it."

Jo can just imagine. "There's a ceremony or something. I'm supposed to be there."

"So you want to stay?"

The question surprises Jo. She assumed her mom would go with Robert's opinion, but that feels unfair, now. There's actually lots that Abigail dictates, like letting Jo have a TV in her room and letting her dress the way she does. She stares across the tile floor out the screen door. The Old House looms darkly over the sunny yard, the door standing wide open. Down below, the awful thing, waiting.

"I still have stuff to do today," she says. "And then, yeah, I want to stay longer. I mean, I should."

There is a silence. Jo waits.

"All right, then. Tell Robert I said you can."

Jo's heart quickens. "You mean it?"

"I don't like it," she adds sternly, "but so long as you know you can call for a car anytime. I mean *anytime*, you understand? Robert will give you the number."

"Thanks, Mom."

"The Subaru can stay there. Then whenever you come back, you have a car to use. That Tom can keep it running, I expect."

"Thanks," Jo repeats, her voice cracking. "I—I'm glad you're OK, Mom."

"I'm glad you are, too, honey. Now, go tell Robert to step on it. If I don't get out of here, I'll literally kill someone."

Jo smiles as her mom hangs up. She's back to herself, which Jo never thought she'd find heartwarming, but there it is. She gets up off the step, and the phone receiver darts out of her hand, yanked by the taut coiled wire. She leaps in pursuit, trying to snatch it as it clatters down the hall, smacking into chair legs and books. She finally manages to grab it, then takes the last few steps into the kitchen to find Mason watching in amusement.

"How am I supposed to know how to deal with this relic," Jo says, fighting the tightly coiled wire that has somehow wrapped itself around her arm.

"Better get used to it," he laughs.

She manages to free herself and hang up. "Is he done?"

"They're still up there."

Jo sinks heavily onto a chair. They sit in awkward silence.

"So it's over, I guess?" He tilts a glance toward the Old House.

Jo nods. "Pretty much."

"Was it hard?"

Jo nods again. A thickness wells up her chest into her throat, choking her. She stares at the swirled designs in the lino tabletop, pressing her hands under her thighs.

"I couldn't do it," Mason says. "It's pretty cool that, you know, you just showed up and took over. Aunt Eeds says you didn't even know."

"I didn't," Jo admits.

"Better not mess with you," he chuckles.

She smiles a little, embarrassed. He drums his fingers on the table, then says, "So you'll be here a bit? I heard," he admits, a little sheepish. "I mean, you were right there."

"It's OK. Yeah, I guess I'm staying. Edie said there was a ceremony?"

"Yeah. The carving." He hesitates. "I play on Wednesdays over in Greensboro. If you want to come." He mimes fiddling. "We're not great, but, you know. It's fun."

Jo flushes. "Sure. OK."

He frowns a little, sits up straighter. "Someone's here."

She follows his gaze out the open door. A blue hatchback is pulling up alongside the Range Rover. "What is this, a convention?" she mutters. She's gratified to see Mason crack a smile.

It's the real estate agent, she gleans from the logo on the side of the car. A few moments go by, then a lady in shorts and a polo gets out, flipping off her sunglasses. She looks all around, taking in, assessing, squinting, and shading her eyes.

Robert comes barreling down the hallway with Abigail's

bags, Hattie close behind. "I forgot to remind you," he says. "Come on, let's go meet her."

Jo registers Hattie's white-faced panic. She reaches out and squeezes her hand. "Don't worry," she whispers.

She comes down the steps to find Robert already conversing with the agent. They're looking up at the house, and he's waving his arms and talking about the peeling paint and how the chimney needs repointing but the house has some fine bones. Robert doesn't know much about houses, other than what he's gotten from fixer-upper shows. The agent listens politely.

Jo walks up to them.

"Ah, here she is," Robert says cheerily. Jo can read his aggravation at her gloomy demeanor. He places an arm around Jo's shoulder. "I know my wife tried to cancel, but you see what I mean, then? Imagine leaving this place to her!"

The agent looks nice enough, maybe even a little put off by Robert's bluster. She says, "Hi, hon. Nice to meet you."

"Mom tried to cancel?"

"She was going on about how the house can't be sold, who knows why, after all this! It's OK, I made sure Ms. McHugh here kept the appointment after all."

"But Mom's right. I'm not selling."

The flat statement hangs in the air. Robert flicks at his neck, chasing an insect. Ms. McHugh says, "Are you sure?"

"It's my house. I'm not selling."

"Josephine," Robert commands, "don't be ridiculous!"

Jo looks at him. "It's my house. Mom agrees."

The indisputable truth stops him. He looks apologetically at Ms. McHugh. "We'll be in touch if anything changes. Sorry you came all this way for nothing."

Ms. McHugh lifts her shoes one by one, examining the heels caked with mud. "Seems you should've listened to your wife," she says mildly. She winks at Jo. "Good luck, hon."

She gets back into her car. They watch her reverse at a pace far too slow, which enervates Robert, who despises poor driving. "Come on, then," he mutters.

At last, she rolls off down the driveway toward the road. Robert turns to Jo, prepared to lecture.

"Don't even," Jo warns. "It's my house. And I spoke to Mom. She said I can stay."

He narrows his eyes, then purses his mouth, defeated. "You'll change your mind when you see how much work it is," he advises.

Jo looks at him a moment, then bursts out laughing.

TWENTY-FOUR

After he's gone, she returns to the Old House. There is an empty feel to it, a silence deeper than anything else in the world, emanating from the dead thing resting in the cellar. She descends the stairs. Waits for a time, adjusting to the dark, and to the deep immobility of the lifeless heap. Then she goes over to it and crouches down. She pulls on its clammy, freezing arm. It doesn't budge.

She can't haul the body. It's just too heavy. She tries, manages no more than a foot before dropping the arm in defeat.

She goes back upstairs. The scrappy yard is pitted with muddy puddles. Her hands are caked with blood again. She stares at them.

Tom approaches, stone-faced and hostile, as if everything's her fault and always has been. She grips her hands behind her back, feeling the sweat slide her palms. She can't be weak.

She says, "You need to take it and bury it."

He receives this without reaction.

"I mean even if you didn't do it before, it has to be your job now, because I can't."

His eyes flicker to the doorway and back, the way a light might flicker with a wire test. He says, "I did the carrying last time. Maur lost her strength. Made her angry, getting sick."

"So you'll do it."

He shrugs assent.

Jo examines his hard face, the bony angle of his forehead. Wonders what he might have looked like, had he never been taken. "Can I ask you a question?"

He nods, eyes slightly narrowed.

"What's it really like there?"

"Don't know what you mean."

"I mean—my dad always said it was sunny and they ran around playing. Hattie says the same thing. But it just doesn't seem . . . I don't know, it doesn't seem like that's how it really is."

"It's a dream," Tom shrugs. "It was real for them."

"What do you mean?"

"They're mostly sleeping," he clarifies.

"So it's not like what they say, not at all?"

"What's the difference? It's like that in their heads."

There is a silence as Jo tries to absorb this unexpectedly philosophical statement. Of course, it's totally literal for him. And he's wrong. The difference is in Hattie's malnourished body, the bones not fed, the mind tangled with loss and sorrow. A murky image comes to her of him as a fairy, scaled and winged, crouched above a trove of dazed, unfed children. The world dismal, dank. A place of no change, no delight.

That's where Edie's daughter is, if she's still even alive. Edie's probably heard Hattie's merry stories, she must picture her child running in the grass, gorging on ice cream. Gammy must have known the truth and kept it from her, just as Jo will have to. A rage creeps up for her dad and Hattie, and all the other Cherished left yearning for a lie.

"It's evil what they do," she says through gritted teeth. "The old fairies, the ones that started it all."

"They're not the ones started it."

Jo tenses at the defensiveness in his voice. *He'll never belong*, Gammy's letter floats back in warning. He may be right, they didn't start it, but still. "I saw one, you know. It tried to pull me in. I had to use my dad's bell to stop it."

He doesn't seem surprised. "They always try if the chance comes."

"Have they ever gotten out?"

"Not that I know."

"Why didn't they make their home nicer? They know about sun and rivers and laughing, that's their enchantment. So why didn't they give it to themselves?" *And to you*, she almost adds.

He chews on his lip, his eyes drifting sideways, seeking an answer. She waits. At last he says, "They got out of their prison, but they didn't, really. The home they made is the one they carry."

Jo stares down at his maimed hands. The mysterious words, spoken in that dull monotone, sink in slowly. The home they carry, she understands: poisonous resentment for the evil done to them. Despair for their faraway homeland, never to be seen again. Tom, for all his detachment and disinterest, understands much more than he lets on. Also because it must be the same for him. She wonders what conversations he had with Gammy, over all these years. If they sat smoking together out near the field, or if they dined together. She wonders if he wishes the old fairies would make it through, come find him. But how can he possibly? He knows they won't want him, not anymore. He's not of them, and won't ever be of this place, either, not really. He has it way worse than any of the other Cherished.

"I'm sorry for what Gammy did to you," she blurts. "It was wrong, like you said. It must be really hard."

She fumbles to a stop, dismayed by her own boldness. He is so still, staring at her. He's like a dark, deep pool, her words sinking slowly to the bottom. Jo scrambles back to what Edie said, how Gammy regretted what she'd done so very much. "I know she never said sorry, but I think it's because she felt guilty. She wanted to make it like it was OK."

He looks at the grass. The muggy sun heats the stillness between them.

"Do you understand?" Jo asks, losing hope. "Tom, do you?"

He gives the slightest shrug. "No matter now."

The sullen response confuses her, pricks her with sadness. He looks out over the yard, his mouth fixed in a hard line, as if waiting to be dismissed.

He must have seen everyone coming and going, she realizes

with sudden insight. He hasn't spoken with Hattie yet; she's inside with Mason. He doesn't know. "Tom, the lady that was here—I'm not selling, OK? I'll never sell this house."

For an instant, she sees bare relief cross his features. Then it is replaced by satisfaction. "Maur said she'd put it in the will."

"She did," Jo agrees, a little miffed that he's ignoring her own role in the decision. "I won't be able to live here full time for a while, though. A few years, maybe even more."

"But you have to live here," he says. "It's you Maur left the house."

She's been so wary of him ever since they arrived, because of what Gammy said in the letter, how she seemed not to really trust him. *He'll never belong*, she wrote, but maybe that was because she never shook her own fear. After all, he did put her in the hospital way back at the beginning. It makes sense she couldn't let go of that, no matter how many years went by. But that's got nothing to do with Jo. Things are different now.

"The house belongs to you, too," Jo says. "It's yours and Hattie's, just like it's mine."

He absorbs this, listening.

"So you'll need to be the one checking the door. Especially the iron if the wings start to go. I don't want those old ones getting through, ever. I won't ask Hattie to do all that. She shouldn't have to. So I'm trusting you," Jo says pointedly. "I'll be here as much as possible, but you have to take care of things when I'm not around."

"You'll be here," he repeats, nodding, as if this is the only thing she's said. At least he seems to want it.

"Yeah," she says. "I definitely will."

"And I'll take care of things when you're not."

"Yes."

He appears to think on this for a moment, then gives her a curt nod. "I'll get the little'un now," he says. He shoulders past her and disappears inside.

She hopes she's not making some big mistake. Probably not. He knows this place inside and out, after all, way better than she does, even after all that's happened. And he knows it's his home now, forever. That has to count for something. Besides, she can call every day to check in, she resolves. It'll make Hattie happy.

She stands in the sun for some moments, feeling its heat sinking into her. Then she gets off the step, makes her way across the yard to the tractor. She drags the tarp out, shakes it open over the bucket. She presses down, creating a bed. She stares at the ugly plastic growing hot in the sun. Her head fills with the dozy summer buzzing of insects.

Tom emerges from the Old House, the creature draped over his powerful shoulder. He walks bent under the weight. Hattie opens the sunroom screen door and stands there, watching, heedless of the flies she's letting in. Tom slowly bends, unloading the body into the tarp. It crinkles loudly as he folds it.

"Wait," Jo says.

He looks up, his hands frozen in the act of folding.

"Just a minute," Jo says, already running toward the house.

She goes up the stairs two at a time, bursts into her room. It is silent and gray and clean. It feels as if she hasn't been in here in weeks. Her dad's satchel is still on the spare bed, the sewing in a pile next to it. She carefully unrolls the stitched piece she was working on. It wasn't ever finished, but it doesn't matter. It makes sense like this, dangling threads and knots, the edges uneven, the materials all different shades of black and gray. It strikes her that the indigo background for the skull, torn from a silk scarf her dad gave her when she was little, might have come from here; it's just like the ones still hanging in Gammy's armoire. Maybe she got it in Egypt, Jo thinks, heading back downstairs. Maybe it came from all the way across the world, then it came to her, and now it will go into the earth.

Tom is standing next to the tractor like he's been placed on hold. Hattie's next to him with her doll. They watch her lift the tarp by the edge, carefully drape the cloth across the corpse. Her fingers brush its freezing, dead skin. She can hardly bear to look at its face, but she forces herself. She's startled to find it changed. The features have flattened, rounded. It looks closer to human. A boy or girl, she can't tell. She wonders if it will change even more, the fairies' awful magic completely seeping away. No wonder Gammy gave them burials. It was a child. It *is* a child.

You had no choice.

She gently pulls the cloth so it covers the face, then folds the tarp back down and steps back. She becomes aware of them watching. "I made it," she confesses, unsure what they want.

"It's nice," Hattie says. "I wish I could do that."

"I can teach you," Jo says.

"OK."

The agreement feels somber, like a pact.

Tom adjusts the tarp, tugging here and there, closing up the package. He climbs into the driver's seat and starts the engine, which is so loud it obliterates all thought entirely for several moments. All that exists is the slow dance of the tractor making a three-quarter turn, then slowly rumbling away toward the meadow. Jo retreats to the fountain and sinks down. Hattie joins her.

"I wish you didn't have to kill it," Hattie says. "Tom coulda had company."

Tom rounds the meadow, following the dirt road toward the forest. Jo says, "It would have suffered too much."

Hattie leans into Jo, resting her head on her shoulder. "Maybe he don't want company, anyway."

"Doesn't," Jo corrects.

The tractor stops at the edge of the meadow. Tom descends and goes around to the bucket. He lifts his load over his shoulder, then walks slowly into the forest.

"We'll put flowers later," Hattie says.

Jo thinks of the clearing, light filtering down to the rolling, grassy mounds. Tom right now is climbing through the underbrush toward it, cracking branches under his boots. "We should put fresh flowers on all the graves."

Hattie likes this idea. "We can have a ceremony."

They fall silent, imagining this.

"You should come to market with us tomorrow," Hattie exclaims. "You can get all sorts of food. Sarah makes cinnamon buns."

Jo hesitates, imagining herself squished between Tom and Hattie in the truck.

"Sarah's in love with Tom."

This is the last thing Jo expected to hear. It is so ordinary, and yet utterly extraordinary. Jo looks at Hattie in amazement. "No way."

"I told him, but . . ." She shrugs, as if to say, *You can imagine how that went.*

"Does she know about him?"

"Not really."

"What does that mean?"

Hattie shrugs. "People hear things. But then they don't believe them. So she knows, but she don't know."

"Doesn't know."

Hattie repeats grumpily, "*Doesn't* know."

Jo stares out at the forest, Tom somewhere within with his awful cargo. A man, but not really human, not anything definable, just moving through this world in sullen detachment, wishing he'd died. She can't quite grasp how this Sarah fell in love with all that, but if it's true, then maybe she's the one who can end Tom's suffering. He just might need more of a nudge.

"OK, I'll come," Jo says. "I think I need to see this."

Hattie grins and hops off the fountain. "Let's go swim. You

need to wash up again, anyway."

Jo stops her from sprinting away. "Hang on, I need to get my bathing suit."

"Why? Race you!" Hattie squeals, and takes off.

The pond is smooth and cold under the overcast sky. Walking into the water still wearing her clothes feels bold, gratifying. She'll never bother to get a suit on again, not if she's already outside and wanting a swim. Her feet sink into the silty floor, one step at a time, the water sliding up her exhausted body until the bottom falls away, and the water swallows her completely. She floats just under the surface, eyes closed, paddling her hands to stay down. All is silent and cool, and for a moment, her mind empties at last. A tiny moment of absolute, breathtaking nothing.

Then something barges into her. She bursts up out of the water, gulping air. Hattie splashes her and squeals. Jo splashes her back. Loco trots the shoreline, whining. The sky darkens, and big fat raindrops start to fall, peppering the silver water all around. In the distance, there is the crack of thunder, so Jo waves Hattie out of the water, and she reluctantly obeys. They start back, their clothes plastered to their bodies. Up ahead, the Old House leans against the sky, darkened by the rain. Jo can sense the place below, silent, orderly, like something folded and stored away. Except it isn't: she recalls with a lurch the viselike grip, her name whispered in her own head.

Stop. The door's closed, all the iron's in place. She has to focus on here, now, her feet slipping in wet grass, Hattie squealing and running ahead. The ordeal is finished. She doesn't have to think about it, not for a while, not until the next time. The rain falls hard and fast, pummeling their bare skin, and they run in circles, screeching and leaping through puddles. Loco takes off at speed to the house, whirls to a stop under the eave to watch. They arrive breathless, burst through the door into the sunroom, spattering water across the tile floor. They twist and squeeze out their sodden hair, gasping and laughing. The storm passes as abruptly as it began, thinning to a drizzle tapping the metal roof, and a motion catches Jo's eye: the tractor coming back across the field. Tom's been working the earth with his spade this whole time, alone in the forest. She watches his slow passage, thinking how she was alone, too, down in the cellar. Maybe that's just how it has to be. The tractor makes a jerky turn, comes to a halt at the bottom of the hill. He swings out with a little jump, lights a cigarette, then plods up toward the greenhouse.

"I should go," Hattie says a little glumly. "There's work needing done after all this rain."

Jo is startled at how she sounds, as if nothing's out of the ordinary, as if it's just any old day. But for Hattie, the door isn't the only thing. It should be that way for Jo, too, she realizes. Just part of all the work of this place, the countless chores and tasks, the planting and growing and markets and cooking.